THE BASSAM SAGA · BOOK TWO

ZAFIR

AND THE SEVENTH SCROLL

Paul B. Skousen

IZZARD INK™
PUBLISHING

ZAFIR

Contact Paul B. Skousen at info@paulskousen.com.
© Copyright 2016 by Paul B. Skousen

Published by:
Izzard Ink
PO BOX 522251
Salt Lake City, UT 84152

First Edition: December 2016
Bassam Saga, Book I: Bassam and the Seven Secret Scrolls (2014)
Bassam Saga, Book II: Zafir and the Seventh Scroll (2016)
Softback ISBN: 978-1630720537
Hardback ISBN: 978-1630720582
eBook ISBN: 978-1630720568
Bassam Saga, Book III: The Search for Rasha (2017)

Narrated by Mark Deakins, winner of "Best Voice of 2010," "Best Audiobook of 2010," and six
"AudioFile Earphones Awards."

Cover by: Christian Fuenfhausen
Design by: Alissa Rose Theodor

"BASSAM" IS PRONOUNCED "BAH-SAWM"

DAWN

Henri let the last of the parchment curl off the wooden rod, disappointed the story had come to an end so suddenly. The ancient papyrus lay to his side, loosely coiled into a cardboard box.

He peeled off his glasses, rubbed his eyes and looked up. The light of a new day was just casting shadows across the floors of the old museum—gray hues slowly taking blurry color and form.

"That can't be the end of it, could it?" he muttered aloud. "What manner of unfinished record is this?"

His back ached from leaning against a display case part of the night, then moving to a hard-backed chair for the rest. It was a good read, he decided. "I must wind the scroll back on its spindle before the morning crew arrives."

He pushed to his feet and groaned, turning his neck and then his shoulders, anticipating those dull pops that signaled bone on bone realignment, and all things painfully back in place.

"Next time, I'm sitting on a cushioned chair," he frowned, rubbing his sore backside.

Suddenly he stopped, his eyes bright with realization that shamed him for not thinking of it in the first place.

Next time? Next time! What am I saying? There must *be a next time!*

He looked at the sarcophagus and rubbed his chin. "There's got to be ...."

Picking up his flashlight, the old man approached the coffin, circling it like a cat testing a new a bird cage.

Stopping at the right side, he bent down and shined a beam into the black hole underneath.

"Maybe I missed it the first time—"

He looked at his hands, still red and raw from the previous work to extract the scroll. "Okay, once more."

He approached the massive clay treasure from the left side and leaned across the back end as he had done before. He pressed his cheek against the cool clay and reached underneath to push his hand into the little opening. His fingers reached far into the black void but found nothing.

And then came an idea—the *mirror*. Of course!

The path through the Great Hall had worn thin over the years, he could walk it in his sleep: around to the back of the gift shop, down a small hallway to the second door on the right, directly to his private domain, his cache of all things neglected, his carefully collected stash of disorder that let him create from anything a degree of order. It was his custodial closet.

Henri's keys jangled as he felt for the old Narragansett, finding it more by habit than by looking. When they came through a few years back to refit the building with updated door handles and locks he had refused to let them change out this old classic. *Why swap out quality?*

The lock clicked open with a well-oiled turn and the door swung wide. The shop was dark but Henri knew the crooked metal racks and rows of bending shelves like his own bald head. They were overburdened with dusty boxes and bits and pieces of discard that collected there over the years—so much a pack rat was he. *And why not?*

Weak bluish light seeped into the little shop from a musty wired ventilation window high up the wall. It's weak glow guided Henri's stumble through the stacks and piles to a certain shelf.

"There it is," he said, pulling down a broken broom handle. Twisted about its end was a crude wire wrapping that gripped the handle of a palm-sized looking glass. It would do. He took another flashlight as he hurried away. "Batteries are short-lived friends," he sighed as the door swung shut behind him.

Henri approached the sarcophagus with curious determination.

"It makes no sense," he thought, seating himself on the cold floor beneath the coffin. "The ancients always finished their records, complete, *inclusive.*"

He shifted position for a better look inside the secret opening. "Inclusive and complete, else why put it there at all?"

It took a moment for a shaky view to come back to him, but it was enough—a fist-sized circle of reflected light spotlighted the inside.

The clay interior was pressed flat by fingers that left small indentations of casual work, a sloppy contrast to the smoothed perfection of the exterior. It was painted over with a stain or whitewash of some sort—cream-colored, an odd expense for something not meant to be seen for the eternities. He saw no dust or debris or mold soiling the little chamber, proving it undisturbed after so many millennia. Where was this stashed away, Henri wondered. From what burial chamber was this first taken? He made a mental note to casually ask about—perhaps such knowledge could shed more light on the mystery of its origins.

Turning the mirror, he saw suddenly the corner of something—an edge of a cloth or such, and an odd-shaped shadow.

"It must be," he breathed slowly, and peered hard over the top of his glasses.

Setting the mirror down, he stretched his hand into the void once more until he could stretch no farther. The edges pulled on the skin of his hand, but then—just then—the tip of his middle finger bumped against the object of his quest—it moved and he smiled.

Whatever it was, it felt soft—soft like leather.

It took but moments and he was back on his feet, cradling carefully in his arms his newest prize: another scroll, smaller than the first, and probably of shorter duration, he estimated. He moved quickly but stealthily to the museum library and felt for his keys. "No cement floor this time," he vowed, and found his way to an overstuffed leather chair. He clicked on the antique floor lamp, and its warm yellow shroud invited him to sit for another long read.

心爱的 **2** 咱爱小

SAND MOUNTAINS

On the eighth morning in the Taklamakan, I awoke suddenly, rubbing the nightmares from my eyes. "Bakra?" I called, and hurried to my feet. Half a dozen startled camels suddenly looked my way.

"Oh, yes," I said to their blank faces. "You are all so ugly. I was having a dream. None of you is as pretty as my Bakra, but you will do."

I shed the bedding, rolled it in a ball, and shook the dust from my coat.

"The evil men that rode with you are dead," I told the animals as I rummaged for something to eat. "They were bad and killed many good men. They killed my best friend. Did you know that? Did you know you carried death on your humps, across these sands, to run his evil errands? I will excuse you for it, *if* you carry me for three or four more days, and that's all I ask."

None were appreciating my excellent speech, and turned their heads the other way as if bored, chewing on cuds and snorting.

"All right then, if that's how you want it, let me make myself clear," I said, holding up the riding stick like a club. "If any of you give me problems I will skin your flesh for the fire and eat you in front of the others, one at a time until I am free of this place, do you understand?"

None did, so I gave up and dressed the train to leave. *My Bakra was much smarter than these*, I thought. *She always agreed with everything I said. She was a smart bakra. These are stupid. Stupid camels for stupid men.*

With the sun on my shoulders I steered my train along the tops of the rising dunes. The air was cold for such a bright blue day. The camels sighed vaporous clouds, and for lack of my movement atop the saddle, I felt the cold magnify. I was pleased that the wind was calm.

With fears of discovery erased and ample supplies for what I calculated to be a manageable journey, I hurried the pace with hope that the desert's end could not elude me much longer.

In the monotony of the lonesome trek, I noticed, as if for the first time, that there was indeed a certain beauty in the sands around me. From the sides of the largest dunes there flowed the softly crafted slides of rippling rivulets, folding away into hundreds of layers like smoothed-over blankets. Beyond them were the friendly intersections of hundreds of smaller dunes—curving, sloping, rounding, and flattening in mazes of texture and form—beautiful, endless, and elegant. Shades of sandy brown faded from dark to light, and back again, into shadows, then into the full blaze of the sun, following thousands of indistinct sweeping carved curves, the works of nature's slow but artistic hand. The whitecaps of spraying dust from the higher dunes rode on currents that dressed the desert and formed the serpentine paths of sterile landscape that rose and fell in rolling rhythm and harmony. The highest dunes wound upwards to graceful peaks that boasted the great magnitude of sands moved about by the Ancient of Days—carried slowly from place to place in a patient act of eternal motion and restlessness.

The camels complained whenever they started up such a climb, knowing it could take half a day to the summit, and the rest of the day descending, before the next rose again to challenge our way. I avoided when possible such difficult climbs and descents, but to expedite my trek south, some of them could not be missed.

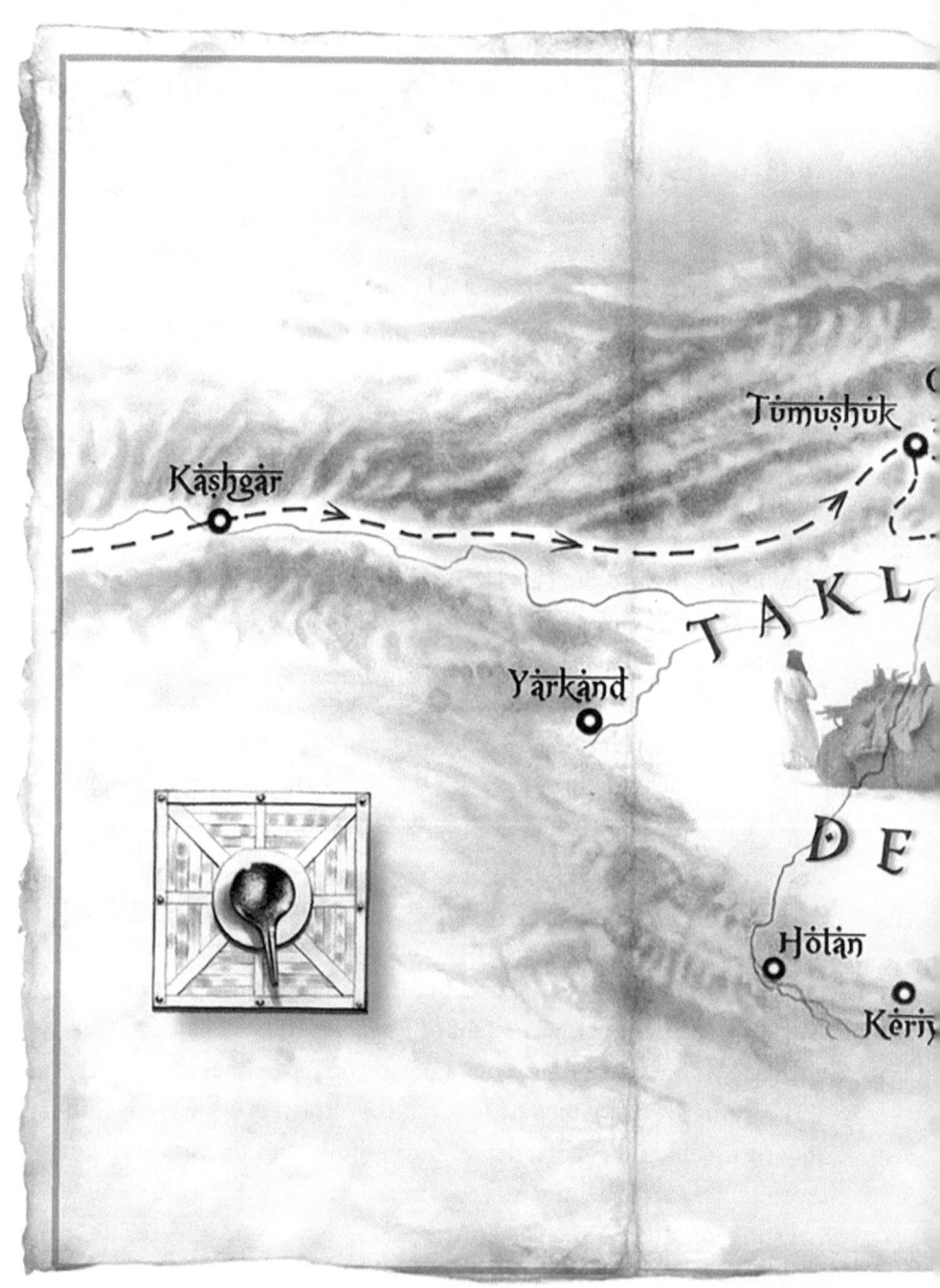

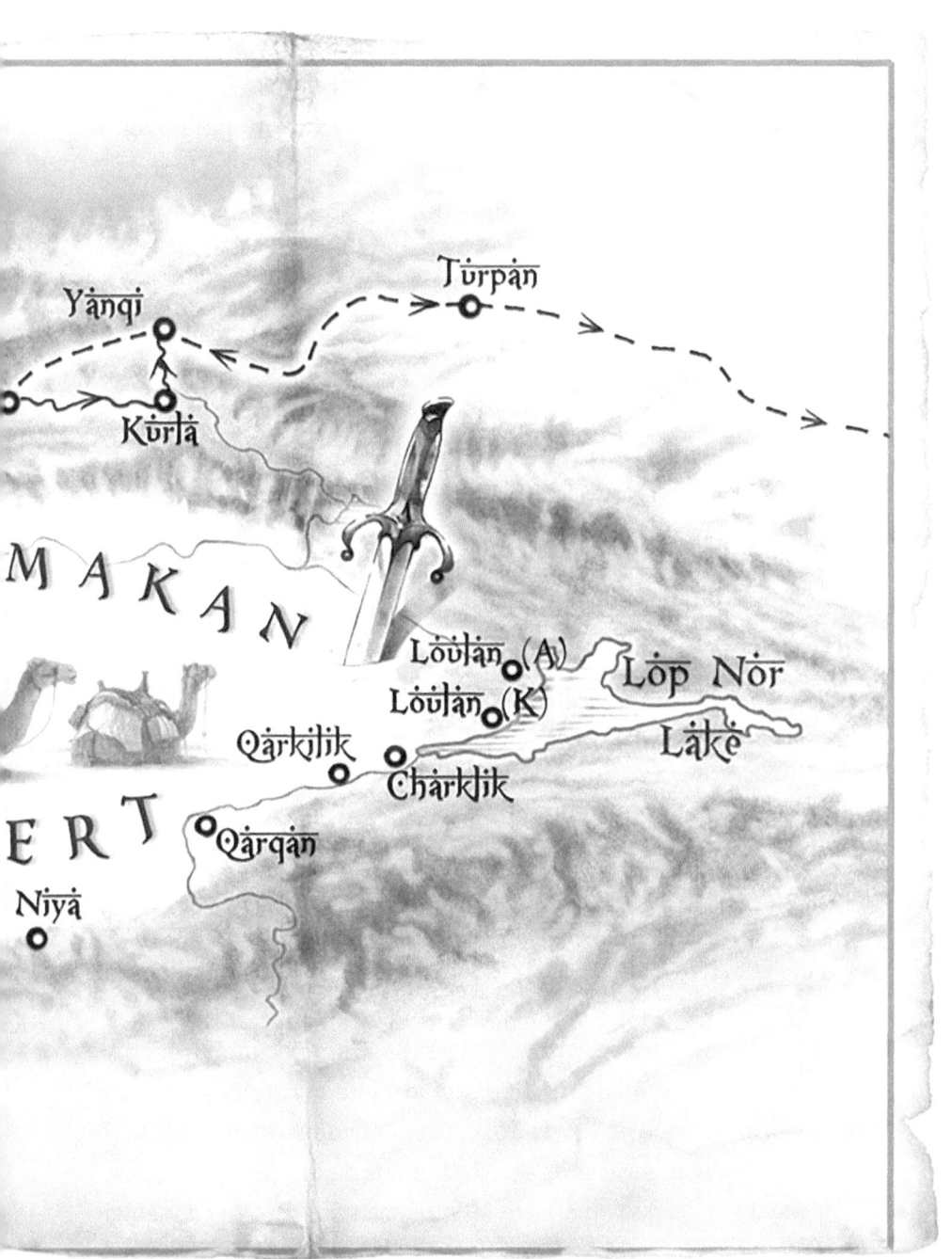

Scaling to their tops at once gave a panoramic view like none other on earth. Even the camels grew quiet at such heights and ceased their complaining, if only for a while. The great reach of sand climbed with a natural harmony that no hand of man could mimic. From those tops, I could see the musical shapes of nature rolling away in all directions, encouraging in their beauty, and discouraging in their expanse. I was as a soul lost at sea—a sea of dry and frozen sand that bode no friendly shore nor island of rescue.

My penchant for numbers and their power of prediction helped me address the shapes of the dunes as we passed them. These mountainous wonders rose and fell in mathematical perfection. The sandy mounds were shallow in the climb, growing steeper as shaped by nature's fixed formula. Their lofty apex leveled for a few calculations more before counting downward to a math of simpler need. Beneath us I envisioned within the dunes the formation of engineered stability, layer upon layer of a thousand billion granules perfectly compressed one atop another, uniquely aligned to answer the pitch of their outward slopes. No man could put equation to their formulations or inject into the harmonious perfection any form of disturbance, except, perhaps, by nature's own tool of recalculation: my desert bakras. They stepped carelessly over the simple arithmetics of nature's balances. Their evenly-paced rhythm of footfalls dispersed a steady two-dozen cascades from each foot-fall that flowed down the ridges in pre-measured quantities. The rolling variables blended into the whole as carefully allocated fractions, completing the equations in shushing whispers.

I had the oddest sensation sweep over me to simply jump from my camel and go running off one of the dunes to race down its long, smooth slope and tumble and roll over the velvet equations that completed nature's untouched perfection—careening through the inviting flat silts of wayward designs that were forever changing and re-changing, sculpting and re-sculpting, heaping up and taking down in a pattern and cycle that marked the progress of eternity already passed and all generations of time forward.

But the urge to spoil the unspoiled no longer held the same allure. I admired the handiwork of nature's forces, and held the immensity of the great desert with a new esteem. It truly was a desert that a man could go into and never come out of—but perhaps such folklore was born not from a lack of water and sustenance, which are the obvious answers to desperate survival. Perhaps it was something more hidden, more tender, more guarded, and more spectacular. Perhaps no man comes out of it for the simple reason that he chooses to stay.

With another long day of riding behind me at last, the sun found his place on the horizon signaling the time to set camp.

I found a protected spot between two moderate dunes and circled the camels about. I unburdened them and gave feed from the stores prepared by Habib and Kahn. The beasts seemed hungry enough but enjoyed making cud and rested there, contented.

I settled down by my sleeping mat. It was shivering cold, and I decided a hot tea would be nice for a change.

Gathering a few sticks from the pack bags, I created a small pile of tinder and worked my bow drill until a curl of smoke rose and a small slender yellow flame stood up. I built it into a modest cook fire and enjoyed a delicious tea, the first in a long while. It warmed me to my toes.

It was time to update my journal.

"Day 341—Dear Rasha, I'm in the middle of the most forsaken place on earth. Dunes climb into the sky all around me, sculpted mountains of pure sand. I cross them at their tops, winding my little caravan twice or three times the actual distance I might go if it was just a straight path. There has been no misstep since leaving my Bakra. I'm cold each day and night, but I no longer thirst and my stomach is filled. The pole star continues to sink as I travel south. I measure half an isba' since the sky cleared, so the end of this desert must be soon. I can see the peaks of snow-capped mountains beyond the dunes so I estimate three more days through the sand. I must be close. —Bassam"

心爱的 **3** 咱愛小

MUD AT LAST

My routine for the last days in the desert grew comfortably regular. By sunrise I was packed and on the road. I ate from the stores with modesty and care, still unsure of my own measurements of time and distance.

Each day south, the mountain dunes were less steep and not as arduous to cross. Nature's amazing equations changed and a more regular pattern in the sand hills began to show as might the choppy ripples of a pond—many smaller dunes perhaps only twice the height of a man rolled in front of me. Like frozen waves on the sea, their crests lined up with the wind and pointed a direct and southerly blow. Ammar told me a secret about the wind—that in the daytime it blew steady toward large lakes or the sea. And the dunes, it shaped the dunes to point in the direction it blew, making a way to find direction beyond the horizon. But the map showed no sea in these parts. To what, then, would the blow point me? I decided to ask Ammar about it the next time we met.

By morning of the fifth day after losing Bakra, my train passed out of the dunes to the flats of a vast plain of featureless, sandy waste. I wasn't confident if the mighty terrain should be a welcomed sight or not. The ground beneath me changed from loose sand to gravelly, hardened soil. My camels paced themselves wearily, showing want of rest, a little food, a little water.

The change in scenery came so quietly that the difference didn't sink into my brain as we passed into it. I was among the dunes for so long my mind couldn't process my reality as before. Was I free? Did I truly leave the lifeless dunes of the Taklamakan? I sought proof in the scene behind me, a disappearing stretch of dunes that calmly marched off north in increasingly lofty perches until they disappeared into the brown haze of the horizon. Yes, it seems the dune desert was behind me, but for what lay in front I could only hope.

By midday we finally crested a long slow rise. From its top, I got my bearings. Scanning the lifeless flat expanse before me, I took a sudden breath of anxious surprise. *What is that I see? Is that not the snaking passageway of a trough, the distinctive carving of a flood plain? Is that not the seasonal remnants of the great southern river?*

"Do you see it bakras?" I shouted excitedly, stirring them to look at me. "Do you see it?" I said pointing. "The river! It's there, the southern river! Water! That means we're safe. That means we are at the end of our great trial! That means we are out of the Taklamakan!"

From my high vantage, I could see the river's winding path cutting through the flat lands like a split in the earth. There were distant patches of green along its banks. The sight of it breathed encouragement into all of us and without even asking, my camels picked up the pace.

"Water is near, my ugly bakras," I said. "Soon I will let you free to drink your stomach's desire, but not until you have carried me close enough to know that it is safe."

By late afternoon we neared the river's bank. Its earthy, stagnant smell was drifting toward us from a long way off. Despite its soiled scent, to a sojourner like me who would welcome any configuration of water, it was the most delicious smell on all the face of the earth.

The camels pulled and growled, their mouths foaming in anticipation. I had fully expected a clean-flowing body of delicious purity, but as I neared to dismount, I saw it was not to be.

"This is a river?" I asked aloud. "Why, it's as thick as the mud in a pottery pit," I frowned as we surveyed from the sandy bank. I scanned up and down as far as I could see the blackish expanse to detect anything potable for me and my beasts.

"It must be the winds, you backward bakras," I scolded. "The winds moved the desert dust to sop its own thirst. The sand has clogged its run—we will have trouble here."

I ordered my beast to kneel and I slid off the side. "It has tricked us into coming here. Do you find any puddles to drink from, you ugly bakras?"

My camels were not listening, but were sniffing at places for pools and puddles, spreading wide a stance that let them bend down to taste it.

I wondered at the circumstance, thinking the same storm that blinded me must have deposited soils upstream, an accumulation that steadily thickened until it reached this lower end.

"If a man was desperate enough," I told my train, "he could capture such filth in a skin and then filter it through his fabric. But how much of this mud would make for even a small cupful to drink?"

To a thirsty man, I could say without question that none of those palatable problems would make the least bit of difference. For such was I but a few days ago, a thirsty man, before God had so kindly spared me and granted me these provisions and skins.

"Ugly bakras," I announced, "I'll wager that after traveling through that terrible Taklamakan, that a man gladly drinks his weight in mud to quench a throat baked dry from a week in such a place. Go ahead and drink all the mud you want—you have earned it."

Laboring with a cloth to quench my own thirst, I finally settled on the ground and watched them take their fill. Squinting to the sun for an orientation, I decided to take a reading on my direction. The pointer proved we were right on course, headed directly south. The problem that awaited me now was to decide how far east I had drifted.

There was no way I could determine to which side of the oasis villages I had placed myself. Had I yet farther east to travel, and possibly find myself in a new place of desolation? Or was it farther west?

The only comfort I found in my new situation was the well-traveled path flattened out not far from the river's bank, heavily visited and worn. I hoped it was near the main route, perhaps the main silk and jade route itself. I guessed we were near the road I recalled seeing on every map I had ever encountered of this region, snaking along the southern boundary of the Taklamakan—but my detailed memory didn't help solve my east-west problem at present.

"Ugly bakras, I know that you're ignoring me, but here is our plan," I said. "You will continue to carry me farther south until we find the main silk road. It must be more traveled and expansive than this pathway. Then we will go east. There must be towns to the east, I just need to go far enough. And when we arrive at a trading town, I will pick one of you to ride. The rest of you I'll sell for meat and leather. The most valiant among you will be preserved, so walk well and live."

The camel's bellies hung heavy behind ribs weakly wrapped with scruffy hide. Only one of the animals looked at me during my speech and she seemed sturdy enough. I chose her, thinking the others too thin for much more than soup bones.

With the afternoon growing old, I thought crossing the river before dark would set me nicely for an early start in the morning. I turned eastward for a suitable crossing place.

After an hour's looking I came upon a broad expanse where the river had spread shallow and brown islands of mud formed a stepping-stone path. We managed to traverse it with no disruption or spill and followed the river's course directly east.

By late afternoon we entered the most unusual terrain. We were in soft sands again but surrounded with the strangest formations. It was like a forest of stacks—columns of rock and earth stacked as tall as a man. These stood like guards, spread sporadically all about us. Small brown dunes were piled around their bases as if to hide their true dimensions. The stacks crowded within arm's reach of each other and slowed our progress. I had to weave around the stumps as though I were negotiating a forest of trees. Atop the stacks grew an assortment of desert shrubs and long tufts of gray grasses. My camels sniffed the greens and I let them nibble as we passed.

With the sun lightly balanced on the jagged horizon, I looked for a nice flat place in the shadows and circled my camels. I made another fire and prepared tea. A few dates and some jerked meat made for a fine meal.

I leaned against my saddle as another beautiful sunset glowed from fiery orange to soft red and then gray and black. I pulled tight my coat and blankets, and prepared my journal. I had so much to say about my lonely trip through the Taklamakan, the bones that were left behind, the many stories and feelings to express. And a deep sorrow that still stung when I remembered Bakra. Oh, that I could express my gratitude to her for her amazing patience with me over this long voyage.

I left my lamp burning late and continued writing until the pitch of black hung thickly overhead. The sticks of the fire exhausted themselves to powdery embers and the evening cold of the desert rolled over my camp. I wrapped my coat tightly about me and pulled my blanket over my ears.

It was the end of second watch and a bright half-moon hung overhead. As for me, I was fast asleep in the soft breeze, snoring alone beneath the stars, with my writing things spread out beneath me, and my bakras resting in peace.

心爱的 **4** 帕爱小

THE FAMILIAR

I slept deeply—my first restful slumber in weeks. I was so wrapped in comfort and ease that the pre-dawn light did little to stir me from the warmth of my bed. Consciousness slowly returned, pleasant and calm. The rising sun warmed my face, caressing it softly to melt away my dreams. Without opening my eyes, I lay there enjoying the smooth touch to my cheek. It was a gentle touch, as the morning should be, hardly stirring, lightly as the light of a new day, a touch that assured with peace of mind that life was good.

In half-asleep half-awake silky dreaminess, I reached up with my hand to touch my face and suddenly felt the delicate fingers of a warm hand pressed against my cheek and a young feminine voice calling me, "Wake up, Bassam."

What!? Am I dreaming?

I squinted my eyes open and saw immediately in front of me the beautiful countenance of a young woman.

Rasha?

"Good morning sleepy head," she said.

"Rasha?"

"What?"

Oh, no—that was not my Rasha—it was—it was … *Kalila*?

"What? What is this? Kalila?" I rose to an elbow, still caught in my sleepy web. She sat right in front of me, a delighted smile spread across her face.

"What?" I stammered again.

And then I saw circled around me a dozen camels crowded in close. Their riders were grinning, looking down at me, and some of them were breaking out in laughter at my confusion.

"Bassam!" a man called out. It was Najeeb just kneeling his camel to dismount. "My boy!"

"Wha-what?" I mumbled, confused and surprised at the same time.

"What in the name of God and all that is good and great are *you* doing here?" Najeeb said. "Here, of all places? You gave us quite the start, my boy."

"Najeeb? What are you … I mean, why? … I don't understand."

I sat up, tugging at my coat and straightening my headdress as though I was caught undressed in front of them all. "Wha-what are you doing here? Wh-where am I? How did you …?"

Kalila put her hand on my shoulder, the first human touch since … since … I couldn't remember when.

"Your journal, silly," Kalila said, gesturing to the pages spread out on the ground in front of me.

"Do you know that you camped right in the middle of the road with your writings all spread out?" she said. "We might have run you over in the twilight had we not seen your pens and your stack of writings."

I looked down at the wrinkled papyrus. Indeed, I had slept atop my pages right there in the middle of a road—*the* road.

"My journals?"

Najeeb stood over me, casting a great shadow. "We all know about your important journals, Bassam!" he laughed. "We were steering past a sleeping stranger when Kalila pointed you out. 'That looks like Bassam and his writings,' she said. None of us believed it, but when we saw your pages and ink pot, well, sure enough, it was you! You're you!"

I stared at him, unbelieving this chance encounter. *Am I dreaming again?*

"So tell me, what has happened here?" Najeeb asked, casting his gaze to either horizon. "Where is Zafir, where are your men, and these camels, where are their riders?"

"Najeeb," I finally said. "I've been lost, for a long time, and there wasn't any river so I kept going and … and …." I looked at the men surrounding me, none looked familiar. "Have you seen them? Have you seen Zafir? How close am I to a village? How did you find me?"

Kalila put her hand on my shoulder. "The bigger question is, how did you find us?" she asked. "Are you not supposed to be north in Turpan? Where is your train? Where is Zafir? And you, you sleepy head, you are a mess. Are you all right?"

I looked down at myself, a dirty, ragged reminder of my former self. My clothes were dusty and stained and ragged with wear, my skin dried to cracks from the hot sun, a sorry sight, and no doubt a smelly one too.

These were too many questions for so early in the morning. I put up a hand to stop Kalila's feminine sand storm and closed my eyes. My whole body ached with pain and fatigue, and my head was clogged with dark and lingering dreams. Her questions swirled around me with so much confusion.

"Wait, just wait, I need to … I need to get up," I said, "Yes, that's it. I need to get up." But I couldn't. She was kneeling on my blanket. "Uh, you're um, on my …."

"Oh, sorry!" she laughed and stood, extending her hand to help me.

I was suddenly embarrassed again. *Should I take her hand? May I touch her, what is the protocol? Will her uncle scold me? If I refuse will I offend her?*

"Uh, um, thank you," I said, and put my weary hand into hers.

She tried to pull but to no avail. I managed on my own, letting the touch linger as long as that awkward situation would allow.

Surrounding me were the other riders, still mounted. They watched the unfolding and looked at each other with toothy grins. I stood to catch my balance and let go of her hand.

Standing tall, a new fatigue suddenly sent my head spinning and I rubbed the back of my neck to bring life back to my brain—I felt weak and tired all at once.

"So, Bassam!" Najeeb said, stepping in front of me and putting a hand on my shoulder. "Let's get you packed and ready, you must come with us!" he said smiling. And then he stopped to look more closely at me for a second time. Concern clouded his face. "Well, maybe not so fast, my friend. You don't look well."

I had stood too fast—my head was dizzy.

"What you need," Kalila said with a wry grin, drawing her veil to her nose, "is to get washed up, *Avenger of Suoud*."

At this I backed up a step and nearly fell backwards over my own saddle. A roar of laughter erupted among the mounted men. Najeeb waved them away.

"Take a break men while we get Bassam ready," he ordered.

The camels turned aside to join the rest, and closer attention was focused on the young hero of Suoud.

Kalila gathered up my blankets and sleeping mat to shake while Najeeb stirred the coals of my cook fire. He shouted orders for food and a tea.

"You had better sit back down, my boy," Najeeb said. "You need something to eat."

He was right. I abruptly slumped right back to the ground and rubbed the sides of my head. Najeeb bent down to examine my desert-burned face. His eyes searched me for answers that remained unspoken.

"Bassam," he said cautiously, "I don't like what I see, my son." I looked up and the old veteran could see the emotional scars of a difficult trial, and that my clothes showed worse—stained, worn and battered, my shrunken sandals and the long, blotchy brown rip across my shirt. Without speaking it, he knew I had endured something terrible, something that needed to be told, something that had taken life out of me at a horrible price.

"Your eyes tell me you carry more than one man's share of troubles, my young friend," Najeeb said softly. "Have you fallen into a difficulty? Do you run from someone or are you chased? You must tell me about it. Whatever it is, we can help you—all of us, you're safe now."

I looked at my old friend for a long tired moment. He was not some phantom come taunting me at my worst time, but he was a real human—warm, understanding, kind, full of vigor and full of love. Gentle eyes smiled back at me, concern shining kindly with seasoned wisdom. *What could I say,* I wondered. It was so long ago—a year? Or had it only been a few weeks? The running, the hiding, the fighting, the struggle, the loss, the sorrow, and the blood—oh, there was blood. And I was lost, very lost, for a long, long time. But now I was found, and my old friend loved me and cared for me. *Had I been lost? Had I killed Habib? Had I survived the test of death?* I was simply too weary and too relieved to feel in me anything but pure love for the goodness and human decency that knelt in front of me, coming to rescue a heart that was crushed beyond endurance and had nearly given up too many times to count. Without thinking more on it I wrapped my tired arms around the old man's neck and hung my head to hide the confusing emotions of relief, of loss, of capture and of rescue—and let the last of my boyhood's tears flow freely in the shadow.

Najeeb reached up and put his arms around my shoulders and wrapped a hand around my head and held me to him. He turned his eyes to Kalila who made an approach but stopped. Both wore a look of worry and knew in the moment that something had happened to their friend—something terrible. Without speaking it they knew this was not a time for multiplying words or breaking the tender moment of rescue. It was a time for coming back, coming back from some dark and unspeakable place. From whence, they knew not—but saw it could take some time. They kept their silence a while longer.

The way of the desert to heal a man, no matter the failing or trespass, is as certain as the endless winds that blow. They stir the grains of time as sand, to sculpt again the perfection that was spoiled, to heal the tired and the wounded, the hurt and the sorrowful, the lost and the forlorn, and grant unto each an atonement that renews itself on the clean canvas of a newly swept dune, and the hope of a newly born day.

心爱的 **5** 咱爱小

RECOVERY

"**S**o, this is Habib's sword?" Najeeb said, pulling it from the leather sheath. The finely sharpened edge flashed in the sun.

"He once had a branded sheath, like most Al Murrah," I said as I gulped down slurps of *mee pok* and broth that Kalila had prepared. "He must have made it after I escaped. He carried another when I last saw him."

"So, let me see if I understand what you're telling me," Najeeb said. "They attacked you at Yanqi, chased you south into a sand storm, and that's when you were separated from the main group?"

"Not exactly," I said. Kalila handed me a bread, my third, and I smiled in gratitude. She attended to the fire. "Zafir divided the group and broke off east. Do you have a map? I'll show you."

Najeeb signaled one of his men to fetch the charts.

"Zafir headed east, but there were mountains dividing us, I don't know what happened. I followed Sofian, and all of us escaped south until we felt safe to make camp. There was a storm and we were separated. There should be a river, but I was there, and there isn't any ..."

The charts arrived, stiff animal skins that yielded poorly to simple rolling as did the finer papyrus maps that Ammar carried. Najeeb looked through them and pulled one to lay between us on the ground.

I pointed to Kurla. "This was our first night, in the mountains here," and traced a line south with my finger. "I woke up in the storm somewhere here and that's how I became lost. And this line here," I said, pointing to the great river. "This river does not flow around the northern rim. I know it for myself—I traveled through there and I *never* crossed a river."

"Never crossed it?" Najeeb said in astonishment. "How is that possible? It's one of the greatest rivers in this whole region. I can't see how you missed it. Trade boats travel all year through here, even in winter."

"Well, it wasn't in the path I was on," I insisted. "Or it dries up this time of year, I don't know."

"How did you find your way in the storm?" Kalila asked.

I grew quiet. The south pointer—*is it a great secret or not? Does Zafir wish me to keep it from these good friends?*

I blanked my face. "I sensed the direction to go," I said. "And I was lucky to find it."

"What you needed," Najeeb said, "was a good *south pointer*. You must have one in these deserts or you'll get lost as sure as dark follows day."

So! He knows it! I shut my eyes and shook my head with an embarrassed grin. I reached into my pocket and pulled out my little south pointer. Najeeb took it and turned it over in his hand and laughed.

"Ah-ha! You have an old one. So it is, my faithful friend, you are both prepared as well as trustworthy about the ways of the Abdali-ud-Din. That's good, my boy, to keep the secrets, I would expect no less of the kin of Zafir."

"I'm not really his kin, I'm ..."

"So, mister hero of Suoud," Kalila teased, "now we must say of you *and* this terrible Taklamakan desert, that this is the place a man may enter but never come out of—unless he is Bassam, the avenger of Suoud."

I felt the blush begin.

"Oh yes, young Bassam, you have conquered this mighty desert," Najeeb said, and pounded his hand with congratulations on my shoulder. "You have gone alone where no other has, and have come out of it alive to tell us about it. You did it alone or you did it with God's help, either way he prospered you! I know of no one who has crossed the Taklamakan. You are indeed the *prince* of the Taklamakan, no one may take that from you, not ever. I'm proud of you, my boy, very proud."

Kalila looked at me, teasing with her smile, and mouthed the new words *"prince of the Taklamakan."* I looked away at the ground and instantly felt the heat rising into my ears.

Girls, I grumbled. *They are so much work.*

心爱的 **6** 的翌小

A SHOOTING STAR

By mid-morning, Najeeb and Kalila had patched me up, fed me and renewed my hope in human kindness. He ordered his caravan assembled, and we were under way on the road that led directly east to Charklik. I rode with Kalila toward the rear of the train.

It was so nice to see people again, especially good friends. I felt rested, had a full stomach, and didn't even mind Kalila's non-stop questions.

"Who was the man who told you to follow," she asked, "to flee into the sandstorm, and then disappeared?"

"I keep thinking back," I said, "trying to remember anything about him, and still, I don't know who that was. All of us were covered with our scarves and coverings, protected from the sand. I could see no face, and the sand was so fine, and blowing so thick, it clung to us like mud. I was as yellow as my camel. We looked like the dunes, little moving dunes. His voice, though, he sounded just like Sofian, one of Zafir's captains."

Kalila smiled. "Your south pointer took you the right way, but there is a river there, Bassam. You must have crossed it—it's a large river, larger than the southern muds you found yesterday."

I pondered the problem. *What reason was there in not finding that river?* I thought. If I had found it, where might it have taken me? Knowing the map, I could have turned east at the riverbank and followed it to somewhere, maybe a village, or perhaps to a gathering of Sofian and his men. But no, it wasn't there, I was sure of it—it wasn't anywhere. But that mistake or oversight, whatever it was, led me to a deadly encounter with two terrible men, and the tragic loss of my Bakra.

"Someday I will understand it," I said. "Until then, I'm content that I was guided and preserved, and that's all I could hope for."

We plodded along in silence, watching the camels in front of us.

"We'll be in Charklik by tonight," Kalila said.

"And beyond?" I asked.

"Miran is another day's travel," she said. "My uncle told me he'll send horse riders to Miran and if any of your caravan is to be found, they will say to them, 'Bassam, the *Prince of the Taklamakan*, is coming, make ye all the preparations.'"

I shook my head. "I'm no prince, and if you don't stop this teasing I'll spread the gossip that you are the Princess of Awakening Bassam—she who finds dirty lost souls, half alive, half dead, and with a magical touch restores them to life."

"You think my touch is magic?" Kalila asked.

"I thought you were the rays of the sun come to warm my face," I told her honestly.

"Then you may treat me to dinner this evening."

"Dinner?" I asked.

"And I know just the place—not as good as my uncle's but it will do."

I panicked inside. *Now what do I do?*

Arriving on the outskirts of Charklik by late afternoon, Najeeb set his caravan in a large field that overlooked the small village. The view was beautiful, with the river flowing beyond and rolling green hills marching to the east. Farmland and orchards were set near the banks, and only to the north did the vapid desert horizon give hint that this place was surrounded by sands and barren stony ground.

Najeeb's train was 130 camels. It was stretched out in clumps, each man finding his friends and setting a camp. The guarded cotton goods with other commodities were moved to the center of the encampment with rotating guards on duty.

A few men took me across the town proper to the river beyond. I changed out of my dirty clothing and waded into the icy waters to wash. The water was clear and cold at this bend of the river. I shivered at the exposure but relished its cleansing power. Except for the mud that washed away from my body, the water was clean—clean enough to drink. And, it refreshed.

After dressing, I caught up with Najeeb and his men who were just then passing through the market square.

"Najeeb," I said, running to his side.

"Why, Bassam!" he said. "You look much better, my boy! Now that's the Bassam I'm used to, though skinnier! You're clean, you're rested, you finally look your age, and you're wondering about Kalila!"

I stopped. *How could he know that?* "Well, uh, yes, she said that I must take her to dinner tonight, at a place she knows, not as good as yours, but good enough. Is it proper?"

Najeeb grinned. "Certainly my boy, certainly! I see some worry in your eyes, young Bassam, but let this be an enjoyable time and not one to spend reading intentions. She waits for her own young man who is traveling for another few months. She is promised to him, so I do not worry for you my friend! But this place is her favorite. I'll take you there, it's not far from here, and you may fetch her when you're ready, and have a good time together. Kalila doesn't have many friends on these long trips—mostly old men like me. It's good you came when you did—she is difficult when she is bored."

"Difficult?"

"Oh yes, every man here keeps his distance lest she catch them unawares."

"Catch them?"

"Oh my yes, and she steals their clothes."

"*What?*"

"Certainly she is most wicked. She will take the very last shirt off a man's back if he is not watching, and hurry it to the boiling pot before he can stop her. She washes and scrubs, and if you don't meet her approval, she scrubs you down as well—like an animal."

"She cleans?"

"Like a storm! And we are old and traveled people, Bassam! We wash every few weeks if we need to, it is the way of old men, and we are comfortable with it. But Kalila? She is a storm."

I smiled. "*A storm.* That explains a lot," I said, and we both laughed.

The diner was much smaller than Najeeb's, and sparsely furnished. Kalila sat opposite me at a small, bare table, awaiting the day's catch from the river. Our escorts watched nearby.

A steaming rice bowl with shoyu was delivered in a porcelain dish. Another bowl with sliced carrots and greens sat to the side. And then a platter was presented to us, holding a large broiled fish covered in chopped spices with sweet onions and leafy greens.

I fumbled with the eating sticks, trying to position them as I was shown before. "I never have understood these," I said, trying to arrange them for eating.

"Then you must do as I do," Kalila said. And taking a stick she stabbed a piece of fish, and scooping it with rice, put it in her mouth.

"That's the smartest thing I've seen in months," I said laughing, and copied her every move for the balance of the meal.

"What I would have given for a bowl of rice a week ago," I said.

"How is it you tried such a risky trip with no supplies, not even water?" Kalila asked.

"I had no idea! I was running for my life," I said. "The Taklamakan was the last thing I worried about. Had I only known ... But there were broad swords everywhere. Were it not for that storm, I don't know that any of us could have made it. They scattered Sofian's men into lands already known to them, hills that they knew the first and last about, but we knew nothing."

"The storm kept them from attacking you," she said, "but they also kept you from Sofian."

"Yes, a strange fate that sent me south," I admitted.

Laughter erupted from another table and we both looked.

"Tell me, Bassam, what will become of you when you find your caravan?"

"I don't know," I said. "We had treasure enough to make the exchanges from Chang'an to places south, but now, I just don't know."

"And if you can't find your caravan?" she wondered.

"Then perhaps your uncle will let me work for him until I can join a train back to Rekeem."

"That could be a long time," she said. "We don't see many western caravans this far east. Zafir is the only trader who regularly comes this far."

"That could be a problem, I suppose," I told her.

"Or, you could stay—I mean, you could stay until you were ready to go west again," she said.

"Yes, I could stay."

We looked at each other without speaking for several long moments. My mind was a million stadia away, wondering about home and my Rasha and the rest of the trip that lay before me.

Kalila finally broke the trance. "My uncle said he was thinking of a caravan west," she said.

"West? How far?" I asked.

"He hasn't decided. But he wouldn't say anything unless he was serious about it."

"Perhaps I could, I mean if I had to stay, I could ..."

We fell quiet again. It was my turn to wonder.

"So, what will you do after this trip," I asked. "I mean, you're just at the beginning, am I right?"

"We've been out three weeks, and we're on schedule," she said. "Uncle had plans for Chang'an. That's where his trade takes him. We delayed our departure so that we could meet up with Zafir and his many swords, to be one large group. It's safer that way, you know. And all of that fighting in the lands north, they say it has been spilling south."

"Yes, so I've heard."

"But now my uncle is not so sure of the plan, not after the attack you described."

"We'll know soon enough," I said, and put my eating sticks to the side.

"You're finished?" she asked.

"That was delicious. I see what you mean—your aunt prepares a much better fish than this, but it was still a good fish, the best I've had in months!"

It was dark I led Kalila back to her uncle's tent.

"You must learn the way of the navigator," I said.

"That's an art that some say is a skill, but it's all confusing to me," she said.

"Not if I show you. Do you want to learn some tonight?"

"It's late already," she said.

"Late? No, not even through half watch! I'll teach you the science of the kamal."

"I must check with my uncle first," and she stepped inside Najeeb's tent for a moment. I looked into the deep night sky. The same lacy, starry formations spread above me as they did during those cold lonely nights in the Taklamakan. Some things remain the same, I thought—no matter if fear or joy resides in the hearts of those who watch, some things always stay the same, like the stars.

"He says fine," Kalila said hurrying from the tent, "but we have an early start tomorrow, so just a few moments, he said." She wrapped a shawl around her shoulders. The cold was deepening.

I stopped at my saddle for the oil lamp and lit it on the smoldering cook fire. I led her a few dozen paces beyond camp, far enough to be in darkness, to see the stars with clear eyes.

Inviting her to sit, I guardedly seated myself next to her to point out the great stars. "These are a few of the 15 guiding stars. They help me find my way when it's dark."

"What 15? Are they all there?" she asked, gazing straight overhead.

"Most of them. If we watched all night, you could see the rest. The most important is the pole star there," I said, leaning close and pointing.

"Yes, I know the pole star, and the two ladles that turn about it every night."

"You can tell what watch it is from the ladles," I said.

"That's not so!"

"It is! All I need to know is how many days since the beginning of spring—the barley harvest—and I can tell you what watch we're in. It's no trick. The stars advance an isba' and a third each night. In a year, their starting place turns around to the same place again on the first day of spring."

Kalila yawned and tried to hide it.

"Sorry," I said. "I had to depend on that to save my life once, I don't mean to bore you."

"You must show me how that works."

"All right, someday I will."

The brightness of the moon was interrupting the night's lesson and we both watched it hang in the sky, waxing toward half. Its muted light bathed the rolling hills and sleeping village in silver and black.

"And what of that?" she asked. "Does the moon guide you as well?"

"No, not as much," I said. "He rises earlier each night, and some nights he comes at the worst time, right when I need to see the very stars he hides."

"It matters?"

"Oh yes, to count the isba, the moon can be in the way," I said.

"Is it any good at all, then?" she asked.

I thought back on the many nights alone in the desert, alone at the hand of kidnappers, alone with Bakra. "Yes, useful and important if you need to travel at night," I said. "I suppose you've had to travel at night?"

"Not at all," she said. "I wouldn't think of it. Is that safe, riding in the night?"

"If the moon is out, yes," I told her. "There was a time I had to pull my beast by rope and the moon guided me. If a road is good, I will ride— but *my* bakra is good, she is … she was so good on her feet. There was one night she missed a rock hiding in the shadow and she stumbled. It is not as easy as daytime."

The reminiscing reminded me of the many times Bakra had carried me safely past sunset and early before sunrise. She was sure-footed, I could trust her always, especially across rocky terrain.

We both sat quietly gazing upwards. A single shooting star streaked across the sky. Kalila took a breath and let it out slowly.

"If you must go, I will miss you," she said.

I felt her hand find mine in the dark and squeeze it. My heart leapt at the unexpected intimacy. Not sure of the formalities in such a thing, I turned over my hand in friendship and gratitude, and squeezed hers gently in return. "And I'll miss you too." Neither of us dared look at the other, not even in the dark, and had no more words to speak. Enough was spoken already.

心爱的 **7** 啪嚓小

LOP NOR

The oasis town of Miran was small but well visited, and it took only a short day's travel to arrive there. A strong river from the mountains kept it watered. For travelers to the desert lands east or west, it was an important stopover. Several smaller trains were already camped when Najeeb carved out a place for us on the east side. He sent runners to ask about Zafir, his men, or anyone western having passed through in recent days. The messengers came back empty-handed.

"We'll sleep here and leave for Lop Nor before day break," Najeeb announced.

I settled my camel close to Najeeb's tent, and sat with him for dinner.

"So, what of those stars, Bassam!" Najeeb asked, passing a basket of breads to Kalila.

I glanced at her and she blushed. I feigned ignorance of the events of the night before. "Ammar is an excellent navigator," I said, "he put a map on my arm. With these winter stars, the map, and my south pointer, I think I could make it just about anywhere."

"I believe you could," Najeeb said. "Those south pointers—around here they are just religious relics."

"So I've heard," I said.

"But my band of traders, we are not so sophisticated. We take the regular roads back and forth. These do not require such things, just a steady camel and a reason to go."

"Najeeb," I asked, "what can you tell me of Lop?"

"Oh, the great desert of Lop and its lake—they call it the Lop Nor. It's a terrible place, probably much like that desert you passed through, but at Lop? There are no dunes. It's a place of sandy plains and sterile mountains. They hide traps of salt bogs and mud. The bogs never dry but can become covered with a crust, a dangerous trap for man and beast alike, Bassam. Many lost travelers are swallowed in the Lop—never again heard from. And because of that you will hear an abundance of legends and stories all through these villages," he said, waving his hand through the air.

"I thought we just passed the worst desert in this region," I offered.

"Ah, the dreaded Taklamakan—a lifeless waste of eternal dunes. No man goes in," Najeeb said. "But the Lop is a great salty flat—stony soil, a few regions of sand hills, but flat desolation all the way from west to east. You'll see it as we near. A great sea once flowed there, filled each season by two rivers that carved a great basin. But the desert, she has her own way, and the lake is all but gone. More of those marshes and bogs cover most of its basin. The rivers that drain the mountains in the springtime always flow into Lop Nor, and she will receive them gladly. But she is selfish and gives nothing back. That is why she is dead. The living give, and the dead do not. The Lop is dead to all who are fooled by her occasional sparkling allure, but it is too salty for fish, too salty for man."

"Are there stopping places there?" I asked.

"Oh yes, several small villages with goat herders. We will stop there before Dunhuang. But the safe time is only in the winter months, when ice forms around the bogs. Ice for our fresh water, salt for the traders. Salt merchants pass through often enough, have you seen them? Have you seen the crystals? They can grow to the size of a man's hand. And larger slabs of it. Around these parts, men cut blocks from dried formations and ship them inland. It's a lucrative trade, Bassam. Your Zafir should consider it."

"Zafir tells me such commodities are for short hauls," I said. "He is working the long hauls."

"So few others share in that trade, that is certain," Najeeb said. "But still, an empty camel is gold left in the desert!"

"I want to learn about that, Najeeb. Our salt at home, crystals from the swamps near shore, sometimes shallow pools cut into the rock for just that—it is not as pure as local salt I've discovered on this trek."

"You should think about salt, Bassam. Abdali-ud-Din moves many thousands of camel loads of valuables, but why not salt? They leave the leftover silvers for traders like me—the cotton and jade, manuscripts, and little religious statues, rugs, the silk, and yes, even the salt. But it's enough, and we make profit on each trip—but these operations *could* be Zafir's!"

Najeeb was right, and the idea left me pondering for the rest of our trip.

The six-day journey to Dunhuang crawled along too slowly for my patience. An overcast gray obscured the sun for most of the journey, and each stretch of desolate flats melted into another with unending monotony. Broken ridges of barren mountains and steep washes penned us in the flats, marching eastward, making any break to the south a climb up and then down, with animals not suited for such terrain.

The cold kept us wrapped and not talkative. When darkness fell, it was a repeat of the prior night—a cold, restless endurance with little protection, and growing doubt about the hope for some village or fortress ahead.

But Kalila wasn't concerned—she said it was this way before on her uncle's prior trips. Perhaps it was my restlessness to get back on the path with Zafir to Chang'an that pinched my patience to such thinness. One afternoon of slow riding I mentioned my impatience to Kalila.

"The total trip is only a week," she said, "and it is, most certainly, the worst part of our journey. It is behind us soon enough."

"Maybe I've become too accustomed to the fight against heat and the lack of water," I said.

"Cold is easier, don't you think?" she asked.

"How is that?"

"When it's cold I can get warm with blankets or a fire," Kalila said. "But in the heat there is nothing I can do except drink water and find shade. There's nothing to escape the heat."

"Even so, I think I prefer to fight the heat than the cold," I said, wrapping my yak coat more tightly around my neck.

"The desert is your home," she said, "so that seems right."

Najeeb's routine was to set up camp near a windbreak whenever the trail allowed it, but was cautious not to stray too far from the main road. The bogs had tripped him before and he refused to risk it again. He told the less experienced members of his caravan that it was always better to bed down in a known place, even on the hard soils with a good bakra blocking the winter winds, than to chance the salty mire in pursuit of a less formidable sleeping place. His warning carried special meaning to me and I nodded sternly in agreement. Caution was worth the inconvenience—*any* inconvenience.

Fires were few, but not for reasons of safety from bandits or robbers. The real problem was the lack of fuel. I managed a few fires from dried manure, but they burned weakly. It gave enough heat for evening tea, but too little to stop the cold. On these nights, my yak coat and blankets made it endurable, and I blessed the name of Tou daily for his wisdom in helping me pick out a good coat.

At the evening of the fifth day when Najeeb's train was a day out of Dunhuang, a pair of riders galloped to camp with grand news. They had met a train on the road, it was headed directly our way, and they said they had seen Abdali-ud-Din camped at Dunhuang. Its chief dwelt in a tent.

"Their chief?" I asked with excitement. "Zafir?"

The riders could offer no more and I was left to fret away the time in anxious anticipation.

"Tomorrow, don't you want to hurry to find camp before sundown?" I asked.

Najeeb smiled and tapped me on the leg with his riding stick. "Patience, my boy! I'm anxious to catch up with Zafir as much as you, but we have a long slow line that can't move faster, and for safety, we shouldn't split up. Don't worry, we should get there before dark tomorrow evening."

I grumbled my impatience and looked around for Kalila.

"So, we find Zafir at last," I told her. "And that means our troops travel together to Chang'an," I said.

"What awaits you at Chang'an?" she asked.

"Zafir will secure a trade route with buyers in that place and with the Hindus to the south. We turn south after Chang'an and secure that end of the trade with Zafir's representatives. It's exciting—he was there a couple of years ago."

"Yes, we saw him."

"Kalila, what will Najeeb do?" I asked. "What work does he do with Zafir in these parts?"

"What he always does," she said. "He'll sell his cotton and trade goods, and see what bargains he can find to sell on the return trip."

"Does he return the same way?"

"Yes, that's all the adventuring he does—Mouru to Chang'an, and back again. Once a year, rarely twice."

"You should think about joining us through the mountains south, it could be a great adventure," I offered.

"I've wondered about that. I'll think on it," she said.

I tapped my riding stick impatiently. "Can't we go any faster?"

心爱的 **8** 咱受小

DUNHUANG

It was shortly after midday when Najeeb's train arrived at the outlaying pasture lands of Dunhuang. The main roads were already crowded with load-bearing donkeys, wagons, camels and walkers, all of them pushing and shoving their wares and concerns along worry-worn ruts and pathways. We watched the congested flow of people converge, some with large bundles of stick cages with squawking birds, others with burdens of straw or firewood, or creaky wooden wagons with winter harvests for market. I noticed the change in culture was much stronger here. An accumulation of the C'ina people busied themselves here or there, barking their objections and taunts in a new and choppy language that sang as much as it confused. But young life among these busied people was no different—children shouted and skinny dogs barked as they raced among the marketplace traffic, playing a hundred games underfoot.

To either side were small trails leading off to settlements or camps, and beyond that, wider roads headed toward herds and farms that could be seen at the foot of the nearby hills.

I was encouraged to be back among people, any people, even if most of them were foreigners, and then I caught myself—"*I* am the foreigner in this place!" The sudden realization made me laugh out loud.

Just then I spotted something familiar. About 500 paces away was a large encampment on the slope of a slow-rising hill, and like a beacon shining its truth for all to see, there stood the tents of Abdali-ud-Din!

"Najeeb!" I said pointing. "Look! Look at that tent, that's Zafir's tent!"

"What? It is? Yes, I believe you're right! Wonderful! Go, my boy!" Najeeb exclaimed. "Perhaps good fortune has smiled on you already, my son! Yes! Those camels are dressed in western drapes. Go! See!"

I kicked my camel to a full-speed gallop and Najeeb followed right on my heels, trying to keep up.

I came thundering into the midst of Zafir's camp, kicking dust and startling all the men who were kneeling at cook fires. Several stood with swords drawn, ready for an attack. And then I saw a familiar face. *Who is that?* Yes! There was Sofian and Humam.

"Sofian!" I shouted. "Humam! It's me! Bassam! I'm back, I'm back!" and I leapt off my bakra without even stopping for her to kneel, and raced to their outstretched arms clasping them firmly. Sofian's stoic face suddenly melted into a broad smile of pure joy.

"Bassam? Is that you? Bassam! We thought you dead," he exclaimed. Others within earshot rose and joined the reunion. Hands clasping, head rubs, slaps on the back, smiles, hellos, greetings, cheers. "You made it! You found us!" Sofian exclaimed. "Whose magic is this thing of wonder? And Najeeb—Greetings, Najeeb! *Salaam alaikum*, peace upon you, my good friend!"

Najeeb halted his camel to kneel.

"Where did you manage to find this young runaway?" Sofian asked." We've been worried about him for many weeks now, and had decided that ...."

"Sofian! *Wa-alaikum is-salaam*, may God's peace be upon you, my dear friend," Najeeb said with open arms. "Thank you, yes! We found this escaped criminal asleep in the middle of the road before Charklik."

"Charklik?" Sofian said slowly, then raised his hands in bewilderment. "Why that's ... that's ..."

And then he looked over at me, his mouth hanging open. "You didn't end up going ... *No*. You didn't! Did you? How could you—?"

"I have so much to tell you," I said breathlessly. "I was looking for you, for anyone, in the blizzard, footprints, anything, everywhere, and..."

"Well, well," Humam said as he approached to greet me, "you have something to share with us, and many questions to answer. We thought you dead! We looked everywhere, we gave up all hope!"

"Me too," I said. "I'll tell you everything, but first, first, where is Zafir? In his tent?"

"Yes, Bassam, but don't go in just yet," Sofian said. "You need to cheer an old man's worried heart, but first you must know why."

"Well, then I'll go!" and I turned but Sofian caught me by my arm.

"Bassam, wait," Sofian said. Najeeb joined the huddle to listen. "Zafir is in bad condition. He has been hurt."

"Hurt?" I gasped. "Badly?"

"It's his leg, and very bad, Bassam. Before you go in, let me tell you first," Sofian said, lowering his voice for only us to hear. "He might lose his leg. It was an accident—his camel fell on him. It was right when we were attacked, after they split us up, do you remember it?"

"Before the mountain pass? Toward Kurla?" I asked.

"Yes, and Zafir took most of Xiongnu and swordsmen with him, and the pack camels, and turned east to the mountains, to lead the bandits away from us."

"Ah, so that explains it," I said. "I looked back and everybody was gone. They must have known ... they had to know, they knew exactly what we would do, and that's why the bandits could leave us, because there were others waiting."

"Exactly," Sofian said. "And while we thought we made it to safety along the river, it was actually another trap they had chased us to."

"A good plan," I said shaking my head. "A perfect plan."

"Almost perfect had the storm not come," Sofian said, pointing across the expanse. "They didn't anticipate the blowing rain and sand that brought confusion and helped mask our escape."

"So what happened to Zafir's men?" I wondered

"The bandits on horses, they chased them to the east. They overtook the camels and then the fighting began. When Zafir saw his men fully engaged and the caravan at risk, he turned to engage them himself."

"He should have kept riding!" I said.

"Well, you know Zafir," he said. "He knows every sword is useful and would choose to lose the treasure than to lose a man."

"Yes, as expected," I said, "the only true asset."

"In that terrific storm, men and beasts were engaged in fierce hand to hand. Swords slashing, that pelting rain, the blowing sand, do you remember it?"

I nodded.

"Men falling, stampeding camels crashing into the bandits' panicked horses, the work of death meted out with every swing of a weapon. I estimated the fighting lasted almost a full hour. Our men and theirs—everyone, we were exhausted toward the end, but it was certainly a do-or-die battle for all of us. I wish I was there to help," Sofian said.

"Me too," I nodded.

"They were on the ground, hand to hand toward the end, all the animals had scattered, and they were in the mud fighting around the fallen bodies of others. Exhaustion came and the strength of Al Murrah brought us a costly but important victory."

"Did we lose many?" I asked.

"Twelve of Moad's men and five Al Murrah, another 30 wounded—a remarkable blessing of God, considering. But of the bandits, we counted more than 200 dead and some 120 wounded, we guessed that was maybe half their numbers. The bandits fled, too frightened to steal our camels."

"But you said Zafir was hurt?"

"We found him lying in the muck. A broken horse was struggling on top of his legs. We pulled him to safety and found his left leg badly damaged, the bone cut through. It held, but there was little we could do. He lost a lot of blood."

"His leg? He lost his leg?"

"Not yet. Humam knows the eastern arts and we carried him here for help. Their doctors cleaned the flesh and positioned the bone. They returned him to whole as best they could, but he is not healing."

I closed my eyes and bowed my head. "Will he continue with the caravan?" I whispered.

"You must remember, Bassam," Sofian said. "Zafir is alive, strong, determined. He is grateful to know you're alive, but this is the end of the journey for him."

"The *end*? What do you mean by that?"

"He commanded it so himself," Sofian said. "He can't ride a camel until he heals, *if* he heals. He has made plans already to travel down river to the sea and take a merchant boat to home."

"What?" I looked up dumbfounded. "Just like that? And it's over?" I couldn't believe what I was hearing. "What of the venture and the treasure and the work?"

"You must speak with him, he will explain it," Sofian said.

I took a moment to gather my wits. A boat trip home, the end of the caravan? What of the great business in Chang'an?

"Then I'll speak with him, and see what can be done," I said, and turned toward the tent.

心爱的 **9** 咱爱小

BATTLE WOUNDS

Lifting back the curtain, a splash of light ballooned inside of Zafir's tent, changing shadow to bright. The old chief was reclined under a blanket on a day bed, leaning on his elbow. He was smiling bright as I walked in, his eyes twinkling in delight.

"Bassam! Bassam! My son!" he exclaimed with joy.

I hurried to the old man and knelt to his side, wrapping my arms about him carefully as he patted my back in loving welcome. "I'm back, Zafir! I'm back!"

"Bassam, my son!" he said. "I am so pleased! I am so glad! We thought we had lost you. But you have returned! You are back! And just look at you—you are much changed, you had a trial! I can see it, you had a trial. Are you all right, my boy?"

"I am," I said. "There is so much to tell you, so much that has happened."

"Indeed it has," he said. "I heard excitement outside and thought I heard your voice. And it is you! You have returned, my son! And your clothes, you are much thinner since last we spoke."

"Many things, hard things, so many—I had to ... I had to do things—things that...."

"It is all right, my boy," he said. "Let us go a step at a time. I expected that some trials would befall you. And so, you endured them. I am so pleased to have you back, son. Come, sit, tell me."

Retrieving a wooden stool, I sat by Zafir's bed and unfolded a story so fantastic that even I had a hard time believing my own words. "I awoke suddenly to a terrible storm, a white-out ...."

It was an hour of private, undisturbed sharing. I told him how I felt someone or something pushing me through the dust storm, knowing not what pursued me or what lay in my path ahead. I told Zafir about my doubts, about my choices, about my quandary over wise or careless, right or wrong, north or south. I told him about my complete dependence on so little but my faith that I was being led by someone or something, and hoped through my darkest hours of despair and fatigue that it would not be my ending. And then to stumble onto a destiny of sorts that I couldn't possibly have imagined.

I told him of my lonesome panic in the dark and the great sorrow of losing Bakra in such a treacherous and needless way, and the miraculous sword fight and the help and training that prepared me for it. I told him about the blue ink on the finger of Habib and his last words of warning and mockery. And then I told him of the unforeseen manna from heaven, the six camels and supplies that stood waiting to save my life and bring me to those I loved. And this because I chose not to abandon my faith and die.

"God blessed you, my son," Zafir said at the end. "He led you where you had to be, and gave you strength to perform his justice."

"I think so," I said. "I hope so. I am not the taker of life."

"He prepares you, Bassam. There is justice in this life and the next. I am proud of you. I know you. I know your questions and your feelings. You acted with dispatch and honor. You are branded with no shame for your actions, but you have learned humility. You are now the student that God wills of you."

The stain of killing still clung to the grip of my sword hand, and would not leave me. I did not know how to remove its guilt and remorse, but talking to Zafir was healing me. "I called on God to spare me," I confessed, "but not to kill."

"You defended moral law, my son," Zafir said. "Remember it well. The labor of justice brings with it a heavy personal toll. Hatred is an ugly emotion that leaves his damage in all of us. But hatred is not what drives justice, my son. It is love, a greater love for all that is good and those who embrace that good. You delivered justice to Habib and the many attackers and bandits."

The old man paused and put his hand on my arm as if peering past the layers of hurt and anguish and disdain that separated me from those terrible acts and the safety of good friends and family.

"Justice, my son, is the end of mercy," he said. "I know this pain, this burden. But when justice must be meted out, you must be willing to carry that for others. It is a duty you owe for the peace of others, do you see it? When you do see it, you will discover that you can carry the cost of justice easier today because of all of your difficult yesterdays."

We both were quiet a moment. My mind was back at the dune, circling my enemy with sword drawn, wondering about the cost of survival, the will to live, the deeds of defense and justice, and my willingness to stand for justice, even at the cost of my own life.

Zafir broke the silence. "You will learn more of this in our next scroll, my young Bassam. But for tonight, will you share your story with the men at the campfire? They certainly want to know what happened to our young Bassam!"

"I'm no giver of speeches," I said. "They are weary of my episodes and foolishness. The caravan has had enough of my travails and the trouble I have caused them."

"Oh no, not at all," he said. "It gives the men courage when justice is served, they feed on stories as yours. It strengthens them for the trials to come. Such witnesses have strengthened you, have they not?"

I nodded.

"That is well enough, then. See here, there's always a feast when Najeeb arrives, it is a good time, a celebrating time with wonderful friends at the fire tonight. After we eat, tell what you learned and experienced. It will do them good, and besides, it will spare you the telling and retelling another 100 times."

I smiled. "I will try my best."

Zafir took my hand and held it. "An instrument for good or an instrument for evil, it is always in the man's heart where the choice is made. You have a good heart, Bassam. You have kept it so. You must keep it so now. Let this comfort your memory, that you were an instrument of good, and never forget it."

Zafir was right. Whatever reason or cause led me to that place and time, I was not the instigator of any evil or wrong. It was justification of the correct kind. It was the return of peace when the trespass remained gaping and begged for resolution, a resolution carried out even by one so young as I. The costs had mounted, and with justice, it was that portion, that chapter, that imbalance to the laws of nature that could at last be rectified, made whole again, balanced as they should be—and many life lessons learned.

I stood to leave.

"Zafir," I said, "there's a tall tale, a lie, that is being passed around that you're finished with this trip. It must be a lie. I laughed at Sofian and Human when they said it. Why would they say such a thing?"

Zafir looked at the ground and a look of pained determination formed across his grizzled face.

"No, Bassam, it is true," he said, pulling back the blanket so I could see his leg. "I'm finished with traveling. It appears my time to rest from these long labors has come at last."

"It can heal, surely it can," I said, gesturing toward his leg as if it was a young sprout that just needed time. "Humam said there's a good chance."

"As much as I disapprove of this setback, I am done," Zafir said. "Look here," and he moved his leg so I could see the heavy bandages and the limp form of his foot covered about with a large towel. "I can't ride a camel like this, and you would need a cart to pull me about."

The flesh of his leg was yellowed—its form was worse. "Humam is cleaning it morning and night," Zafir said, "and he's concerned the slow mending could be undone from the rigors of the trail."

I knew Humam was right. I knew Zafir was right. I just wasn't sure yet if I thought it was right.

"Our enterprise will continue just fine without me," Zafir said. "This isn't the first time something like this has forced a change in our plans. The enterprise is not one man, Bassam. I have Sofian, Ziyad, Rakin, Malik, others. They will continue to our stops and trades, just as we planned. They will probably arrive back home about the same time that I do."

"Home? And how will you make that trip?" I asked. "You can't go it alone."

"That's right," he said. "I can't. That's why I want you to come with me, back to Rekeem. And Fawzi, as our lead sword—Ammar to navigate our way, and me, a one-legged anchor should the boat cast adrift."

"A boat? We're returning by sea?"

"It's the only way," he said.

I sat up shaking my head. "If it must be, and you order me so, I will help take you back to Rekeem. I will do my best."

"It's not the end of anything, Bassam," Zafir said smiling. "We will plan the next adventure and you will lead it without me ...."

"Oh no, I could never do that," I protested.

"Yes you will, or I will have wasted my time teaching you the scrolls. We have one more scroll to read and then you are ready to lead this great enterprise yourself," Zafir said.

"I couldn't know what to do, I don't know the routes and ..."

"And you will learn them, with the help of my faithful friends who are now your friends as well—you will learn them well enough soon enough."

Zafir groaned as he sat up. He labored to swing his legs around to the ground and tried to hide a painful grimace, but I saw it on his face. "If you'll get me that walking stick, let's go greet Najeeb."

"Can you walk?"

"Not without my stick—or a good shoulder. Humam has me walking as much as I can. 'Keep the blood moving,' he said. And so, I do my best."

I helped Zafir to his feet and held him until he was steady.

We stepped into the bright of day, and there stood Najeeb in conversation with others.

"Ah, my friend!" Zafir called out upon seeing him. "You old desert fox, you made it! We've been waiting, you're late, but it was a lateness worth waiting for. I am so glad to see you!"

The men embraced like brothers.

"I see that you carry a battle wound, my old friend," Najeeb said. "Will it heal?"

"Ah, yes, I am in good hands," Zafir said, "but look at this, this is how far I must go to get a leg up on you, old friend."

They laughed like old times.

"Sofian, spread the word," Zafir said. "Our feast tonight must be an extra special one. We welcome Najeeb and his men, and we welcome home Bassam. Build a large fire. Let's eat well and hear strong stories of faith and courage. Spread the word."

心爱的 **10** 的爱小

SUOUD'S NO MORE

Dusk came quickly and the men gathered in clusters of exchange and discussion. The large fire burned hot, casting yellow warmth across the faces of some 700 travel-weary traders. With the addition of Najeeb's company our numbers were large. We had become a regular army of friendly swords—now clustered together on mats or logs or blankets in a large, tight circle surrounding the fire. Watching the flames licking at the fading deep blue was mesmerizing—ideal for the telling of tales both true and imagined.

Zafir seated me at the front next to Najeeb. I had not found a free moment to finish my meal with so many dozens of well-wishers stopping by to speak, and was still chewing rice and meat when the call to order came. Fawzi finally stepped in to guard for me so I could at least chew and get some nourishment. "Let him alone, you dung droppings of sick camels," he commanded. "Get away you fermented goat guts, you'll starve him to bones with your empty chatter—get away, you *bedawi*."

With the last stragglers finding a place, Sofian raised a hand for silence, called our meeting to order, and invited Zafir to the forefront.

Upon seeing the old man hobbling, Humam took alarm. "Zafir! This cold air, this excitement—no," he said shaking his head. "Not good, I'm telling you, not good."

Zafir looked back at him and frowned. "Let me talk to my men, Humam, this little bit can't hurt," he said. "I'll be finished in no time—you said walk, I'm walking! And then I will get off my feet, I promise."

Kalila sat on the other side of her uncle, watching me gulp down the last of my meal.

"As you know," Zafir began, "we have great reason to celebrate together this night. We have as our honored guests and wonderful friends, Najeeb and his men, and his niece Kalila, safely here for our joint trek to Chang'an. Welcome old friend," he said, turning, "and welcome to all your associates. You will always have our swords, our brotherhood, and a place at our rice tables."

All the men clapped their approval.

"Some of you are asking, so let me tell you at the start. My injury, you are all aware, is not progressing toward healing as expected. Humam advises, and I agree, it is best I bow out at this point and see all of you back in Rekeem in five or six months."

A grumble of disappointment spread among those seated.

"I am leaving the care of our enterprise in the capable hands of Ziyad as head, Sofian, and my other captains of 100. Modu has agreed to remain with his men as escort to Chang'an, and I fully expect an excellent report, brilliant trading arrangements, and an enormous profit for Abdali-ud-Din. I may need it sooner than later," he said as he glanced toward me. "I fully expect I may have to afford a dowry or two when I get home, you never know what happens to daughters when their favorite beau is out of sight for two years."

There was laughter and clapping and it seemed everyone was looking at me. I blushed. Kalila leaned forward to look across at me, but I didn't dare look back at her, and kept chewing although my bowl was empty and there was no more food in my mouth.

"We are also pleased to have one back with us. One dear to me who we thought certainly had fallen somewhere between here and a faraway place. But God has heard our pleadings and has returned him to us with tales to tell. Bassam? Could you come join me here for a moment?"

The men all clapped and cheered. Fawzi shouted "Don't bore us like last time, camel breath"—it was like old times. I joined Zafir at the head and he put his arm around my waist and held tight for support.

"Bassam," Zafir continued, "could you please take a moment and share some of what you were telling me, the adventures you experienced for these many weeks past?"

With that, Zafir patted me on the shoulder and returned to his place. I waited while he arranged himself to lay down and, brushing away the help of others, he propped his leg on some pillows and got comfortable beneath a blanket. He glared at Humam who frowned back. With everything finally settled, and I was left all alone in front of 700 men.

I looked around a few moments before speaking. Almost every face was familiar, some more than others. Each man gazed at me warmly, with encouragement in his eyes, smiles of admiration, friendship, genuine affection. I felt among family, among my dearest friends in the world. Oh, how I had missed that warm embrace of human contact, human love and even Fawzi's relentless teasing during the past weeks. Such a contrast to the black evil shadows of darkness and hate that I saw in the eyes of Kahn and Habib.

At first, no words would come and there was only the sound of the crackling fire speaking its hiss and pop into the cooling quiet. As my silence grew awkward, a few of them started clapping, others calling out encouragement, others thumping their feet. They knew I felt embarrassed and anxious, and they also knew that I hurt. They knew my feelings and wanted me to know I was back among friends.

I acknowledged their support and they became silent. My emotions lay just under the surface as I gathered together my thoughts.

"I don't know what to ... um ... Thank you, my friends, my wonderful friends ... Thank you, Zafir. I suppose this robs me of the chance to exaggerate the details of my story because tonight you'll all hear the first version without me having a chance to craft it into something truly fantastic!"

The men laughed with growing empathy. I could read in their eyes that they were surprised if not shocked to see firsthand that the vibrant, healthy Bassam who had left them more than a month earlier was now a thinned, weathered survivor. I could see in their faces that they sensed from the tone of my voice, the way I stood, my choice of words, my wearied face—that I had endured something terrible, something unspeakable, something many of them knew from firsthand experience. For that brotherhood of experiences, they nodded softly toward me— genuine, honest, wanting to lift it from me but understanding at the same time the wisdom of allowing these, the means of building boys to men, to unfold in due course.

"I am nothing that God should notice me," I began, "but you must know that for reasons I don't understand, God protected me those many weeks in the desert in a way that I will never be able to express or repay or explain. I've never been happier than to be here among my friends, with you this night."

The words suddenly choked in my throat and I had to pause. Dancing past my memory were desert images of evil incarnate, images that already found a way into my idle waking hours and my restless churning at night to haunt me for my choices. But to see, contrasted to *that*, these friendly faces of good people who smiled with warmth was nearly too much to absorb and express back, to convey my profound sense of appreciation and love. May an inexperienced young warrior love his companions as this, as brothers and fathers?

"For the goodness of friends who cared enough about me, I was provided with the right tools to flee the dangers that followed us from Yanqi. Pursuing a blind path that in some mysterious fashion was laid out for me, I hurried through a blinding sandstorm so severe I could not discern at what part of the sky the sun shone. At night it was the same, no stars or moon to guide, but complete and total blindness. And upon awaking, I found the world about me was walled in with the same, and only a dim light diffused through the brown blowing haze in such a way I could discern no direction to travel. And so was I led by powers and passions unseen, and into a place where cowards go to run, a desolation of dunes with not a living green thing to be seen. After many days with no water or food remaining for my care, I came to the end of my despair and the start of my ending—"

I spoke for three quarters of an hour, sharing what details I could recall, the run, the hiding, the chase, the cold, the deprivation, my Bakra. At last I came to the end of my telling.

"I left the bodies of Kahn and Habib there, to the elements, to the sand and to legend, caring not for their memory among men, or my own. I have cut them loose in my heart, though they sometimes shout at me in my dreams. I take comfort, though, that they lie there still, in an unmarked pit among the dunes, probably blown over into forgetfulness by now. It was a proper ending for those doers of evil who were bent on doing so wickedly against so many of us. For their families, my heart aches. But better for this life that they are gone. And for me, I am deeply moved to see that in their dispatch, at the end of that labor in the desert dunes, an important work was finished. Suoud's sword that had laid restless could come to its rightful ending place to complete his last and most important work that had yet to be done. To execute with justice the unrighteousness of a year ago. It completed its work among the lost dunes of the Taklamakan. To that I am witness."

Not a man stirred, all eyes were on me.

"I have something that is good news," I said. "I've not yet told *you*, Zafir, but it is some good news—for me, anyway."

Reaching down I picked up a sheathed sword I had brought and held it up for all to see. Not saying anything I tied it to my belt in the usual place.

"This is the sword of Suoud," I said, placing my hand on the handle. "I keep it with me always, with Zafir's permission. It never leaves my side. I didn't know Suoud well before he died, but I knew him enough to trust him as a friend. Zafir has kindly allowed me to carry his sword—Suoud's sword, that has the honor of his many years of valiant service. And a short while ago, it served him again this one last time, in justice. I keep it sharp, as Al Murrah would expect me to."

I bent down and picked up another sword and held it high.

"Here is another sword of Al Murrah. It belonged to Habib, a man I am told many of you knew. When I was kidnapped many months ago, the killer Moluck was assisted by our Habib in a deed of treachery. They were conspirators in the crime to murder Suoud, and to take me for ransom. But you should know that during that ordeal, during the long march across the desert as their prisoner, Habib kept me safe from Moluck, and for that I do owe him. But it was this same Habib and Kahn, two wicked men, who plotted the great attack at Yanqi that cost so much blood and suffering. For whatever reasons, and I still don't understand them, I found myself wandering into the Taklamakan. I did not plan that, but it happened. I was lost. I couldn't see my directions. I headed south, and some tell me I crossed over a river. But I crossed over no such river. And without sun or stars as a guide, I stumbled along, two days in a blinding storm, me and my Bakra—"

The words tightened in my throat again. *This is too fantastic*, I thought. *What did God have me do, or was* He *the benign observer, wondering just what* I *would do?*

"I struggled through the sandstorm, wishing I still had Humam's goat fat, or any fat! Must it be goat, Humam?" Humam smiled and shrugged, and the men politely laughed.

"I made no plan for anything except to run away from danger, you must know that. It just happened and turned out that way. But one night, when I was out of food, out of water, and certain I was a dead man within a day, maybe two, I saw as I laid down to rest, there, on the distant dunes, the light of the fire of Habib and Kahn far from my camp. I went immediately and spied on them. They found my trail the next day and came to kill me. Suoud's sword kept his honor in the work it did that day. First it found Kahn, breaking his sword to get at him, and he died. And second, it found Habib, who betrayed his weakness by his footsteps during our standoff. I told him before he died in whose name I finished the work of Suoud. All that he could say to me was that there is no honor, no honor in the service of Zafir, no honor in the death of his fathers. I told him that the only honor he needed to secure was Zafir's, and his only duty was to be worthy of that trust. I told him he had failed in that because of his greed, and that he had no integrity or trust."

The memory of it brought so many discouraging moments back to my recollection. The desperation, emptiness of hope, the death of faith. I had not forgotten God, but I was also ready to die. I hung my head and wiped my eyes with my sleeve.

"And Suoud's sword was both mercy and justice that day in the desert—mercy and justice at the throat of Habib."

I walked to Zafir and offered him Habib's sword. "Zafir, this is yours. I return to you the sword of Habib that I took from him just a few weeks ago. He will not need it again. This belongs to you."

Zafir took the sword and pulled it partway from the sheath, and turned it to read by firelight the names inscribed beneath the hilt. He pushed it back again and closed his eyes, shaking his head slowly. And then reaching out to me for help, he struggled to his feet and turned to the men to speak.

"I have exposed this boy, the only heir of my most faithful friend, to dangers that most men during their natural lives won't ever experience. In each instance his judgment has been balanced, honest, and correct in those terrible situations he was compelled to engage. Bassam, do you remember what I told you about the sword of Suoud?"

I bowed my head in thought. "Yes, I remember the words exactly. You said that when a man takes up a warrior's sword he takes up the responsibility of that man—his honor, and the responsibility for others, to retain its honor with strength and mercy."

"And what did I say about using it to take the life of another?"

"You said I must know when death is certain or life just the same, that I must be able to decide."

"Bassam is correct, my men. That is what I told him. Your swords are emblems of honor, the mace of justice in the hands of the loyal guard of Abdali-ud-Din."

Zafir turned to me and putting one arm on my shoulder to steady himself, he reached down to my belt and pulled the sword of Suoud from its sheath. He held it up high, pointed to the heavens like a torch reflecting the fire in glimmering shafts of yellow and silver, flashing across the faces of those assembled.

"Men of Al Murrah, after the order of Abdali-ud-Din, I present to you Bassam, son of the desert, survivor of the evil designs of formidable enemies, a student of the arts of navigation, swordsmanship, the bow, living by one's wits alone, who bested the strategy of more seasoned assailants, who endured the great Taklamakan alone, a student of all things good, penitent, and humble before God. I present to you not a boy but a man, whom I judge to have earned the right to bear this sword no longer as the sword of Suoud, but as the sword of Bassam— *Bassam ibn-Kateb*. If you agree, please stand to honor Bassam, a valiant new warrior of Al Murrah, and a true son of Abdali-ud-Din."

And with that, the group rose to their feet clapping their hands, shouting my name, and smiling one to another. Fawzi elbowed the man next to him and shouted, "I taught him all of that!"

Kalila remained seated—proper and dignified, smiling with bright eyes for the honor this clumsy boy had earned in the heated battle of a winter desert.

"This sword is yours, Bassam," Zafir said as the men again seated themselves. I stood awkwardly, embarrassed by all the attention. "You have earned it in battles that few of my best warriors could have judged as well as you. I have great affection for you, my boy, your father is proud of you. Please, take this sword and have the engraver place your name below the others. It is no longer the sword of Suoud. From today forward, it is known and always known as the sword of the avenger of Suoud, the sword of the lone conqueror of the wicked ordeal of the dreaded Taklamakan. It *is* the sword of Bassam."

心爱的 **11** 的爱心

CHANGING GUARD

The next morning was spent reengaging with friends and survivors, exchanging stories, and piecing together the events of the past month. At midday, I finally caught up with Ziyad with a hundred queries about how the company would continue forward without Zafir. He must have stayed up too late as he was short with his answers. He kept shooting an impatient glare at my non-stop questions.

"What do you mean 'new elder'?" Ziyad asked. "I'm not the 'new elder' for the rest of this journey. Zafir tells his Captains of 100 all that he knows. I am a captain of 100, I will simply fill in for the duration of the excursion while you take Zafir home, and I will help bring the men and the treasure back to Rekeem, as planned. There is nothing new here."

"But who will trade? Who does the bargaining?" I asked.

"Oh my boy, you insult me! Who do you think trained Zafir?"

"No! *You?* I don't believe it."

"Believe it you should," Ziyad said. "Don't think we Abdali-ud-Din are so foolish as to pretend that any one of us is indispensable, my young friend. No, we have many men trained in the ways of the caravan lest any drop out along the way. Zafir was my student years and years ago, and he is a better trader than me. It is now I who learns at the feet of him. He is missed but not forgotten."

"Does this problem come often?" I wondered.

"No, not often. Even so, Zafir is the greatest among the traders, it is his gift. He is known east to west, north to south. All men know the man Zafir, his kindness and fairness, his wisdom in the trades. Yes, he is missed by us, but not at the table of negotiation."

"It seems to me he would be missed there too. Isn't he the master of completing a deal with the buyer thinking he has bested Zafir?"

"And that, my naive friend, is exactly why he is so revered. Men know they are dealing with the master trader, but Zafir understands the many values of the coin. That is why we will miss his wisdom and friendship. But as to the value of gold—well, gold wears the same on all men."

I knitted my eyebrows in thought. Something suddenly caught my attention. "What do you mean about Zafir knowing the *many* values of a coin?"

"Really? Do you really want me to explain it now, here, with a thousand things for me to do?"

I stood there unflinching.

"All right, all right, the short version—*really short*. It's actually simple for those who take the time to understand it," Ziyad said. "A silver or a gold is really of no more value than what men make of it. And they make of it many different things in different lands."

"Yes, so we have talked."

"Then he has told you it is as simple as this—" Ziyad said, holding up a skin partly filled with water. "How many silvers is this worth to you?"

"An eighth, maybe less."

"But two weeks ago, when you were in the desert?"

I smiled. "*All* of my gold."

"Yes, a treasure spent to save a life is a treasure well spent."

"Yes, well spent."

"Zafir is a master of the value," Ziyad said. "He knows the value of the goods he brings in the different lands where we trade. He knows when to ask for top value in a trade, or expect less. Most other men do not. They are too fixated on the value they themselves put in the coins, and this is an error. Zafir lets the greed grow in men's hearts—and like those in need of a skin of water in the desert, they will pay high prices. The trick is knowing in what part of the world a skin of water is worth its weight in gold."

"So he lets the buyer set the value?"

"They set the value."

"And if it is not enough?"

"No, you misunderstand the principle, Bassam," Ziyad said. "Zafir lets them set the value and he negotiates the trade. The buyer bargains as best he can, offering less than what he values it for, hoping to get it cheap. But given enough temptation, he will pay more than it is worth in Zafir's estimation. In the end, a wise seller will let the buyer pay what he thinks it is worth."

"What is so clever about that? Don't all buyers want this? I don't understand."

"In one place our frankincense will fetch its weight in silver. In another place, its weight in gold."

"So, Zafir sells only where it is worth its weight in gold?"

"No, don't focus on just the coins. No, Zafir still trades in lands where the frankincense sells for its weight in silver, he simply offers smaller tears. They pay their silvers and Zafir adds them up to gold. In the end, it comes out the same."

"Do the buyers know it is the same rate?"

"I suspect some of them do. It is a matter of honor, to buy from the great Zafir for less than a going rate. Zafir is good with such trades, asking at first for their gold, surrendering for their silver, but at the same time, charging the same rate. Each goes away with what he wants and does not feel cheated."

"It seems a great waste to me," I said. "Why not just pay the gold and be done with it? It's a child's game to divide up a gold's worth just to hand over a gold's worth in *silver* coins."

"And that is how Zafir allows men's greed to spend itself. Many silvers seem easier to spend than a few golds. They put down a few for a few. And then the greed begins to work on them. They put down a few more, and more, and before they know it, they've put down the same as a gold. The only difference is the color of the coins."

I shook my head. "It still seems a silly game to me."

"When you stop looking at the coins and see the trade, then you will see the wisdom."

"And you—*you* Ziyad, will become that man in Zafir's stead?"

"Certainly."

"Then I suppose the train is in good hands. And the Hindus had better hang tight to their silvers."

"They trade in gold, Bassam—pure gold. And we will bring it with us, bags of it, when we see you in back in Rekeem."

心爱的 **12** 𠯘𢙢小

THE RIVER BOAT

Leaving the caravan in good hands wasn't as complicated as I had anticipated. In a quiet moment I thought it through more carefully, and it started to make good sense—here go many dozens of my greatest friends to carry the trade east to Chang'an, and then to the routes south, before heading home again. I could not join them but the plan was good. They would trade along the way, magnifying Zafir's treasure with each stop, and leave behind business contacts and stewards from whom an accounting is had at the next visit.

As for the men of Xiongnu, they had performed their duties and had delivered the expedition safely through the Jade Gate and into these southern lands. It was agreed to release them from their oath early even though Modu had promised protection all the way to Chang'an.

Zafir paid them in gold and arranged for the next rendezvous some two years hence. For now, they planned to remain longer to usher the caravan beyond the towers of the Great Wall east before returning to their homelands.

Without saying it, Zafir bid his good friend a goodbye while hoping inside that some of Modu's men would remain as escort—*all* Modu's men. And without saying it, Modu intended to do exactly that. He planned to remain as escort all along the way to Chang'an. It is what friends do.

"I will meet your train at Mouru, two years and the same day as before," Modu said as he clasped Zafir's hand in final goodbye. "Who will you send?"

Zafir gestured directly to me. "He will lead it, look for my young steward Bassam."

"You have given him the scrolls?"

"All but the last, my friend," Zafir said.

"The last? Then he is not yet ready," Modu replied.

"But soon," Zafir said. "He will be, soon enough."

The morning was bright blue, a glowing sun climbed slowly into the sky sending his warmth to those who stood at the river.

The river boat waited impatiently for the men to finish their farewells. The crew loaded wares below deck while Ammar talked to the river guide to estimate the added time delay from buying passage aboard a merchant boat. "More stops, lower ride in the water," he said. Zafir just nodded as though he didn't need to be told something he knew already.

I watched the men of Xiongnu and Al Murrah at their parting. Each man knew the dangers that were held mysteriously in the hands of time, and the unpredictable nature of fate. Some faces they would never see again, and every man knew it. With each hand extended and each farewell granted, they wondered without speaking it—might it be *you*, or might it be *me*?

The trials of the journey had brought them close to each other. They had become more than hirelings and more than friends. They were brothers.

Modu saluted me.

"You can count on loyal service from the swords of my men in two years when your caravan once again travels east," Modu said.

I thanked him and assured him we would rendezvous as anticipated.

Tou came next, standing before me and smiling. This time he did not look down at me, but across—as friend to friend—peers, and extended his hand in full fellowship.

"I am honored to know you, Bassam. May God protect and preserve you until next we meet. I will bring my best swords for you."

"Thank you Tou, thank you for teaching me the ways of your fathers. I'll never forget you. May God watch your step and give strength to your arm in all things."

Tou tipped his head in a polite salute and pulled from behind him his bow, handing it directly to me as a gift.

"Your father's bow?" I asked, my eyes widening in surprise.

"It will protect you my friend," he said. "Your sword will serve you first, it is best, but when the time comes, let the bow take his turn. It is a gift from our people to yours, from my father to yours, from me to you."

I took it carefully and gently stroked the fine workmanship of the polished wood and layered bone. It pulled heavy and firm.

"And this quiver of twelve arrows, one each for the number of children I expect you to bring to this world, and to teach the ways of the caravans, and with whom we will create friendships during the years ahead. I'll look forward to meeting them each."

"Twelve?" I stuttered in exasperation. "You are more hopeful than I, Tou! But I'll use these to serve the cause of peace—in your name. It will serve the cause of justice, my friend. Safe journey until then."

The little dock seemed to strain as the men of Modu and the men of Zafir crowded together for our send-off. With our supplies finally loaded and our small bags accounted for, we were ready to go.

Zafir stood on the dock, fondness for his men warming his countenance.

"You, the faithful of the Abdali-ud-Din," he said, "I leave you in the able care of my captains of 100. Ziyad will stand in my stead where there is a need—he is the first of my captains. Follow and support him. Your journeys will take you to Chang'an and then south past the great mountains. I am pained that I cannot be with you, but the trade will prove profitable. Safe travel to you all, God-speed in your journeys, and may His benevolent hand guide you in peace, in dispatch, and in safety."

And with that, he turned to the boat, hobbling across the plank with his walking stick. Two Al Murrah warriors helped him on board. He limped to the bamboo canopy spanning the width of the boat where he found shadow, a pillow, and rest. He laid down with his leg propped on a box and smiled bravely back to the others, giving them a friendly salute of farewell.

Ammar followed, taking a place aft, near the boat captain, to study the direction and to chart their progress. Fawzi boarded near the bow, taking hold an overhead rope that lashed the fore-mast sturdy. He scanned the waters, keeping ready for dangers. The other men of the boat stood, waiting for me because I had one last goodbye. Najeeb politely stepped back. He knew his young Kalila was hurting.

"The months and the years are easily numbered," I said to her. "Modu was wrong. It's not two years. It's one year and ten until we are back in your Mouru."

"A year and ten."

"And it will go by like that shooting star we saw the other night."

"I won't forget that shooting star," she said.

"Nor I," I smiled.

"And you are coming back?"

"Oh yes, it's my work and my greatest wish. I'll return. And find you and your warrior, I look forward to meeting him."

"All right then, sleepyhead," Kalila said. "You must take this," and she handed me a small tied cloth. "Don't open it until you can no longer see us, and then you may open it."

I closed my hand around the small gift.

"I'll be back to Rekeem in a few months' time. I'll recover from this journey, discover my place with Zafir, learn more about trading and prepare to come again. I'll see you then."

"Or the next year," she said "It's the way of Abdali-ud-Din."

"Yes, but I can ..."

She shushed me. "I know them better than you, Bassam. You must be patient. And should your journey bring you to our diner again for a meal, I'll be there, waiting with one of mother's wonderful recipes, as you found me before."

Waving a warm final goodbye to my friends, to Kalila, Najeeb, and so many smiling faces, I climbed onto the boat and found a place to sit by Fawzi.

Sofian untied the last rope. With six men leaning into the boat's side, they gave it a hard push and it slowly drifted out toward the current.

"I expect to see you in Rekeem in six months," Sofian called as the oarsmen pulled against the water. "Bassam, you take good care of that old man, he thinks he's still in charge."

I smiled and waved. The oarsmen found the power of the rush and pulled us toward the swifter waters. They wouldn't deploy the mainsail yet, the swift waters that flowed so quickly would do more work than could the wind.

Fawzi and I watched our smiling friends crowded on shore waving goodbye. Except Kalila. She just watched, not looking away, her hands folded in front of her.

"How long on this river?" I asked.

"Four weeks," Fawzi said.

Neither of us spoke as the vision of our many hundreds of well-wishers became too small and distant to discern—and finally fell from view in the gray horizon of the hurried river.

By early afternoon, the image of Najeeb and Kalila still clung to my mind, their smiles unchanging, and hope forever painted in their eyes.

Zafir had fallen asleep and Ammar was busy with his charts. Fawzi watched the horizon ahead and was trying to communicate with a man who didn't speak the language. I settled comfortably against the railing, accustomed, finally, to the swaying of the boat in the currents. Ahead of us I watched new vistas open, like lifting the lid on a treasure box with every turn through the channel, new sights, new smells, new harbors and villages. The river banks to either side were flat with distant brown hills rising above, some green shrubs were visible but they were mostly barren. The sky above quickly grew overcast but remained calm, and the air was cold.

And then I remembered.

Reaching into my pocket I produced Kalila's gift and untied the small threads that held the little cloth folded. Opening the corners with deliberate care, I turned it around to read the beautiful embroidery in red silk thread. I smiled at the familiar words that once again were prayed in proxy for my well-being: "Be safe and well. Peace. Joy. Courage. And remember me." It was thoughtful, and left confusion in my heart until I reached for the other, the small veil that showed so much more wear and handling, but it was the one I treasured. As the boat hurried downstream, my heart was venturing far, far to the west.

"Day 374—Dear Rasha, Today we begin our river trip to come home. Your father's leg is suffering. We will find a place down river where those who are expert in medicines will try to help. The river is much faster than

land, and the sea much faster than our river, but between the two there is a large distance to cross. It will still take us many months to travel it. — Bassam"

心爱的 **13** 咱爱小

DOWN RIVER

Our river boat was unlike any I had seen. There was no keel or beam beneath to protect against rocks or collision. The nose swept up to a blunt square, the slats of the decking and the outer planking were polished smooth and varnished with a glossy wax of something mysterious. Water beaded up on its surface to add buoyancy, and wiped off just as easy. There was nothing like this in the west.

The gray current carried us easily, steering us down the middle of the river with hardly a movement from the oarsman who guided with deftness and skill. The water splashed at a few of the turns where rapids churned white, but it was a steady ride all the way.

There were three masts, a mainstay in the middle with a smaller lateen to the front, a square to the back held taut by lines. The canvases now deployed were ribbed with long staves, and roped to small, metal pulleys tied to the decking. A little jib gave alignment to the opposing currents from the wind and water.

When the water smoothed to calm, I took a short walk around the deck, checking the hold, observing the strain of the shrouds against the masts. I noted the creative construction of the sails and the pulley systems that kept everything tight against the wind.

"This boat sits heavy, Zafir," I observed.

"And that explains the smooth ride," he said.

"It looks to me like such boats could move a great deal more than our camels could."

"Yes, they could, they have for a thousand years," he said. "The maritime trade is a lot older than our caravans. Small dhows were plying the large rivers for ages before we came along."

"So tell me something, why continue overland? Is not this the better way?"

"Yes and no. There are limitations," Zafir said. "They can't sail through shallow rivers or into the desert sands. And the quantity—we can carry many boatloads of some products in a long line of camels, and deliver an entire shipment. Lose one camel, maybe ten, and it is no great loss that we can't recover from. But lose one boat and it sets a man back a lifetime."

"Then more boats with smaller loads?" I asked.

"Make them small enough and you're back to a camel," Zafir said. "They've been working at this for a long time. When the harbors and trade arrangements are safer, it is more profitable. And they'll put our long camel treks out of business, giving their business to the shorter runs. I believe that day is coming."

"Have you ever considered navigating your trade instead of carrying it overland?"

"Not me. But you should, Bassam. The sea routes are tried and true, and the risks are well known. If your enterprise can make a sea-going circuit without incident, the profits are enormous. A year's profit in a single voyage—think of it."

A light drizzle had accompanied our journey, and after several hours the sun finally broke through the gray. We felt the cold of the morning melt away, and toward the afternoon temperatures more tolerable gave us a brief respite. And then the sun began to sink from the sky, returning a chill to the air.

The oarsmen said something about a village on the river banks some distance beyond, and wouldn't stop until we arrived there at day's end. As the sun made his nightly descent into the western horizon, the men slowed the boat and directed us towards torches lighting a long dock. We pulled alongside, cast ropes, and secured to some old posts.

It felt good to be back on solid ground, and the four of us linked arms and staggered to an inn. Between keeping Zafir off his leg and getting our own land legs back beneath us, people who saw us probably thought we had started our drinking too early that evening.

The captain was kind enough to translate the fees for a stay plus meals before leaving us for some friends he had in the village. We found a nearby diner and sat to eat around a small wooden table. We broke bread over bowls of mee pok, chicken, and vegetables with a curried gravy.

"We have sat at many such tables on this journey," Fawzi said.

"But none like this," Ammar replied. "This place—so peaceful, quaint. Here a man could enjoy the quiet life. Step out back to fish for food, a clean river to wash and drink ..."

"And die in the ambush," Zafir said with a twinkle. "You can have your serenity—I'll forever be restless in one place. You're all too young to think of retirement. And look at the opposites—you could rest, I could not, I am old, you are not, your life is long in front of you, mine is long behind me, our paths demand the opposite of us."

"Zafir, tell me about the boat trip home," I asked. "How long will such a trip take us?"

"Several months," Zafir said. "And it's good we are not in the stormy season."

"Have you ever made that trip?"

"Not from this far west. I've taken their rivers before, but always closer to the ocean. This river takes us on a long detour before joining others, and then the Huang He."

"And that is ...?" I asked.

"A large river," Zafir said. "The land is drained by many rivers that drain the high plateaus. This is the Danghi[1] Its mouth is near Dunhuang and it points us toward Chang'an. It should take us ten days or two weeks, and then the tributaries take us to Huang He. After that, it's a long sail to the open sea at Zhigu."

I shook my head and covered my ears. "Sorry, Zafir. Too many new names. Where is Zhigu?" I asked.

Fawzi looked over at me with a big laugh. "Bassam, don't try to quiz Zafir—he speaks the language, he knows the land, and they're all his friends. Just listen, and when we get there, I'll let you know."

Zafir laughed and slapped his leg, suddenly groaning. "Ooooh," he said, forgetting the wound was still tender. "Zhigu is a large trading center on the coast," he said through clenched teeth while rubbing the pain away. "We'll need to change there to a larger boat. The oceans are much rougher than these rivers. I imagine they'll take us to the trading villages all down the coast. Learn their names, Bassam, you may one day employ stewards there: Ye, P'anyu, Kirti-nagara, the others, all the way to the straits of Kantoli. I've been to these places in the past—good people, good trading stops. After that, it's an open-sea voyage west, with stops along the way."

"Are these recent trips or when you were with your father?" I asked.

"Five times if you count the trip my father took me on when I was a young boy."

"Five times? That's a lot of long camel trips to get all the way out here," I said.

"I've never started down the rivers from this far away," he said. "But from Chang'an to the sea, yes, five times."

"So, how long to sail home?" I asked.

"Probably five months, maybe more. My return trips were always by land. I imagine by sea it takes about the same time because we must travel so far south, and then the stops along the coasts."

"*Five?*" I gasped.

And that's when Fawzi leaned in close and stabbed his finger onto my chest. "Get used to it, fin face," he said. "There's a lot about Zafir that you don't know."

心爱的 **14** 帕爱小

SHEN NUNG

Our boatmen would not let us sleep on the river. By sundown each day we pulled off to a new village, a new town, a new trading center. It was an intimate tour of a magnificent land.

The closer we sailed to the larger cities, the more intense became the poverty. We floated past dozens of small, coastal villages sharing common farmlands without much of a market to profit by. And those who worked the rivers ate as much of their catch as they could sell. At least they had *something* to eat, if daily fish was to their liking.

The natives welcomed us warmly each evening. This was a pleasant change from the badgering of the desert villages. At first I thought this attention was simply their unique way of lusting for our coins. But after the first week I learned it was in the nature of the C'ina people to be kind, to offer their goods and to welcome strangers to their part of the world.

According to our maps we were only a few days out of Lanzhou. That's when I noticed a distinct change in the density of population and dwellings. The prosperity didn't seem to improve with the increase in people, but their shacks were tighter together, and the crowding was more concentrated. I couldn't guess how many people lived in these places—tens of thousands? More?

It was the 16th day on the river and I found Fawzi at the front of the boat.

"What do you know about this man who we are supposed to meet, this Shen Nung?" I asked.

"Not a lot," Fawzi said. "He's a friend of Humam's, some kind of healer."

"And he has some magic cure for battle wounds?"

"I suppose," Fawzi said. "Humam said he's good with the needles and we should let him work on Zafir before we go farther."

The needles—I had heard of them. Some secret technique that only this people understood, some mystery to work with the body itself to cure whatever problem might be afflicting it.

Since leaving Dunhuang we did not see Zafir's injury improve. But neither did it get worse. Humam and Ammar had talked at length about what to look for should the wound show signs—redness, whiteness, seepage, bleeding, growing tenderness, growing numbness. And should any of these become severe, only removing the leg could spare Zafir from a certain and painful death.

On the 18th day, we arrived at Lanzhou. It was a large and busy city with many boats clogging its harbors.

"It was the gold," Zafir said.

"Around here?" I asked. "Why then do I see so much poverty?"

"It was the discovery of gold that built the city," he said. "At one time they even called it the Golden City."

"They must have run out," I guessed.

Fawzi rolled his eyes and shook his head. "Oh bait breath," he said, turning away in a huff.

Zafir smiled and reached out for a hand to stand. "Its gold ores were well exhausted long ago, but the local economy was what created this problem," he said. "We can discuss it more, but just remember that where great wealth is to be had, there arises as if by magic a great population of needful people. The leaders could have handled it better but tried instead to take from everyone a tax to support the impoverished. This encouraged more desperate people to move in for the handout, and discouraged the poor from working for their own bread. It creates an attitude of 'why work when it's free?' Why work when a sad countenance while begging can win a day's supply? It's an old story that plays out here for you to see, and that's why the many shacks, the street people, the great pain."

The crew tied off the boat to a large and ancient-looking dock, and we excused our way through the harbor crowds. Ammar waved a couple of carts into service, both pulled by men.

"Humam told me that Shen Nung lived just beyond the foothills, to go to the foothills," Ammar said. "That must be over there, through the village," he said pointing.

"It shouldn't be far," Zafir said, peering off into the crowded market center. "These foothills, they must be hidden away in their forests. Let's ask in the market."

I could tell Zafir was more at home than the rest of us in this strange place. He didn't hesitate to approach an elderly man selling fruits to request some directions. An exchange of gestures and rough pronunciation of Shen Nung's name led to hand-waving and more pointing. Zafir had the man tell the directions to our runners, and we were off.

"I guess they know him," I said.

"I think so," Ammar said. "That's a pretty good reputation to have if all you need to do is ask any man at random to get directions."

The men pulled our carts through the village center, cursing others out of our path, until we had passed the hazards of road traffic and trade, to finally escape beyond into the quieter part of the village. Soon they had pulled us up gently rising slopes into the rural neighborhoods that hugged the tree-shaded hillsides beyond.

As the din and ruckus of the trading fell quiet behind us, we soon found ourselves traveling down a level, tree-lined path. I could see that a different sort of person lived in this part of Lanzhou. The homes and estates showed a prosperity unlike most of what we saw everywhere else. I guessed these were the earliest settlers, or their descendants, living off the wealth that once gave the city its name.

We passed single-level mud-brick homes with spacious and well-tended gardens. Running brooks were diverted to create ponds near the houses, and birds flew to and from, a beautiful setting.

"Look at all of this lush greenery," I said. "And trees shading grasses and places where people just lounge and watch us go by. They must be rich."

"Remember," Fawzi said, catching me looking with too much interest. "A house is only a grave for the living."

"But what a pleasant grave," I said in return. "I could endure such a grave for forty or fifty years."

Our runners stopped in front of a modest, simple house of many windows, surrounded with tall gardens and flowering trees. The men motioned to us that this was the home of Shen Nung.

It was a long pull for our runners, and Zafir rewarded them nicely for the work.

"I'll check that it's safe," Fawzi said. He stepped out of the cart and felt about for his knife strapped beneath his shirt. The front door was wide and painted red. He approached it and looked back before knocking. "There's gold leaf decorations on this door!" he said in a hushed voice. "I wonder what's on the *floor*?"

He was just about to raise his hand to knock when an elderly woman opened the door. Fawzi was startled but lowered his hand and gestured a greeting. She smiled as if she had greeted strangers in this fashion a thousand times, and then waved a friendly beckoning to the rest of us, inviting us in.

We helped Zafir get out of the cart. "I don't need help," he said after we got him on solid ground. "Get me that walking stick."

As we approached the house a new figure appeared at the door, an elderly gentleman whom we guessed must be Shen Nung himself.

"You are most welcome here, my friends," he said in our own tongue. I looked at Fawzi with a surprised smile and he just shook his head. "There's a lot of people in this world smarter than you, fish lips," he muttered.

Shen Nung had a calming accent that made him a genuine master of congeniality.

"My physician Humam sends you his warmest greetings," Zafir said.

"Ah! Humam, my great friend. A friend of Humam is a dear friend of mine," Shen said. He extended a slight bow, and with a gentle sweep of his hand, invited us inside.

Shen was a frail, balding man, perhaps in his mid-seventies. A flowing white beard and lively black eyes smiled at us. He wore a loose brown robe with drooping sleeves, and light woven sandals.

"Humam speaks highly of you, Shen," Zafir said. "He expresses his regrets that he was unable to be with us."

"I understand," Shen said. "Other friends of his have come to see me over the years, and it is with great pleasure that I make your acquaintance. For a friend of Humam, I am at your service."

I expected the inside of Shen's home to be rich with gold, jewels and fine furniture. Instead, it had a special charm, a comfortable elegance found in its simplicity of design and decor. Bamboo furniture with soft silken pillows dressed the various rooms, with small end tables that held vases or polished rocks.

"Look at that," Ammar said, pointing to a tall, ornate table that stood sun-bathed by a window. "A south pointer!"

Indeed, there was—an elegant brass heaven-board with a large, gray south pointer standing perfectly still. On the wooden floor around it lay several large and richly woven carpets with signs of the stars and heavens, with lines and symbols, woven directly into the mesh.

"Is that their worship of the sky?" I asked.

Ammar nodded. "So much red means prosperity," he said. The diffused sunlight fell on it from the open windows giving it the appearance of honor, almost worship. "The light is important for their worship of energy," he said.

We could see that the various adjoining rooms were all dressed in reds and blues—on the walls, the ceiling, the window openings. A generous flow of light poured in from the large openings. "Look at that garden," I said, walking toward one of the windows.

"Don't be rude," Fawzi scowled. "Come back here, you haven't been invited to go snooping around someone's home, fish head."

I took the rebuke but couldn't prevent myself from looking at the beautiful scene outside. There was a sky-blue pond and a dozen floating water fowl watching us, curious, drifting slowly in our direction looking for, perhaps, a piece of bread. They had long necks and beautiful snow-white feathers. I could see dozens of birds in the trees singing assorted tunes. I smiled to myself. There was an abundance of natural peace in this quiet place.

We took our seats as invited, just then noticing the sweet perfume of blossoms carried into the room by a gentle breeze, a strange contrast to the winter-like weather was had experienced just days before. I looked at the others and none of us dared speak a word. It was almost reverent in that place, simply beautiful because it was so simple.

"May I please offer you some tea?" Shen asked.

I was ready to politely decline but Zafir accepted with gratitude. Shen motioned to the elderly women. She stood in the back wearing a simple floral silk dress that draped from her shoulders to sandaled feet.

She nodded with a smile and with graceful motion well-rehearsed over the decades, she turned from our view into a back room.

Shen looked at us, smiling. Tiny clean wrinkles framed his soft eyes.

"I see you are suffering from an injury," he said, directing his attention to Zafir's bandaged leg. "A fall? A battle?"

"A sword that almost finished its job," Zafir said. "Humam has been cleaning it with an herbal wash, but the mending is slow coming."

"Very well, let me look," he said standing. "Will you please join me in the other room? You may use your stick and my shoulder. And you, gentlemen, please wait here, my bride will have the tea here shortly."

"Bride?" I whispered to Fawzi. Shen heard and grinned back at me with a twinkle in his eye, "Oh yes, young master, for sixty-four years," and returned to helping Zafir to the back room.

Fawzi had ignored me and watched Zafir being led away. He sat up—his *Al Murrah* training didn't like the removal of his charge from his immediate jurisdiction. Zafir saw the reaction and gestured with a wink and a turn of his hand that all was well. Shen led him to an adjacent room and they disappeared behind a blue and green silk curtain.

Shortly afterwards the woman came to us carrying a tray. Her silver hair was wrapped in a bun with a scarf, and she smiled sweetly as she set the tray on a table in front of us. There were four carefully painted porcelain cups and a round tea pot that steamed from its mouth. A small loaf of cake bread was cut in even slices.

In broken words, she smiled another greeting. "You are welcome to our home," she said, pouring the first cup. "May I ask your names and how you came to visit our country?"

心爱的 **15** 馅爱小

NEEDLES

We must have talked for close to an hour before Shen reappeared from the back room. He held the curtain open. "Will you join us, Bassam?" he asked.

I looked over at Fawzi and he furrowed his brow and whispered: "He likes you better than me."

I smiled and nodded. "Yup," I said.

I crossed the room and ducked past the curtain. The little workshop was brightly-lit but sparsely appointed. Zafir was lying on a white sheet draped over a long, tall-standing table, smiling at me. His leg was illuminated by a broad shaft of bright sunlight beaming through the large window. Shen began to explain.

"I know the problem with your Master," he said. "I want you to see this," and drew my attention to Zafir's open wound. It was undressed and opened—no, it was more than undressed. The skin, a small section of the skin, was folded back and the bone shone white and shiny. A towel beneath was changed—the bleeding was stopped.

I hesitated, took a short breath, and then forced myself to step closer and pretend it didn't bother me.

Zafir saw me react and smiled. "Bassam, I don't feel a thing. Not a single thing," and pointed to several long, slender needles poking directly into his skin—two in his side, three in his upper leg, two in his lower leg.

"What are those?" I asked.

"It is the art of zhenjiu," Shen explained. "As I was telling Master Zafir, the needles stop the flow of qi moving through the body, interrupting at different layers in the pathways. As you can see," he said, pointing to the needles above the wound, "I have stopped the qi here, here, and here."

Zafir's leg was tied to a board with white strips of cloth above and below the wound.

"This is an old art," Shen said. "Not many know of it, that is bad. But I use it to stop the pain, and that is good."

"Amazing," I said, thinking I was in the presence of a science that was so far ahead of anything I had ever heard of. "Does it last long, these needles? Will Zafir feel the pain later?"

"After the needles are removed, he will feel the pain return, but not for some time. It is delayed. By then, I want healing to begin."

Shen walked around to the far side and motioned me closer.

"I want you to see what is happening here, things to watch for on your trip home."

I approached and bent down for a closer look.

"The reason your Master Zafir has not healed is because the wound was not cleaned correctly. It is a difficult thing to do, to open it up like this and clean, without the zhenjiu, especially with a wound so deep as this. But now look," he said pointing again. "I have cleaned the break and removed some splinters of broken bone. When he finishes healing, your master will have a limp but he is strong. See here? I have removed dead tissue. When I sew it together again, it should heal normally."

"Then what do I look for?" ——

"I want you to see how this has been done. Should the humours fall from balance again, I want you to open the skin like this, and wash it with the herbal wash I will give you."

"But, those needles, I don't know how to work them," I said.

"Yes, and that is unfortunate for Master Zafir. But pain for a short time is better than no pain ever." The old man smiled as if the logic should speak a thousand words to me. It didn't.

"And the sewing?" I asked.

"If you must open his wound, cut the threads carefully. The herbal wash must be boiled first, allow it to cool so it is warm—but not hot, we do not want to kill the healing," he said. "Bind it up as before. Without the sewing, it will not heal as well but it will heal. And when that knitting of the flesh has started, you will not be able to open the wound easily—that is a good sign. Never use plain water, Master Bassam, only the herbal wash, boiled and cooled, as I have told you."

"Zafir, shouldn't Ammar also be here learning this?" I asked.

"I agree," Zafir said. "Shen? Will you also show our friend Ammar this same process? It is safer to have two who know."

"I'm happy to," he said, and I was led out of the room.

When Zafir emerged from the curtained room, his lower leg was immobilized with six slender boards embracing it and strips of white cloth binding them firmly.

"Five weeks, keep it on," Shen said. "But watch the incision for the signs I told you about. In five weeks, the bone healed if the incision is healed. The bone will not knit completely for another year—you must remember that. But you must exercise the muscle, gain your strength back, return the harmony within you."

We helped Zafir from Shen's front door and down the walk. He expressed doubts about the confinement. "I'm not convinced I can accommodate you for five weeks," Zafir smiled.

Shen smiled and nodded. "I know exactly what you mean. And I am glad that you are anxious to get your leg back. If all goes well, and you follow my counsel, you will be weak and tender for two or three more weeks. That is still too soon to use your leg without help. After another four weeks, you may start limping around without your stick, and you should feel strength returning. When you get home your leg should be strong enough for you to walk into your house and bless the hand that brought you there—if you are kind to yourself."

Zafir paused and moved his leg. "Your treatment is already at work," he said. "I can feel the healing has started already."

Shen smiled and bowed in humble acceptance of Zafir's gratitude. Zafir offered coins that were refused, so he asked that they be given instead to someone Shen knew who stood in great need of such help. Upon that condition, Shen was willing to accept the coins. We finished our farewells, promising to extend to Humam the warmest regards of Shen, and boarded the carts for our return trip to the docks.

I saw that Zafir was much more at ease. The ride back to town was not as difficult as the one coming out. I put in my journal Shen's name and the location of his house. There were things taught there that I wanted to know more about.

"Day 410—Dear Rasha, I found a new tool for the physical arts that is popular in this part of C'ina. They insert needles in your body to stop pain, improve health, cause healing. An old master named Shen said it will bring other imbalances into proper form such as bad feelings and evil dreams and turmoil and worries. I have a pain that cannot be stopped with needles. It is my longing for you, until that time that we are together again. — Bassam"

"Dear Bassam, A messenger came, my mother has taken ill. My sisters have called for me to help. I will leave Rekeem for a few weeks but I will continue to write. Faris said his whole family will miss me and asked if he should accompany me for safety. Kateb and Dalal think that is a good idea. I said yes. — Rasha"

心爱的 **16** 咱受小

WEIQI

After a night in the village we were back on the river after sunup, later than usual because the captain had to wait on a shipping arrangement. The men on the boat told us another seven days to reach the Huang He, the direct passageway to Chang'an and beyond to the open seas.

"Seven more days?" I complained to Ammar. "How far away is this place, anyway?"

"Not to worry, Bassam," he said. "It is still faster than by land. The time will go quickly. And see Zafir? He is impatient but trapped with us. He is more at ease with his pain."

Ammar was right. Even so, Zafir still broke the rules. Fawzi and I nagged him like nanny goats every day, anything to keep him off that leg—not an easy chore for either of us as he did not take kindly to our attentions. As for the wound, Ammar was best at administering the needed care so I just watched. Whenever Zafir tried to stand or walk without his stick, or tried to overdo it, I told Ammar who delivered the reminder with sharpness and alacrity, and Zafir obeyed.

And then one afternoon, suddenly, we broke free from the narrow waterways. Our oarsmen negotiated us into the swift waters of the confluence with Huang He. It was a mighty waterway indeed, heavy flowing, fast, and filled with silt. That's when everything about our trip changed. Zafir's wound stopped bleeding, our spirits were energized for the trip that lay before us, and our swift and new water path carried us forward.

The Huang He was massive. It was a yellowish muddy color, and grew so wide in a few places that we could not see the other side. There were boats so distant they almost made us believe them to be on the open sea instead of a river.

It was in these shallow flats that the current slacked and our forward progress came nearly to a stop. The crew compensated by hoisting a full set of sails, rigging it for wind power. Watching them work the lines and fasten off the canvases was an amazing rush of harmonious cooperation. In just a few minutes the sails were set, a course taken, and the moving air overcame the slower current. In just moments we were skipping along leaving a wake behind us.

I had never seen a river so enormous. "It's like a giant lake," I said, scanning the horizons to the far side.

Fawzi looked at me like I didn't have an intelligent thought in my entire head.

"Just like a lake?" he said shaking his head. "Yes, just like a lake that *flows exactly like a river, moss mouth.*"

That first day on the big river was peaceful and new. Hundreds of boats of assorted sizes and sails moved past us going both directions. The shores were clogged with docks in constant service—loading, unloading, preparing and repairing. Our drivers sailed right past, stopping at none. It seemed they had a certain dock in mind.

As the passageway grew more congested I turned my interests to Ammar and his maps.

"That's such a long trek," I said, pointing at the river's cumbersome loop northward. "Three whole weeks? Just look how far north then south, such a waste of time, why not take this more direct way," I asked, pointing to the dotted lines on the map, a river valley between the mountains. "Lanzhou to Chang'an, just a week or so—?"

"Don't think of risking it," Ammar said. "See this dotted line? That means seasonal travel only, Bassam. These rivers don't run all year, and we're not in the run-off. They're shallow to start with—we'd run out of river for sure."

"But why not stay here another week, let Zafir's wound close up? And we could take a camel trip east. Surly that would be faster than the loop, maybe even catch up with the others."

"Oh no, my impatient friend," Ammar said. "Do you know where the caravan is by now?"

I shook my head.

Ammar drew a line across the map with his finger, south and east of us.

"Another month for them," he said. "We'll be in and out of Chang'an and into the ocean before they make it half way. No—we must stay with our plan, and Zafir is not out of danger yet, don't forget that part."

Eighteen days on the river, Ammar said. I was terribly nervous for something to do. It would be the hardest 18 days of the entire trip, and my greatest enemy was boredom. After just three days on the Haung He and I was already fully engaged in a battle with monotony—the monotony of a daily routine that convinced me that a house truly was a grave for the living, but this boat was even worse—being trapped on its course with little agency to move except forward or back across the deck. And the only break was a meal of dried fish, or maybe fresh if we caught one. Or fruit. Maybe bread and a mug of brackish river water that was not always to be trusted. I wanted to return to the road with the others, riding our beasts through trial and hardship, surprise and success, where each step forward created a chance with the unknown, a daily jousting with death by bandit or cobra or quicksand—and meeting all those different people, and their voices and faces, their foods and wares, their hardships and joys.

But *this trip*—on the river—it was the same each day: sitting, standing, walking, eating, never a change. Each day the same, every day.

I didn't do a good job of hiding my impatience, and that prompted Ammar to action. He showed up one morning carrying under his arm a surprise he brought back from market.

"Bassam! I have the perfect solution to your pacing and complaining," he said with a guarded smile. "Have you ever heard of Weiqi?"

I shook my head, unimpressed.

He brought forward a leather sack in front of him. Reaching inside he produced a flat board with thin, black lines evenly crossing one another to make hundreds of small squares.

"A heaven board?" I asked.

"No, it's a game," Ammar replied.

"I don't play games anymore," I said.

Fawzi came along side and wrapped an arm around my shoulder and gave me a crushing squeeze.

"Sit down and listen, fish breath," he said. "Weiqi is not a game. It will teach you things. Keep your fish lips closed and listen to Ammar. All three of us are tired of your constant pacing and whining. This will hook you like we hook fish for lunch. And if you don't listen, we'll pull out the net and keep you there, it works just as well."

I sighed and sat down by Ammar, leaning my back against the railing and crossed my legs. "Okay, hook me," I said.

"Weiqi is an ancient game," Ammar began. "More than two thousand years old. It was invented in this very land."

"They invent everything here, the south pointer, the—"

Suddenly Fawzi stomped on my foot. "HEY!" I yelled.

"Yes, Bassam," Fawzi growled, not lifting his foot from mine. "We know all about inventions. We'll give you your lesson on inventions later. Right now, just be quiet and listen."

Ammar ignored the rebuke and kept talking. I kept quiet but my suspicions were aroused. Was there was a conspiracy afoot between my two friends?

"They say an emperor was worried about his bored son," Ammar said smiling, "much like we worry about you, Bassam. So, he asked one of his best generals to invent a game that could teach his boy the creative disciplines of tactics, strategy, and concentration. The general came up with an idea that is simple. Its name is Weiqi."

With that, Ammar pulled from his leather bag a much smaller leather pouch and poured out hundreds of little stones. They were polished and flat, some obsidian black, the others marble white.

"Black and white," Ammar said. "That means two players or two teams. It's best with just you and me until you learn it. Interested?"

"Okay," I said. "I'm interested. What's the strategy?"

"That I will leave up to you," Ammar said. "But these are the rules. Very simple, really."

"Okay, I'm listening," I said.

"This is not a board of little squares—I want you to look at it as lines crossing each other. A grid with intersections—each crossing place is called a point."

"All right, a point," I said.

"There are 19 points across and 19 down, that's—"

"That's 361 points on the board," I announced, interrupting him and stealing a sideways glance at Fawzi.

"I was just going to say that," Ammar said.

"Showoff," Fawzi drawled.

"The black always starts the game," Ammar continued. "You may place your black anywhere on the board on one of these points, and then it's my turn to place a white, and we go back and forth. Your goal is to cover as many points as you can. Do you follow?"

"I follow, but what's so exciting about that?" I asked.

Ammar looked up at Fawzi, and Fawzi grinned back. They both nodded their heads as if agreeing to something secret.

"That, my young friend, is where all the trouble lies," Ammar said. "You want to protect as much of the board as you can by lining up your stones next to each other. Connecting them—up, down, diagonally, in a tight circle, a big circle, any possible way so long as there is no point or opposing piece in your line."

"And if there is?" I asked.

"You want to surround it with your pieces and continue building your wall. If you succeed in building a wall around my pieces, then you have captured those points and any of my pieces that are in there. You may take my whites off the board and all the points inside are yours. At the end of the game, we count and see who has the most points and he is the winner."

"Sounds simple enough."

"There are three or four other little rules I will teach you as we go along, but that is the game."

"All right, let's play."

After two hours of feverish tripping into this trap or that, I was mad, I was frustrated, I was determined to beat Ammar at his own game.

"Should we stop for some food? It's time, you know," Ammar said.

"No, you go ahead," I said. "I'm going to look this over some more. Somewhere, you've made a mistake and I'm going to find it."

"Don't touch any of those pieces until I come back," Ammar warned.

"I won't."

As Ammar and Fawzi stood to join Zafir and the others for food, I overheard Fawzi hush his voice.

"Better watch it, Ammar. I've seen Bassam, he won't let go until he's bested you."

"Do you think I'm worried?" Ammar asked. "We've knocked off most of the day without one of his whining complaints. Don't you see? I've won already—it's been peaceful and quiet!"

I overheard but didn't care. I was determined to figure this out and sat there with all my brain power churning and focused, searching and concentrated.

Indeed—I had become hooked.

心爱的 **17** 咱爱小

THE ROCK

It was the morning of the eighth day. I had just set up my Weiqi board and was about to scout out a companion to play when a powerful crashing jolt suddenly threw me sideways into the railing and tipped the boat sharply to its side, almost capsizing. Everyone shouted and grabbed whatever they could as supplies and some gear slid down the deck and flipped over the railing and into the water. I was hanging onto the rail, more worried about my Weiqi game than anything. The board had flipped across the deck, scattering its pieces everywhere. The captain instantly shouted commands and on the other side I saw Fawzi and Ammar bracing Zafir to keep him slipping down the deck, and other passengers holding to anything that wouldn't move. No one fell overboard, but it was precarious for several long seconds. Crew members crawled to the upward side with ropes and long poles and began pushing to dislodge us.

I saw Ammar with the captain. "What happened?"

"We hit a rock," he shouted back.

The swift water that was so calmly quiet and peaceful before now roared past us in a torrent of foaming fury.

"What can I do?" I shouted again.

"Stay there," he said, waving me down to remain. "They're pushing us off."

A few moments later the boat was dislodged. We quickly uprighted, drifting uncontrollably back to the heavy water flow. The current grabbed the bow and snapped us back into the middle of the river. The captain shouted to a man and pointed to the deck hatch, directing him to check for damage. He emerged again and chattered away faster than any could translate.

Fawzi helped the little man from the hatch and exchanged some gestures.

"What did he say?" I called.

"We won't sink," Fawzi answered, "not yet anyway, but we're taking on water. We need to dock as soon as we can find a suitable place."

It was good for us that this part of the river was not deserted and there were others watching our distress from shore, calling to lend aid if needed. Some manner of construction project was underway on the north side. There were many boats and docks on that side that gave haven if we could but steer to one of them. Dozens of men had stopped their unloading to call encouragement and point our way to safety.

The captain steered our crippled ark toward an open dock where we found many hands pulling our ropes to secure us at last.

"Here you go, boulder brains," Fawzi said, "an unscheduled stop. Now's your chance to tour this place and I can have some peace and quiet for a change."

A delay was the least of my concerns at that moment—I was too busy rounding up all the pieces to my Weiqi game.

"An uncharted shoal and large rocks," Zafir said as we helped him from the boat. "The captain said the river is running low, rocks that normally are deep now pose a danger, and we found one."

The crew helped us disembark, and started the work to remove personal belongings. We gathered our supplies and packages and hired a man with a cart to help.

"Wait here, Bassam," Zafir said. "Watch our things, we may be here a while. I will be back."

He took Ammar and Fawzi and hobbled with his walking stick, as best he could, and followed the boat captain up the grassy bank and out of sight.

I was left alone. With guarded suspicion, I turned my attention to the mass of workers around me—hundreds of them, maybe thousands. Whatever work they had fallen upon, it was a large and exhausting labor. Men were scattered in lines all over the river banks, the hillsides and up the slopes of the foothills. Most of them carried loads, baskets in their arms or shoulders or suspended from a pole between two men. Some were numb to their labors, I could see that, while others are dragged down with exhaustion. Few noticed me waiting there with our coveted supplies until one of the workers stopped in his place and looked hard in my direction. We locked eyes. He smiled and waved and broke ranks to approach. I immediately grew concerned and stole a quick glance around for Zafir and the others. *Now what, I wondered?*

心爱的 **18** 咱爱小

BANG

"You," he said with a broad smile, extending his hands, palms up. I looked around checking for another he might be addressing. "Me?"

He nodded and came closer. I could see he wasn't more than four or five years older than me—about my same height but hardly half my weight.

"You! You are western, no?"

"Yes," I said cautiously. "I am western, and you know my language."

He grinned. "I do, I lived in your world for many years."

"You did? Tell me!" I asked.

"Leuke Kome, I was a boat loader for most of my boyhood," he said. "Do you know it?"

Hearing that name again was the most wonderful pair of words I had heard for a long time.

"Know it? I know it well!" I exclaimed. "It is not far from where I live, Rekeem."

"Rekeem? Why, yes, yes," he said, "the city of caves for homes and mysteries for truths, a wonderful place I have visited two times."

"Twice? That's wonderful! When were you there?"

"I was a boy, fifteen, twenty years ago, a long time," he said. "My name is Bang, what is yours?"

"Bassam," I told him.

"Ah, yes, he who smiles," he said.

And that made me smile. "You know our language well," I said.

"I grew up with it," he said. "Made friends, but not for long. Then my father had to return to here."

Here seemed more along the lines of a punishment or exile. I could see no redeeming value in this mountainous region where misfortune had abandoned us.

"So tell me," I asked. "What is this place, this great building project, do you live here?"

"Oh no," he said shaking his head. "This, you can see, is not a place to live, it is my job. My home is not far from here, across the river, but this is where I work. We come by boat each morning and go home by dark. I'm a worker on the Great Wall, we have no villages here."

"A wall?" I asked. "Why do you need a wall? Are there floods?"

Bang laughed and looked up river. "They come from the north, bandits, armies, bad men."

"You mean the Xiongnu?"

"Yes, but others," he said. "For many centuries. Our walls keep them away. Too many of them—Tuyuhun, the Khitans," he said. "Khaganate, Nanzhao, others. They invade through these valleys," he said pointing away. "We have no defense but these walls—they are old, maybe five hundred years, maybe more."

"It looks like repair work," I said.

"Yes, we make them taller, stronger. Today there is peace in the land," Bang said. "A long time coming, too. Many fightings, many dead, many people flee for help and protection. The emperor did it, he fought them and brought peace. We are one country now but the enemy remains."

"I didn't know," I told him. "The Xiongnu are friends to us, they escort our caravans, I didn't know they were your enemies."

"Not all Xiongnu are enemy," he said. "Many factions. They struggle for power among themselves, too. Many dark forces."

"Yes," I said, "many."

"And you?" Bang said. "For you the Great Wall is also help, to protect you from bandits, have you seen it on your journey here?"

I had not, although everyone talked about it. "They make for safe journeys," I said. "I am glad for that."

"You bring business and news from the world," Bang said. "It is good for our people to have your trade here."

Just then Zafir appeared at the top of the pathway, returning with the others.

"Bassam!" Zafir called. "This is a friend of yours?"

"Yes sir, meet Bang, a worker on this project."

Zafir extended his hand in greeting. "Bang, my pleasure. This is Fawzi and Ammar, two of my associates, and Bassam you now know."

"Yes, we've talked," Bang said. "It is most unusual to have Westerners this far north of Chang'an. The caravans travel south—it is most unusual seeing you so far from the routes. I wanted to discover what brought you."

"Indeed it is off the beaten path," Zafir said, "but we are indeed traveling to Chang'an just as soon as our boat is repaired."

Bang looked toward the river, spotting our boat being pulled to dry dock. Ammar told of the surprise collision and of our good fortune to come upon work crews with the wherewithal to give us aid.

"That work on your boat, it will take a day?" Bang asked.

"That is what the captain told us," Zafir said. "We were looking for accommodations."

"Then you must come with me, I will show you, but first let me show you what we do here," Bang said.

"Our things?" I asked Zafir.

"We have a place, a watched place for supplies and such," Bang said. "Fetch your bags and come with me. We will make them safe."

心爱的 **19** 咱爱小

THE GREAT WALL

The climb up the river bank was a challenge for Zafir's sore leg but he took it bravely with his walking stick, and stayed abreast with Fawzi and Ammar. I walked with Bang who led the way to a grassy plateau that suddenly opened with a grand vista of the whole river valley. Bang directed our attention to the starting place of the wall's march up the barren mountain slope. It straddled the crest from foothill to summit with perfectly engineered balance. At the peak stood a stone signal tower. The wall continued farther up the mountain side, levelling for a stadion before rising again to another tower, and so forth, far into the rocky crags of taller peaks beyond.

It was a lonely outpost standing solitary among the rolling barren foothills. From our vantage, we could see the land was coated in ancient clay, hardly a green thing to be seen. The soil under our feet likewise was hard, embedded with gravel, and baked solid in the heat of many summers now lost to history.

"This would make for terrible plowing," I said.

"Yes," Bang said. "A hated ground for grazing, and worse for building, as you see."

Sparse smatterings of scrub trees, dried or choked to brittleness, were clustered in scant patches across the lower foothills. The mountains rose from there, piled up in slabs like great stone tablets layered one atop the other. But rising atop these lifeless slopes, like a crown on a corpse, was this amazing Great Wall. We beheld with astonished respect man's puny labors to fortress off the land with such labor.

Bang led us close to one collapsing section of the wall to give us a closer examination. The structure stood twice my height and revealed layers of tamped earth. I counted at least two dozen such layers, each denoted with a layer of sticks and twigs about a palm's depth. The tamped soil was not pure—chipped stones and baked gravel-clay revealed the secret to its longevity and strength.

"Armies of men have worked these walls—you can see it?" Bang asked. "They make it with some water that dries. The sun bakes them hard, hard like a rock."

We saw that the passing centuries of wind and weathering had exposed the ancient labor with patient erosion.

"Those cliff canyons," Bang said pointing, "they are formidable passages. Large armies may pass through only with great effort and risk. It is told that the blood and bones of a hundred thousand enrich this rocky clay. See how they nourish desert plants to life! It is difficult to assault the Great Wall from this place, and difficult to invade our lands. Beyond these mountains the vast southern He-tau region stands between here and many cities south and east. It is not fertile ground, and attacking us here weakens their resolve. Our desert outpost has proven worthy for many centuries, and we make it even stronger today."

From this vantage, it seemed the cliffs, canyons and valleys would prove foolish in any assault—impassable even for a mountain goat. The wall itself stood four times a man tall and thrice a man thick, easily wide enough to allow wagons and large garrisons to man a protected position from the enemy's bows and arrows. The towers were of a different construction, made of brick with protected windows. Every stadia of twisting, climbing, descending, and curving construction was so protected. We stood in awe.

"Some men call it the purple frontier," Bang said as he directed us toward a bleached-dirt pathway that turned to another plateau. "In these parts we call it the earth dragon—do you see how it snakes across the mountain just waiting to awaken? It slumbers, you know. It is a mighty work!"

I didn't know what to say. From this higher view the great work presented itself a fantastic wonder unlike any we had seen.

"How far does it go?" I asked.

"No one really knows," Bang said. "For many centuries they were enlarged, added, strengthened to protect us. Parts and pieces stand throughout for long distances—mostly to the north and west, but the emperor seeks to join them into one. It is part of his government of the provinces. Did you not see any of these along your way?"

"I was told about it," I said. "After Dunhuang, they said there were many stretches to be viewed, but I was—uh, detoured, and missed them. This is my first."

Bang was pleased to share his knowledge of the Great Wall and anxious to tell us more. "It is a work you will never forget," he said. "The emperor extends it many *li*[i] to the west, new constructions to the north, and some south. We work this frontier, adding to older sections. Can you see it? Five, maybe six hundred years it is here, other parts much older in the west. It is a great work," he said pointing, then turned uphill to resume the hike.

Bang stopped at a flat field so we could catch our breath. All around we saw their great activity underway. Thousands of load-bearing workers moving materials and laboring in lines along the nearest points of construction.

"This is where I must leave you, I must go to work," he said. "That is the way down," he said pointing.

We stood at the broken ending of an ancient section that terminated on this slope. Hundreds of men trudged in swarms like ants busy at their hill to build and repair. They were stripped to loin cloths and wore on their heads pointed straw hats or cloth turbans. Some were movers of material—others were the actual builders who stood in lines atop the sections of wall. Many of the movers bore two baskets balanced on poles across their shoulders, laden heavy with gravel from the riverbed below. Others pushed strange carts with a single wheel in the front and handles behind to carry a wooden box of dirt or stones. It let one man deliver many times the basket loads, yet the carriers shouldered their own, continuously—without break.

"Slaves or workers?" I asked.

"Both," Bang said. "We obey the emperor's command, but we do it for a wage. The emperor united the land but demands a tribute from his conquered. Their tribute is labor, mostly young men—and for that, you could call them slaves."

"Lonely work," I said, watching the long lines snaking their way from the river to the hillsides. "Is their term of service long?"

"A few months, sometimes longer," Bang said. "Many die, many more go back to their homes. It is good work for our country."

"And he feeds these workers?" I asked.

"That is a chore almost as great as the construction," Bang said. "The many boats docking near you are supplying the men with breads and rice, sometimes fruits and water. It is expensive work, but so is the Great Wall."

Ammar was studying his map and joined us making notes with his charcoal scribe. "Tell me, Bang," he said, "where does the emperor build his new wall? I've got it running from the western desert, and then it spreads into several sections, does this look about right?" and handed over the map for clarification.

"No, not here," Bang said pushing it away. "There are spies, they will think you are spying, put it away. We will talk of it, yes, certainly, but not here."

Ammar folded the map and sheepishly put it back into his bag. "Just visitors," he said looking around, "just visitors."

"You will need to stay the night. I will invite you to my father's home, you will stay with us, a great honor, and then we will look at the map." Bang smiled and looked around. "Not to worry, now you are among friends. Many of us have dealings with the great trade routes and the Westerners who trade. You are welcome to stay, to visit, to watch, but the emperor has his men watching."

"Thank you, Bang," Zafir said. "It would be our honor to accept your hospitality, thank you. Those must be ferries to the other side?" he said pointing. "We will await you across the river—and, that must be your village?"

"Yes, our village named Fuping, across the river—very good place. You will find a diner to rest and watch our work, but evening meal is with my father and mother," Bang said. "I will find you at fànguān *Liang*, they will feed you midday meal. Westerners are welcome there."

"Very well," Zafir said, "Thank you, Bang, we will look for you there."

Bang smiled and turned to join his fellows.

We stood and watched, spellbound at the sight of workers crawling over the hillsides and covering the wall like insects on a crust of discarded sweetbread. The many sections under construction had tall poles straddling the wall with legs to either side and joined at the top.

I stood by Ammar. "Do you understand what is going on there?" I asked. "Those poles are not being used like a crane to hoist, what are they for?"

"Do you see the piece of rope tied a few cubits from the top, stretched tight as if to hold the legs from spreading?" he asked.

I did—such a rope was on each set.

"That keeps them at the same isba,' can you guess why?" He asked.

"Not really," I said.

"Look at the wall, do you see the long boards?"

"Ah! Yes, now I see," I said. "The poles give the angle on either side to build the wall, so it is the same slope?"

"This is what you missed in Dunhuang," Ammar said. "They use these poles to measure. The poles hold boards to contain the earth while the workers tamp it down. I measure about 20 cubits along the wall from set to set. See how they pound the clay and gravel between? When they reach the top of the boards, they remove those below and place them on top for the next layer of earth, and so it grows upward."

We watched in silence as a steady stream of laborers marched past the section nearest us, dumped their loads and left, while others on top tamped it tight with heavy logs and big rocks lashed to short poles. A layer of dried reeds was laid between each layer of earth, some water, and then more soil pounded again. A dozen workers at each location followed behind one another in short circuits, chanting a tune as they dropped the logs, lifted and stepped forward, dropping, stepping, repeat. Their motion was set to lyrics, a song— monotonous, regular, laboring. I was captivated by their rhythmic action, calculating the thousands of millions of actions—tamping in unison, a heavy thud, packing with each hit, a half step forward, thud, again and again. Across the valley we could see the same actions repeated—for thousands of stadia and hundreds of years. Was it worth the toil and the life lost?

Their only break came when a group finished a layer and moved away so the boards could be pulled to ready the next layer. When they finished a section the workers dismantled the poles and moved to the next section to erect them again. The finished sides were beautiful— symmetrical, measured, balanced, engineered and artistic. Other workers smoothed away the seams and flaws with some water and a trowel, leaving a hard-flat surface the sun could bake dry and turn into a rock-hard wall. And thus, they fortified their construction against attack and destruction.

"You could drive a wagon across the top of those walls," I said. "Do you think an enemy could dig through it?"

"Not through those slabs," Ammar said. "Any attempts would have to be attempted with arrows raining down on them. It is foolish to try. There would not be enough time to do any real damage," he said. "Near Chang'an these walls are made of baked bricks and stones— much taller, stronger, with towers and fortifications. An enemy would need a much longer time to breach such barriers. That's what the emperor seeks to build across the northern frontier, a very important work."

We watched another hour as section after section slowly rose a cubit at a time. With each section finished, the men changed their song as they dismantled the poles and boards—a new chant, a victory chant of celebration. And then they moved to the next section.

I traced the snaking structure with my eyes, from ridge to ridge and higher, to the tops of mountains, past steep cliffs and dangerous drops.

"Look at that cliff," I said pointing to the top of a steep cliff, I would not want to work on that section, what if you fell?"

"I've heard one of every four men dies," Ammar said. "These mountain passes are not so severe as Jin City or parts northward where the work is certainly more treacherous. Maybe we will see them, Bassam, maybe we will get close."

In my imagination, I projected the labor required to perform a similar project around the plains of Rekeem. Could we be successful at that desert location with such a wall and fortification? I decided against it. The sand would not agree to such boarding up and pounding because we are a free people who must be allowed to flow freely across our desert lands, like the sand.

心爱的 **20** 陷爱小

LU ZHI AND BAN CHAO

The family of Bang was as generous as they were kind. They welcomed us with open arms as if we had all been friends from long ago. Their knowledge of our language was fluent and relaxed. It did not take long for them to share knowledge of Abdali-ud-Din and all the goodness that its vast networks had produced. They knew people familiar to Zafir, and he knew people familiar to them. Zafir was flattered to learn they heard speak of his own name.

Bang's mother was called Lu Zhi, and his father, Ban Chao. They shared stories of their adventures on the trade routes, to the west and back, to the sea, the mountains—they were well traveled. They had visited Rekeem and lands farther west: Egypt, the islands of the Greeks, and yet they had many dreams unfulfilled. Their zest for travel burned as warmly as ever—but for today, for this late time in their lives, they faced their more cautious years and resigned themselves to this riverfront village. It had become a place to rest and provide work for their adult children.

"Your son Bang," Zafir said during meal, "he is your only boy?"

Ban Chao shook his head and smiled. "Bang has two older brothers, workers in another province, doing the bidding of the emperor. We have two daughters married, and Bang will soon marry."

We smiled and offered our congratulations. Bang grinned.

"Her mother and father are the owners of fànguān *Liang*," he said. "You might have seen her this afternoon when you dined there."

Just then Fawzi kicked me under the table and looked at me grinning. "Were you shopping again, wall eyes?" he grinned. I ignored him and kept eating.

"This is wonderful news, Bang," I said. "When do you marry?"

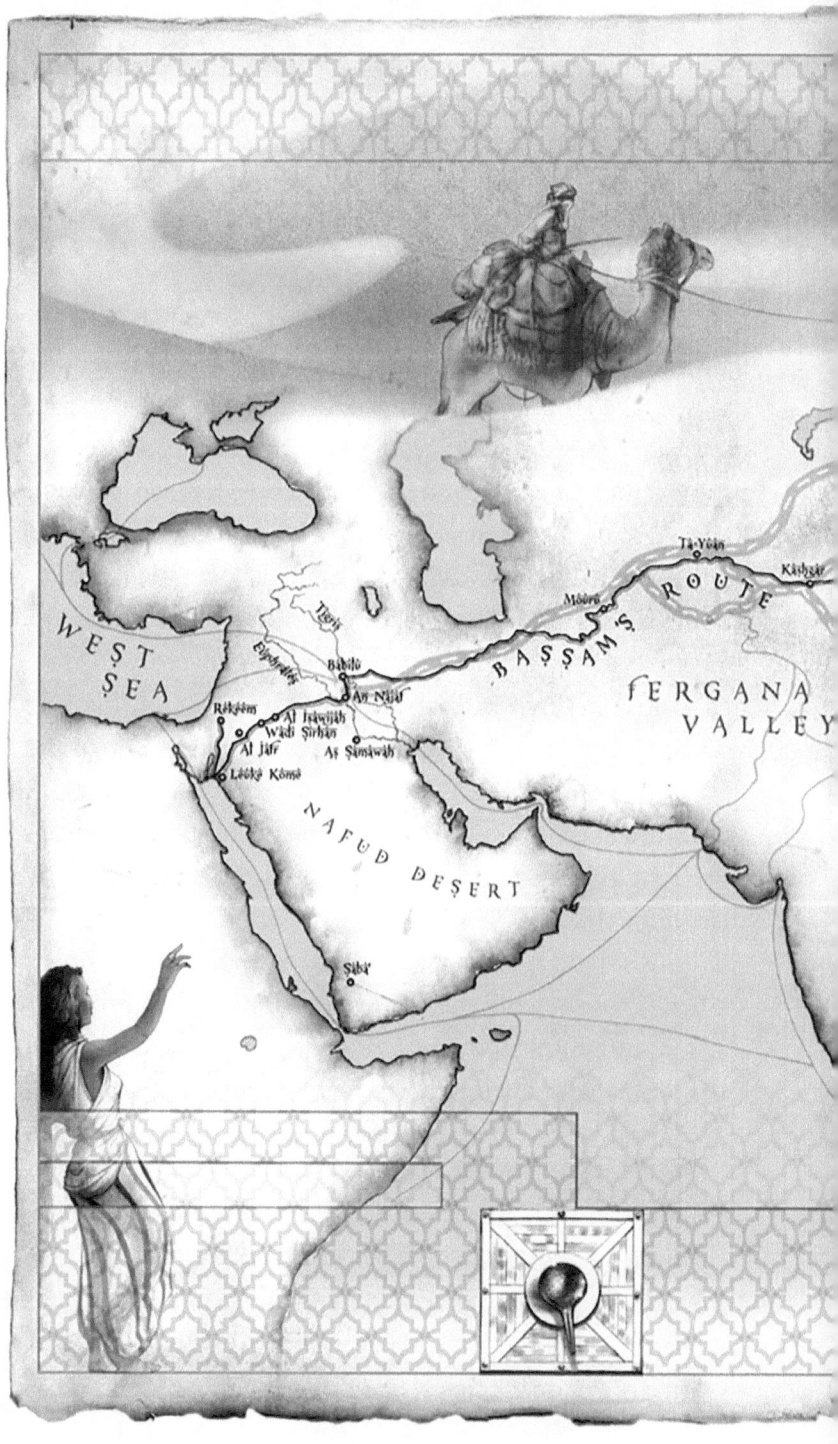

West Sea

Tigris

Euphrates

Babilû

An Nûû

Rekêm

Al Isawijâh

Wâdi Şirḥân

Al Jâfr

Leukê Kômê

Aş Şâmâwih

NAFUD DESERT

Şâbâ'

Ta-Yûin

Kâshgâr

Môôru

BAŞŞAM'S ROUTE

FERGANA VALLEY

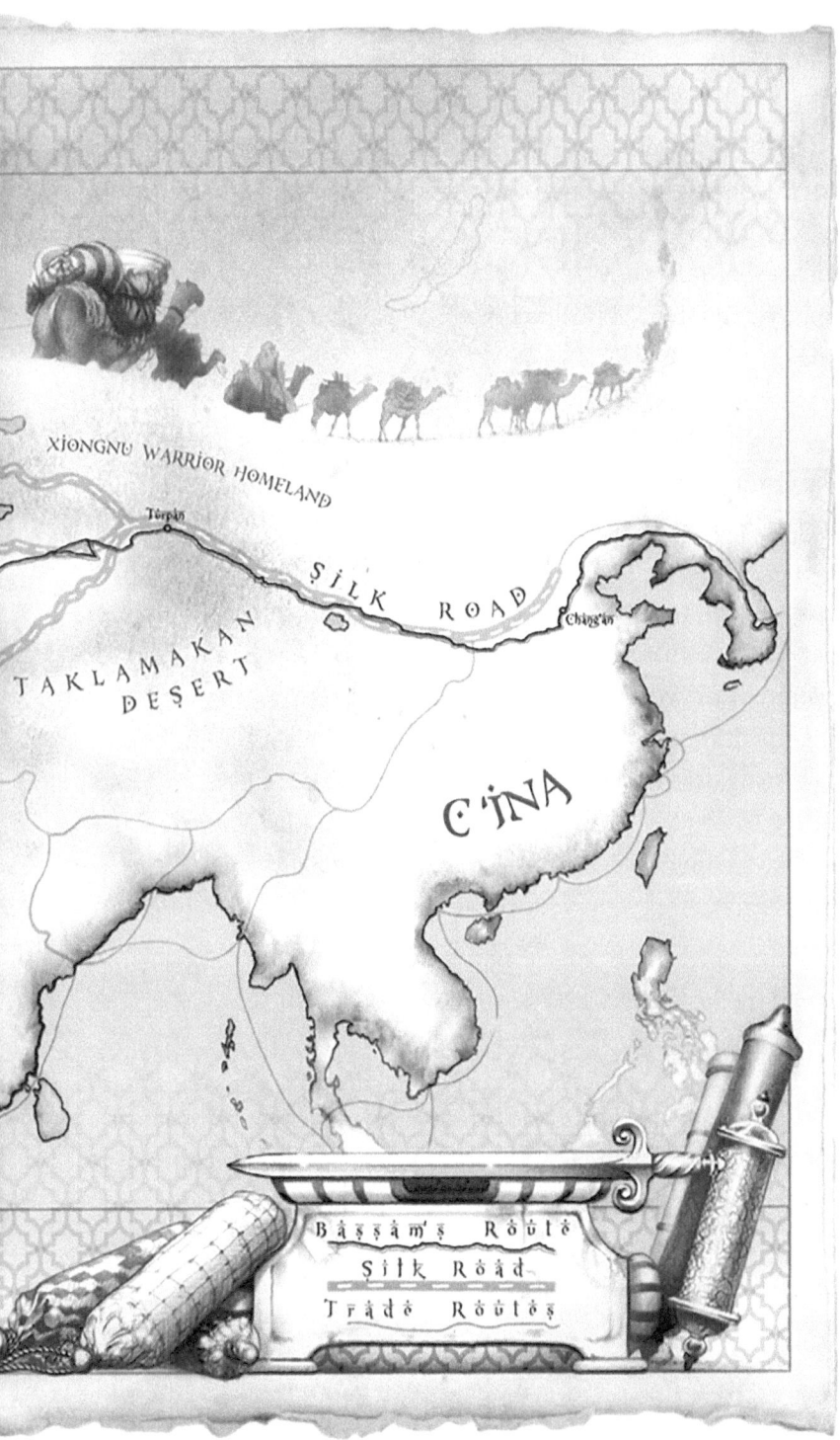

XIONGNU WARRIOR HOMELAND

Turpan

SILK ROAD

Chang'an

TAKLAMAKAN DESERT

C'INA

Bassam's Route
Silk Road
Trade Routes

Bang put another rice and pork on his sticks and ate with a smile. He looked to his father. Ban Chao seemed pleased.

"It is a match!" he said proudly. "The *méi shuò* has taken the tea! We visited for the telling of the suàn mìng zhê, and her name harmonizes with my son's birth in all five colors and all five sounds—it will be a grand marriage! Many sons!"

"Or many daughters!" Lu Zhi chimed. We laughed and nodded our glad tidings.

Bang was all smiles. "We have presented the betrothal gifts and the letter. Her parents are pleased."

"And you too, Bang?" Zafir asked with a happy nod. "Did you know this young woman before?"

"Childhood friends," Ban Chao said. "We told the matchmaker the young people were strangers—it was not a whole truth, but true from our hearts—and a good match they would make, we told her. She wondered why the ceremonies went so smoothly. It is our secret!"

Bang gulped another bite to agree. "Oh yes," he said humbly, not wanting to bring disenchantment to the coming bliss.

"Then we toast you," Zafir said, lifting his cup. "May your new life bring joy and prosperity to Lu Zhi, Ban Chao, and all of your kin. May the bright stars rise on you every night and your shadows fall behind you in the day."

We all lifted our teas for a sip.

As promised, Lu Zhi and Ban Chao put us up for the night. The guest chambers were well furnished and it was clear to me that even though our newfound friends lived modestly they were successful. It was a large and well-appointed home. Fawzi and I shared one room with two nice beds.

"Did you sit on these beds?" I asked, trying the one nearest the door. "They're warm. I like it!"

"Not everybody is as dense as you, sledge brain," he said. "These people will surprise you. Look here, I will show you," and he crossed the room to a thick-walled clay box between our beds. There was a tea kettle quietly hissing on top. A small door in the front had a latch. Fawzi opened it and a small pile of coals glowed warmly.

"Do you see it?"

"See what?" I asked. "The stove? Yes, I see it, what about it?"

"No, the chimney, *ash head*," he said.

"No, I don't see the chimney, where do they hide it?"

"It flows under your bed, under mine, it makes them warm—do you see? It's an old idea we don't have yet. The pharaohs did, the C'ina do, and now Bassam the shopper of serving girls has, too. It's called a *kang*. The smart people have them, you don't."

Ingenious, I thought—*every* problem solved. Vent the smoke to pass under the bed to make it warm, brilliant! This is a wonderful land of inventive people, I decided. Zafir *must* spend more trade time in these parts. If he won't, I will. I wrote into my journal the details, and began to create some applications of these ideas in my imagination.

Fawzi extinguished the lamp and I closed my eyes on the day's labors. It took only a few moments for a combination of fatigue, warmth and comfort to overtake my best labors to resist and I fell into a deep sleep. It was the warmest bed ever.

心爱的 **21** 咱爱小

HUANGDI

At sun-up I awoke refreshed and staggered into the kitchen to find Bang looking at Ammar's map.

"It is all named the He-tau," Bang said, pointing to Ammar's map. "A great land, everything south of the river." He circled with his finger the vast empire below the great northern loop. "Much rich soil, many people, good roads, this whole region, the heart of our country. It is on maps and important in history. You see?" Bang asked. "Many sections of the Great Wall run here and here," he said. "You will not get lost if you use our map—yours is not good, ours is good."

Ammar wasn't as convinced but assured Bang that we wanted one. With breakfast completed Bang saw no reason to dally. He jumped from his place at the table and headed to the door.

"Follow," he said, "we find maps in my village, no need to search. They are good for you to have—for now and for future," and led us out the door toward a neighbor's. Zafir and Fawzi didn't follow and just waved us on our way. Ammar and I stepped into the brightness of a beautiful morning. I took a deep breath and let it slowly escape. The fresh air smelled of cut grasses and mountain streams. I felt rested.

"Ling-he is my friend," Bang said. "He draws maps for the Great Wall, he will help, he draws good maps, follow me."

Back in the kitchen Zafir and Fawzi were steeped in conversation with Ban Chao.

"The emperor is building a world," Ban Chao said. "The Great Wall is its boundary, its protection, its employer. It will make safe trade. But Chang'an is his great jewel in the crown he seeks—a center place, the center of world trade, have you seen it?"

"Yes, two years ago," Zafir said. "We will stop there soon. Is it much improved?"

"Yes, much improved, all the time," Ban Chao said. "The emperor has ordered the building of many cities and roads and monuments and buildings. We think maybe twenty or thirty thousand temples and fortresses, from here to the sea—Qin, Zhao, Yaqn, to the Yùménguān Pass and all the provinces. Since peace has come he turns his warriors to workers to do this great construction."

"The Jade Gate, yes, we've traveled it," Zafir said. "A great work indeed."

"A vital pass," Ban Chao said. "Your trains pass through the Gansu Corridor, and the road to Chang'an. The Great Wall is a protection to you, a protection to your trade, from attack. Very important," he said.

"This is an industrious people," Zafir said. "I see more construction here than even among the Greeks and Egyptians. Very inventive, very creative people!"

"They are," Ban Chao said. "The emperor inherited much of this, he did not build all of it, but he adds."

"Is he a good leader?" Fawzi asked.

"No," Ban Chao said shaking his head. His eyes furrowed to an angry frown and he looked about as if in a habit of checking for listening spies. "He was born under an evil sign and took power when his father died. He was 13. The great war raged across the land many years before his birth."

"That is a young age to lead a nation without wisdom," Zafir said. "Did he have advisors?"

"His father's chancellor served him, a man called Buwei. But he also was a secret lover of the young prince's mother. The king did not know it when he died. It is a sad story but Buwei became chancellor and regent to the young prince," Ban Chao said. "Later Buwei surrendered his place in the queen's bed to an impostor eunuch named Lao Ai. This new suitor fathered two boys with the queen, in secret."

"And they ruled behind the throne," Zafir said.

"For many years," Ban Chao said. "A bad demon. A much dark time."

Lu Zhi stood to clear the table and patted the knee of her husband. "And you, my dear," she said, "are weaving dark clouds to cover this beautiful morning." And she turned to her guests. "More tea and cake?"

Zafir looked at Fawzi who nodded.

"Thank you," Zafir said. "Your kindness is a welcome change."

"Change?" she asked. "You have fallen on rude times?"

"Yes, outside the Great Wall, outside the land," Fawzi said. "But here we find only friends, good people."

Ban Chao nodded. "The wicked, the nomads from the north, they attack because they cannot forge the sword and craft the crossbow or build the cities as do we. They are wanderers and must come and take the labors of others, plundering and building their empire on destruction and ruin. On theft. They are too lazy to build but strong enough to take. It is their culture, for a long time."

"Tell me about this great war," Zafir asked. "Is it settled now? We hear rumors along the road but it is difficult to know what is truth."

"Yes, it is much quieter now," Ban Chao said. "The young emperor grew to become a man and led armies to the warring states and conquered them. He conscripted the conquered into a large army of warriors and slaves to build an empire impervious to attack. The plan was not new, it was a long-time plan from his father and the father before him," Ban Chao said. "As the young emperor grew strong he feared assassination more than he feared the armies north. He feared his mother and her lovers. With an iron fist, he ruled with death. He forced all people to obey him. He forced them what to speak, what to write, what to believe, what to work, and who to marry. With that he built a massive army that defeated the rebellions and united the country as one."

"What did the people think of him?" Zafir asked. "Did they go along with this? I can't imagine they would for long."

"At first, no choice," Ban Chao said. "Later, very angry. There was conspiracy in the emperor's own court. His mother's two sons by Lao Ai that I told you—the emperor discovered it and sent for five horses to pull Lao Ai apart as punishment, in the palace courtyard. He had the queen, his own mother, killed for her indiscretions, and sent his guards to strangle the two boys. He took pity on Buwei and banished him forever, a terrible disgrace. The emperor killed them because there would be no ruler over his kingdom except the emperor's own son."

"It is a familiar story to us," Zafir said. "Greece, Rome, Egypt, it is the bloodbath of tyranny, the assassination of one tyrant to replace another."

"Yes, we learned of it on our journeys," Ban Chao said. "Just a time ago, not long, our emperor stood before the people with his armies and declared himself the beginning of the new history and then he destroyed the old."

"It is the same with all tyrants," Zafir said. "And he burned?"

"Yes, he burned the bamboo scrolls, the writings of the ancients, the schools of thought," Ban Chao said. "Many of them centuries old. *Burned.* If a man had them hidden, he was put to death. If a man taught them to his son, both put to death. This history he burned because he wanted history to start new with him so he had to burn the memories of the old. He was not completely foolish. He kept alive the scholarship— the works of numbers and alchemy, astronomy and medicine, the catalogs of the body humors and metal works, the art, these he kept. It is why your man Ammar must keep his maps guarded, to himself. The emperor has spies."

The guests were silent, considering the heavy hand that stretched over the land to stifle and smother this creative people.

Ban Chao thought a moment and then shrugged his shoulders. "But he has done good as well," he said. "Our land is one, and he fortifies it. He abolished the lords and divided their holdings into 40 prefectures with districts and counties—wards of families, one hundred of them to be watched. It was well organized."

"Like father Moses and the children of Jacob," Zafir said.

"Yes, like Moses, I have heard of him," Ban Chao said. "And he was wise with the children of Jacob. The emperor tried to be wise. He brought a common language and writing, a common money, and standards for weight and measuring, like your Moses. Peace and prosperity came and the emperor felt free to begin building the infrastructure and the roads and expand the Great Wall. For this he appointed a new name for himself, Huángdi—the conqueror. Have you heard it?"

Zafir and Fawzi shrugged and shook their heads.

Lu Zhi was sitting quietly through the exchange and suddenly spoke up. "Not exactly, my husband," she said. "It was *First Immortal Emperor*."

"Ah, my wife, she is right, she is good at this," Ban Chao said. "Yes, the emperor thought himself so powerful that even death could not conquer him. He sent through the land an announcement declaring his new title, but to the people, *First Immortal Emperor* was much too pompous and long-winded, even for our language," he smiled. "A shorter name came of it and soon the decree—he was to be called Huángdi."

"Huángdi," Zafir said, letting the last syllable linger as if in judgment against the tides of history. "A new name for Ruler's Law, but a law that is not new at all," he said. "Shāhanshāh, pharaoh, rajah, monarch, Huángdi, all of them sounding different but the same in tyranny. First he must weaken the people to control them, and then unify them as one, after much blood is shed. It is the work of such rulers everywhere. Different names, same man, same terror against his people."

"Indeed," Ban Chao said. "It is ten years that he has put all the people to work to glorify himself. We pay heavy taxes and carry heavy burdens. It is commonly voiced abroad that the Huángdi builds an empire on the backs of the poor because there is no end to the poor—and therefore, no end to his building."

"How much longer will the people suffer this, before they right themselves abolish this tyranny?" Zafir asked.

"These many wars, these many projects, there is no dissent from the people yet, but they are growing angrier each day. The Huángdi wants unity but he creates dissent by his heavy hand. He is corrupted. He is a mad man. No one speaks it but all the people know it themselves—there is revolt in the minds of many. When this wickedness rules, the people mourn. I am not a prophet but I will foretell that an ending will not come from within before an ending comes when he dies."

心爱的 22 咱爱小

SWEETBREAD FAREWELL

When word came that our boat was ready and was waiting on us, we hurried a goodbye. We could see the captain standing impatiently for us while the crew loaded passengers and their supplies. Ammar waved and he waved back, pointing to the sun.

"It is time," Zafir said, and together we all walked down the footpath to the nearby dock.

Bang pulled me aside for a last look at the Great Wall.

"When you come again, I will take you on a trek atop the wall, up the mountain, to the top tower, it is a pleasant walk," he said.

"I won't be arrested as a spy?"

"Even the Huángdi sees value in friends who bring trade to our cities!" Bang said.

"Then I will come," I said, "so you and your wife and son can show me the top tower."

"Or daughter," Bang said laughing. "You will enjoy it—not even a half-day walk. The return is downhill, much faster."

"Do your warriors live in those towers?"

"In times of tension," he said. "If we see signs our enemies are gathering, our warriors live in those towers to prepare to send a signal."

"I wondered about that, with fire?" I asked.

"There are two," he said pointing. I scanned the misty blue backdrop of mountain peaks walling off the northern horizon. I finally found them, two square towers distinctly perched atop the summits of distant mountains separated from each other by a dozen valleys between. "They keep a large store of sticks and reeds and brush for three fires. By day the smoke and by night the bright flame, sometimes both. It is fast, very safe."

I measured with my eye how much alarm such a fire would bring, and turned about to see where the answering towers might stand.

"They tell the numbers with flags," Bang said. "It is a code that changes, but tells of the strength of armies. Smoke is seen from far but flags cannot so other towers watch and send along. Very ingenious."

I stood staring thinking what terror such lights might announce, and what scurrying about it would mean for people like Bang and his family. Would the Great Wall detain the invaders from destroying their families and farms, their peace and prosperity? Could enough bows and arrows arrive in time to thwart an attack, a scaling of the Great Wall?

The boat crew completed their tasks and helped us board. I turned to my new-found friend and extended my arms in farewell. He clasped them and smiled.

"You are good people," he said. "I miss our trips to your desert land but we will come again someday."

"And I expect to visit you soon, Bang," I said. "Zafir will mount another caravan and we will come. Thank you for your kindness, thank you for finding us and sharing your home."

Zafir and Ammar extended their hands in departure to Lu Zhi and Ban Chao.

"We owe you a great deal for your hospitality," Zafir said. "As we discussed, Ban Chao, we will bring our trade to your village and hope to help you prosper. I will bring gifts. And then I hope to find you well—and with many grandchildren," he said, winking at Bang.

Bang smiled. "If the gods be willing," he said.

"You bring good omens to our doorstep," Lu Zhi said. "You are always welcome, and you may be our guests always."

Ban Chao took Zafir's hand and placed a small wrapped object. "For the blessings of a safe trip, for healing, for your home—that there is peace when you find it again."

"Thank you my friend," Zafir said, "we will meet again soon, and it is good."

We boarded the boat and the captain ordered his crew to release the ropes for departure.

We smiled and waved as oarsmen pulled the boat from the shallows. Soon the current caught hold and the captain ordered more sail. The men worked the ropes and the great ribbed fabric unfurled and billowed out against the breeze. The lines pulled tight lurching us to the side and the boat gained speed. A small wake formed behind us, and at last we were moving again. The Great Wall and its thousands of laborers quickly disappeared.

Some minutes later I found Zafir in his usual place, just settling down to take weight off his leg.

"What did Ban Chao give you?" I asked seating myself next to him.

"I don't know," he said. "Let's see what it is."

Ammar and Fawzi joined us as Zafir produced the small package. It was wrapped in cloth. He peeled back the corners and revealed a sweetbread baked crisp to a golden brown.

"What is that?" I asked.

Zafir smiled warmly. "It is one of their wonderful traditions," he said. "It is the food of haste, the food of revolution. It is their version of the feast of Father Moses on the night he led his people to escape the criminals of Egypt, the bread that was not leavened."

"Does he know that story?" I asked. "Can you eat it?"

"Yes, I'm sure they know that story, but I don't think that is where this treat comes from. Here," he said, breaking off a corner to share around. "You may well eat it, my hungry student."

I tasted mine. "This is good!" I said.

Ammar tasted his. "Yes, I thought I recognized this, I've had it before. It's baked from a paste they make from the lotus nut with honey. Quite unique, Bassam, and a special treat."

Zafir broke off another piece, and there, hidden in the crust was a small piece of writing folded over.

"Ah! Just as I expected," he said, and separated it from the treat.

"A hidden message," he said with a grin and looked up at Ammar and Fawzi. "It is written for us," he said smiling, and opened it to read.

"It says, 'Be safe and well. Peace. Joy. Courage.'"

"The blessing of the traveler!" I said, reaching instinctively into my robe to find Rasha's veil.

Zafir smiled. "These are good people," he said, and tucked the small writing into the folds of his robe. "Bang and his family do know the traditions of the west. It was a thoughtful gift, you must write it in your journal, Bassam."

The workmen had prepared our boat well for the river. New planking freshly stained was laid below deck, and more to the side where the planks were cracked in the accident. The new planks were neatly knitted to the old, and a black ooze bulged from the seams. The mineral smell of the caulk was strong and none of us liked the odor. We hoped the sun and weathering would soon bake it away.

When we settled back into our routine of waiting, I engaged Zafir for a moment. "They are a warm and kind people," I said.

"I find that such good souls may be found in every port," he replied, "and I count their friendship sincere and mutual. You will visit Ben Chao on your next trip, Bassam. I sense more than a business opportunity here," he said. "I sense friends we will want to keep."

I nodded and leaned back to enjoy the refreshment of the cool river air. The swirling gray current welcomed our return. The captain was alert and cautious, and worked quickly to steer our boat beyond the narrow turns and bends of the shallow waters to the deep again, keeping a strong sail to push us along.

We passed many construction sites for the rest of the day. On either side of the river, from the banks upward, more workers were engaged in great labors—more building, more hauling, more towers and walls. At each place as those before, many boats crowded the occasional docks with ferry workers to deliver food, supplies, and laborers.

"The emperor does indeed try to build a whole world here, doesn't he?" I said.

Zafir nodded but didn't speak. I could discern from the look on his face that his thoughts were echoing my own. From all that we had learned on this trip, the emperor stretched his shadow over these activities to saturate his own delusions of grandeur and greatness. I decided the man must view himself standing alone with the earth and her treasures, bent on keeping them greedily in the hollow of his blood-stained hands. But the true greatness hoped such aggrandizements might bring still eluded him, a truth he couldn't possibly realize. The reason was only recently made clear to me, that despite Huángdi's tremendous power and wealth, he remained an ordinary man who was *not* of the scrolls. And thereby would come his self-fulling prophecy of corruption, decay and collapse.

"Day 419—Dear Rasha, Your father told me to learn of the C'ina and their many creative ways. Today we did. We made new friends and saw the largest wall in the world. I think their leader drives the people to waste their labors to adorn his tomb. What do the dead need of such treasure, is *it not better for the living to live? We made friends who know our Rekeem, it was a chance encounter. They made me promise I would return. I told them I would bring my bride. — Bassam"*

心爱的 **23** 的爱小

CHANG'AN

The captain said two more weeks on the river if the wind remained in our favor, and that gave me hope this eternal river run would finally end. Despite the encouraging news for our hastened journey, there was still too much time to think. For me, I couldn't push Huángdi out of my mind. The increasing congestion of boats and workers that passed led me to wonder if were we not sailing away from his abusive ways but right into the heart of it.

A boat is a clever master. For the abundance of time and water that tests a man's patience, it offers needful chores as a distraction that never take a holiday. Our chores were many, and the captain made of us a disciplined crew. On the third day, our monotonous diet of fish and nightly docking at tiny villages took their toll on our spirits and our health. It put a drag on us as we felt the drag on the people from Huángdi's demands. Could the people ever escape him?

Ammar rescued me on one of those hard days with a new set of playing pieces for my board game. I was thrilled and wanted to play so much I quickly wore out my welcome with anyone on board I approached for the game. Ammar, Fawzi and even Zafir found easy excuses to leave me abandoned, to fight boredom's heavy test alone. Weiqi was a wonderful confluence of strategy and intrigue, but only if someone would walk into it with me as a playing partner. It was a world that could easily swallow the whole of the day for whoever would join.

On the fifteenth day after the accident, the captain steered us out of the main river and into some detours that did not appear on Ammar's maps. That kept Ammar scurrying with his scrawl trying to capture the new routes as accurately as he could. The steady southerly sail changed over the course of the day, several times, with side routes that required oars and patience, sometimes for many hours at a time. With that came more river traffic, a hazard that required a steady hand on the direction and a refined trim to the sails. The number of boats steadily increased. This unusual river traffic disturbed the otherwise calm waters and our deck started to roll gently in response. Several waves washed beneath us, unsettling my game and our passengers' patience.

And then a voice called out: "Chang'an!"

Everyone turned to look.

Over the tops of tall trees lining the shore we could see bright red flags in gold trim waving atop towers we could not yet see.

"Is that it?" I asked Zafir.

He smiled and nodded. I jumped up and joined the others at the railing to watch. The anticipation was exciting. I could almost feel the energy radiating from the obscurity as the din of noisy people and animals and traffic suddenly came to life, rolling over us like a warm breeze that grew stronger and louder as we approached. Moments later the river took us around a lush growth of trees and finally—there it was, the majestic city at last revealed itself! Massive grey walls stood up instantly like manmade mountains towering over us with painted reds and gold across their faces, looming over swarms of people shrunken in their shadows who scurried about in a multifarious swarm of melting cultures and voices. Colorful towers with flags rose high in the background, glistening and golden, casting reflections onto the waters and trumpeting into the smoky blue sky its expansive, sparkling, magnificent, bustling, crowded, modern, rich, beautiful, and eternal center of the world's eastern trade, the incomparable *Chang'an*!

All of us stood silent but smiling in awe.

The crew mechanically dropped sail and slowed the boat, navigating with as much rudeness as they did skill through the thick congestion that engulfed us—hundreds of shouting, noisy men maneuvering their boats and rafts and ferries and small craft with large sails and poles and oars, many of them sitting heavy with bundled loads ready to topple, others with mast arms nearly clipping our bowsprit, while the smaller and more mobile craft skimmed between us with anxious fishermen returning with loads or departing with hope. We wove through the traffic of their haphazard harmony of docking, launching, loading, unloading, scrambling here, butting in there, pushing away others who shouted in strange tongues and waved their clenched fists. Our crew guided us fast and hard, steering away from sure collision—not once, but many times as we steered for a port.

"Stay close," Zafir said as the river led us close to Chang'an's magnificent walls. "I'll tell you about this amazing place, the massive portal where the great Silk Road ends and commerce begins."

"The walls!" I exclaimed, pointing.

"Chang'an has been their capital for a few years now," Zafir said. "Those walls are new, built just this past decade according to the commands of the emperor, and enlarged in recent times—thirty cubits high and thirty-five cubits thick, more than 10,000 cubits long—that's thirty stadia."

"*Thirty stadia*," I breathed, "why, that's more than an hour's ride by camel. That's a lot of bricks, millions of bricks," I offered.

"No bricks in these walls," Zafir said. "These are rammed-earth walls, great blocks of it built up as you see them, the same idea as their Great Wall but in much larger dimensions. A hard facing prevents attacking armies from pulling them down. And then there's the moat."

"I don't see it."

"You must stand high, but chances are you won't see it from the river. There's a moat twenty cubits wide that circles the entire enclosure. Very formidable. The natives swear there live man-eating beasts there that swim just below the surface, so stay clear of it."

I didn't know if he was teasing me or warning me, but I decided I didn't need to find out for myself.

We floated past an expansive confusion of people calling from every boat and raft in languages I had never heard, standing out from others in the dress of strange and foreign colors and expressions. The multi-colored sails and flags heralded their origins from places both far and near, a confluence of noise and color and culture that mixed with smells equally foreign—the rot of sewage and stagnation, wafting clouds of burned grease and hot spices from stacked-stone diners. It was a sudden and overwhelming cacophony of noises, aromas and odors mixed with color and activity that drifted across the smoky, traffic-clogged river. Only the stink could drift freely through this noisy confusion. For most of our passage past the great central gates our little boat was blocked nearly to a stop many times, adding to the discomfort from the sticky humidity and the profusion of excess that fed the fire of excitement, commerce, exchange, competition, and so many anxious rigors of prosperity.

The three towering gates stood ten times taller than a man, elegant structures of giant wood frames and swinging doors of dark, weathered oak. Over the tops of the walls I could see buildings even taller, with fluted roofs of rich red, all of them boasting golden dragons or assorted designs swirling in circles, with odd lettering and emblems in glittering gold.

"Do you see the towers of the three palaces, Bassam?" Zafir asked. "These are famous around the world. The Weiyang Palace is surrounded by another wall about a third this height and more than fifty stadia around all four sides."

I whistled aloud. *"Fifty stadia,* that's a two-hour ride—just to go around *a palace?"*

"There is more than one building inside, and many palaces, it is large," he said.

The gates facing the river were open. Thousands of people flowed in and out with carts pulled by horses and donkeys, camels by rope, merchants, men with helmets and spears to keep order, children, dogs, animals on spits and sticks, others in cages, most of them butchered for sale—a great flewage of motion, action and noise.

"It would take a month of weeks to see this place, to see it all!" I exclaimed.

"A lifetime, indeed!" Zafir said. "Here in a while we will dock."

"And see the city?"

"Not me," he said. "I couldn't negotiate their streets in my condition, so you must go and I must stay."

"But I'll see Chang'an?" I asked excitedly.

"If there's time," he said. "We are not trading and we are not here for a sight-seeing journey, either."

"But I can go ashore?"

"Ammar knows the way to Zun," Zafir said. "Fawzi is a good sword, he is patient and will sit this one out with me at the docks. Zun is a fine man with a brave, wise wife who runs a goodly household."

"I can do it," I promised.

"Yes, yes, I know my son," Zafir said with an impatient smile. "Now, here's what I want you to do. First, locate Zun and check for messages, and then if you have time, let him take you through the city. I expect you back tomorrow night. If you are longer, I will stay till the next midday, but that is all. Don't be late or you'll have to hire your own boat to catch us."

"Then I will look forward to meeting him," I said, "and if there is time, to see this magical place."

"If you have time. Zun won't show you the city from this side, so watch with me as we pass."

Zafir began pointing out details I had missed because of the excitement—forms of architecture and construction, the history, the builders' careful planning and good management.

"Do you see the open gates?" Zafir asked pointing. "This is the starting point for all trade going west. This is the great terminal of the twelve routes. Here begin the roads for those trading with the Hindus south for their ivory pearls, cotton, gems, exotic spices, polished agate, carnelian cloth, even works of iron and steel and other metal works. And from the west, wine, copper and brass, glass, papyrus, dyes, ceramics. And from the sea, ebony, cinnamon, ostrich feathers, strange animals, the giraffe and tiger, the leopard. And overland the frankincense, dates, jade, tortoise shells, porcelain, fine glass and dinner works, scrolls of paintings, seeds, incense, slaves. These thousands of enterprises congregate here for trade, purchase and exchange. The Great Wall is a blessing to us—it protects our trade so we can grow the wealth of the people here. And for this we take away gold for ourselves, Indus ivory, south seas coral, and C'ina silk in all colors and textures. It is a rich market for things bought or sold in Chang'an. If there is another trip in me, I will show you it myself, as I promised."

I admired in silence as the busy throngs hurried here to there, in and out, scurrying about the grandeur and glory of industry and trade that magnified itself right before our eyes.

Zafir told me that the city layout and the buildings themselves were influenced by the C'ina peoples' religious beliefs and study of the stars.

"You see that awkward bend in the city wall that follows the river?" he asked, pointing along the banks where the mighty foundation stones came close to the water.

I saw that it seemed to do just that, make seven distinct turns, each spaced evenly.

"They are students of the stars, Bassam. They govern their lives by them. The seven points on the wall give honor to the large ladle that circles the pole star. Do you see it? Do you see how that wall inscribes that shape in the sky?"

It was the Big Ladle, copied exactly.

"Look closely and notice that all of their important buildings face south," Zafir said. "And do you see they are placed in the south of the city?"

"I've heard this," I said. "When Ammar and I bought our south pointers, I heard all about this."

"An old shopkeeper told the whole story," Ammar said. "He gave Bassam an entire lecture on their religion in something like half an hour. Bassam should be our local expert."

Zafir smiled while the excitement and noise drifted by. A passing boat hailed them and Zafir returned a wave.

"It's one of the largest cities in the world," Zafir said. "Their people are at least four times as many as Rome, four times the land also, and in those villages beyond, more than a million live there. All that you see, everything as far as you can see, has been doubling since I was first here with my father years ago. It's an old but growing city—a city being renewed." Outside the great walls were crowded and rundown dwellings. I tried guessing their number—thousands of little shacks—no, *tens* of thousands, pushed together in tight configurations. It was an untold number of stone houses, most with tiled roofs, piled one atop the other, side to side, edge to edge, with small alleyways threading their way into darkness. The great mass butted up against the enormous city walls like a frozen ocean wave, as if to beg entrance. The narrow pathways that I could discern from so far away were clogged: people and animals of burden, coming and going, carrying things, pulling carts, sweeping, talking, living. And hanging above it all, like a foreboding storm that did not descend, was a continuous gray cloud of stove smoke blotting the sun and choking the air.

"They are superstitious," Zafir said. "You can see from here that they build their cities with nine streets that run north and south, and nine that run east and west, in clusters. Many of the neighborhoods inside those outer walls are also walled, a barrier to separate them from others, and the pattern repeats. It's not just for local control or privacy, it's also for their religious beliefs."

"Just like the game!" I said, realizing it suddenly. Indeed, this city *was* the game.

Zafir looked at me, puzzled. "Weiqi?"

"Weiqi, a most horrid game," I said pointing to the board still in play at the front of the boat. "Fawzi and Ammar got me hooked to it. I can't leave."

Zafir smiled as if remembering. "Yes, just like the game. I don't play you anymore because you've mastered it. Perhaps you could negotiate the city yourself after all. You do know these people invented it, to teach strategy to their warriors?"

"So I've heard," I said. "At least I know now whom to blame."

心爱的 **24** 饷爱小

HOUSE OF ZUN

Ammar and I left Zafir and Fawzi at the boat to locate an oxcart for hire. An old man with time to spare agreed to a price and gave us a bumpy ride through the wards of Chang'an. It was slower than a horse but horses were highly valued, the driver said, and horses were refused to any except the royal guard or the military.

"I could walk faster than this," I complained, watching people on foot pass us by. Ammar rebuked my murmur.

"You would be good on foot for an hour," he said. "After that, you would be happy to get back on."

"All right," I said, resuming my stupor of silent boredom.

The home of Zun was beyond the villages of Chang'an on the low-rising hillsides to the south. For more than two hours I sat cramped inside the planked cart, flies bothering me, the humid air stagnant with the sweat of our unkempt beast wafting through the slats of the cart.

We plodded through busy streets and into the pathways between so many shacks and dwellings leaning into each other like so many boards of an old tired fence.

"How far must Zun live to serve a business," I asked. "I would want to be closer to commerce than here."

"It is just to those hills," Ammar said pointing. "The foothills."

The green rise was thick with grasses and low-standing shrub trees. Runoff had carved a path now shadowed by taller trees where the rains could reach deeper roots. There was a perfume of farming blowing off the great spreads of grain fields. A few rice paddies were reflecting the sun from the terraced slopes of the nearest hills. It was a pleasant change from the city's congestion. We could see teams of beasts patiently dragging plow sticks through lumpy red soil. Farmers wearing round straw hats walked alongside to guide the work.

Just then a refreshing coolness washed down the hillsides and passed through our cart, taking away the sweltering heat, the smell of the ox, and the persistent flies. The ride suddenly felt smoother.

"Maybe I spoke too soon about this hot place," I said.

Ammar nodded. "There's good reason most people live outside a great city as this, if they can afford it," he said, and then let his eyes return to sleepy slits in pleasant repose.

These homes were nicer, reflections of greater means. Most of them were squat three-bay structures with a nice courtyard in the front. Pillars and beams supported the pitched roofs and interlocking clay tiles sagged on ancient trusses to funnel the rain to the drip tiles on the ground, neatly aligned in the soil to catch the falling runoff. Gutters and gardens received the torrents beneath.

Advancing farther into the costlier areas we passed the nicer homes. These were more colorful, with large courtyards and nice front quarters for servants. Ornate gates leading to their trimmed entrances hung beneath large wooden archways meticulously carved to stand guard with graven images of their gods, their symbols of protection.

The less-blessed families in this same area had smaller courtyards with simple gates, or none at all. Their roofs were sometimes thatch, sometimes bamboo. But each that we passed, rich or poor, was neatly kept with a garden, flowering trees adorning the sun-side for shade. I could see fruits of flat colors hanging from leafy trees and wondered if these were ready for harvesting or new on the branches. It was, I decided at last, a harvest time after all.

"There is Zun's home," Ammar said, pointing. "The red door and brown tiled roof, do you see it?"

I turned to see a street of nicely aligned pavers packed together with red dirt. More of the three-bay houses were here, evenly spaced, squarely built, with their doors opening to the south.

"Look over there, Ammar," I said, "they all face south, is that more of the same?"

"Not exactly," Ammar said. "Those choices are guided by another of their superstitions. Did I mention their arts of wind and water?"

"Don't tell me, it's more of their religion, right?"

"It's their art of placement," Ammar said. "Their art of living in harmony with their surroundings, with wind and water."

"Now you're talking like that shop keeper in Kashgar," I said.

"Had you been listening, my forgetful student, the layout of these farms and homes would make better sense," he said. "It all comes from a book you should see one day, their Book of Rites, an ancient script, a sacred book. Maybe Zun will find us one, a cheap one on bamboo slats, something durable for the travel, and you can learn their language. It teaches them how they may keep the balance of nature intact and how they may create scenic formations for their graves."

"For the dead?"

"Is there any other?" he asked.

"What does that have to do with farms and houses?" I asked.

"The ancients used this art to place their graves where the wind and the water would not disturb them," Ammar said. "No wind to blow away the soil, no water to wash the dead into the light of day. The concept of wind and water grew into a science that was intertwined with religious beliefs and superstitions. Today you may hire a consultant to help you lay out your farm or your home—very ingenious, Bassam. When you look at what they can do it makes good sense."

"A consultant? Who needs a consultant?" I said. "I don't need some expert pretender to tell me where the wind blows and the water flows. I can do that on my own."

"You should learn more of it," Ammar said. "Such balancing can become complex. It's like the game, they control the ch'i, the energy, so it flows naturally around your land, around your home, around your life."

"That's too much ancient philosophy for me," I said.

Ammar shook his head and looked the other way. "So much to learn, young Bassam, so much to learn."

The driver turned onto the red-dirt road and stopped in the middle to let us off. He accepted a coin for his time.

I was happy to escape the confines and stood to stretch my legs and bend my back. It popped into comfort while I rolled my neck back into place.

"Another half-day ride like that and I'll need those pain needles from Zafir."

"We have a return trip to make," Ammar said, stretching out his back. "I'm sure we can round up some needles when we get back, I'll put them in you myself, without charge," he said, rubbing life back into his back parts.

Zun's house was neatly coated in stucco and whitewashed. Green overhangs decorated the edges of the roof, and a beautiful red polish covered the front door, giving it a fresh, kept look. Above the door hung an image of a tiger and eight trigrams.

"That's to ward off the evil spirits," Ammar said. "Usually all things are done in threes or fives, but never even numbers, those are unlucky. You can see it is unlucky for the evil spirit to find the eight trigrams, an even number—it is bad for them so they leave and don't enter the home."

I saw wavy glass panes of greenish tint fill the windows, veiled behind beautifully carved lattice works. Earthen pots overflowing with blossomed plants cascaded down from the window ledges.

"Those windows are unusual," Ammar said. "Very rare. The C'ina almost always allow no openings in the outside walls except a door. The walls keep out evil spirits and sticky-handed prowlers at night. You can probably figure it out that our friend Zun is not restrained by these spiritual traditions."

I nodded my interest, and decided regardless of what their spiritual dictators asked of them, it must be good because this was a pleasant place, well-tended and well loved. Maybe the art of the wind and water wasn't such a bad idea after all.

Just as Ammar raised his hand to rap, the door suddenly opened. There stood an elderly woman modestly dressed in a blue robe with long sleeves that hid her hands. White stockings covered her feet and toe-thong sandals kept the red dirt from soiling them. Her long graying hair was neatly tied behind her head, and her eyes were kind and lively. There was a brief pause of wonder showing in her face and then a warm smile as recognition replaced suspicion.

"Ammar?" she asked. "Is that you?"

"Pingyang!" he said smiling. "Yes, fresh from the trek and come to visit a good friend!"

"Ammar! This is a surprise! This is quite the delight! Why, I had no idea!" and extended her arms to a kind embrace. "You are many weeks early," she said. "We were not expecting you yet, welcome, welcome!"

"Yes, and a surprise visit we did not want to make," Ammar said. "But we find ourselves out of sorts, and have made our visit early just the same."

Her smile changed to a look of helpful compassion, and gestured us inside to the main hall. Chairs with pillows awaited.

"Do I find Zun at home?" Ammar asked, turning to look.

"He's in the fields. I will send a messenger, he will be happy," she said, and then turned her eyes to me, tipping her head with a smile. "And you...?"

"This is Bassam, Zafir's young student," Ammar said. "Bassam, meet Pingyang, the most beautiful woman and best cook this side of the ocean, our wonderful hostess for many years past."

"It takes a well-traveled student," she said, "to find our humble home so far from your own." She smiled a warm greeting and I accepted her offer to sit.

"You must tell us all of the news, how is Zafir? Is the trade going well?" she asked, then stopped to offer. "My husband will come shortly, but let you rest, I will bring food, you are hungry? And while we wait, you must tell me of your sorts, the sorts that you are out of," she said.

心爱的 **25** 佀娈小

THE MAD MAN

Zun stood taller than most men, a head above the workers laboring in his newly plowed field. A thin, wiry fellow not yet weighed down with years, Zun had a full growth of black hair tightly knotted atop his head. A pointed moustache and beard speckled black and gray finished the face of a man who walked toward us with purpose. He had large hands accustomed to manual labor, and took great strides with each step.

"Ammar!" he called upon seeing us, and quickened his pace. We had ventured into his field to meet him part way. The two men saluted warmly, and Zun's firm jaw revealed healthy white teeth when he smiled. They laughed and talked, then Ammar made the introductions.

"Pingyang was gracious as always," Ammar said. "She has not changed a day since we last left you. And I'm afraid Bassam and I have come visiting without warning. Please accept my apologies for this intrusion."

Zun waved away the formality and looked at me.

"Bassam?" Zun repeated, and looked deeply into my eyes. He wrinkled his forehead in thought. "Ah, yes, Bassam, 'He who smiles,'" he said at last.

I was pleasantly surprised. "How would you know that?" I asked.

"I know just enough of your words and ways to keep me in Zafir's good service," he laughed. "You are most welcome to our home, Bassam, and I am so pleased you have come! Both of you! But where is master Zafir, does he watch for us at the house?"

"He is well enough but not with us this time," Ammar said. "He awaits our return back on a boat at Chang'an harbor. We fell to some bandits many weeks ago. Zafir was hurt, we are returning him home to heal."

"Hurt? Should I go to him? He must not travel. Bring him, he can heal here for as long as he requires. Tell me the whole story over a tea. Let us get out of this heat," and turned to lead the way across the field toward his home. As they exchanged stories and news, I was careful to step over the young greens neatly spaced in the furrows, admiring the rich plenty that thrived in this faraway place. The adjacent farmlands marched up a slow slope to the green foothills. A gentle wall circled the whole valley. In each field was manifested the wonderful cycles of growth—new plantings underway in one, workers tending to mature plants in another, harvesting in yet another—all of it tuned to the regimentation given them by their religious beliefs governing such things—and, also, to their philosophy of the wind and water. I felt an ancient recycling at work, a process that was millennia old, a hundred generations at work. The earth feeds her children, I thought, and more abundantly for those who will work it. And here? Here they work it well.

The story of Zafir was sufficiently told when we reached Zun's house. The afternoon sun slumped low, signaling to the farmers that the day's chores had come to an end—the resting time for both the fields and the backs that tended them had arrived. It didn't take long for Zun and Ammar to complete their reunion and create plans for future business ventures, as if the two years' separation was but a night's interruption.

When we arrived at the house Pingyang met us at the door and invited us to join their meal. As we sat to dine, bowls were set and a simple but delicious C'ina cuisine was presented—along with those dreaded sticks for eating. I struggled to remember their utility without abusing them with Kalila's short-cuts, hoping to honor my hosts with exquisite manners. The servant brought the main course—slender strips of chicken ladled over a steaming scoop of wild millet and cucumber. A small white cup of mellow rice wine warmed the palate for dessert. The meal finished with ripe peaches and apricots sliced in cream and honey.

As we ate and talked, Zun revealed a particularly strange task that was sent to him by one of the emperor's royal messengers, a task he promised to show us in the morning. He related in full his excitement and bewilderment about the strange politics of recent times that imposed so many "voluntary" tasks on the peoples of C'ina.

"The man is mad," Zun began. "Huángdi rules the commandries and thinks he is a god."

"A god or *the* God?" Ammar asked.

"A god on earth," Zun said with a wry chuckle. "He heard rumors and sent expeditions for an elixir that gives immortality, thinking to be a god on earth. It is rumored that some islands guarded by large fish were the dwelling places of those immortal ancients and their elusive elixir, and try as he might, none of his faithful could reach the islands. The man worries for his future."

"What makes him fear?" I asked. "He sounds powerful and yet has fears?"

"It is the afterlife," Zun said. "He is wise in his organization and plans, but foolish with the lives that bring it."

"He is your king?" I asked.

"A king, an emperor, a dictator," Zun said. "But a ruthless man. He executes those who challenge him or fail him, in a most terrible fashion. Even his prime minister was torn asunder by horses, his arms and legs parted."

We both nodded at the retelling of the horror, thinking the fear of this tyrant was well engrained across the land.

Zun's wife frowned and hushed her overly-descriptive husband with a wave of her hand and a mild scold. Zun nodded an apology.

"I have heard that he dispatched a royal servant with ships and soldiers to find the legendary islands of the immortals and their elixir," Zun continued. "Fearing for their lives should they return empty handed, the men simply vanished, taking their wives and families with them. Word on the docks is that they settled other islands, large islands with tall mountains suitable for living and raising their families. But for Huángdi, they are lost to places unknown, and that is good enough for the rest of us."

"Is this also a project of his, the rebuilding of the walls and fortress of Chang'an?" Ammar asked. "We saw it from the river. Beautiful work, lavish work. Was it many years and slaves in the process?"

"Oh yes, and with slaves from all his conquered lands," Zun said. "I would like to take you there if you have the time," he offered.

"We would be delighted," Ammar said, "but Zafir awaits us at the docks and our errand must be short."

"Ah, yes, so it is," Zun said. "Then I will fetch the message bag and return you to your way tomorrow, is that your wish?"

"Thank you my friend," Ammar said. "I'm sure Zafir will be pleased to hear that all is well with you and Pingyang, and I will relay your kindness to Zafir and look forward to our meeting again soon."

Zun looked over at me and smiled, "The rest of your band, master Bassam, are they also waiting at the dock? A formidable fleet that would be!"

"Actually, it's just us," I said.

"Fawzi waits with Zafir," Ammar said. "You should see the rest of our train come through soon. We thought they might have come already."

"Not yet, it will be good to see them," Zun said. "So, you are returning to Rekeem?"

"It was quite the sadness for all of us, to end our anticipated labors so near our final destinations," Ammar said. "But for the duration of this wine, I will share this amazing tale in chapters. And you will be pleased to know that our young Bassam is a large part of this story because of his trip through the Taklamakan."

"Where?!" Zun dropped his chin in astonishment and looked over. Pingyang turned quickly as well.

"The Taklamakan?" she asked. "Our horrid waste place where prisoners are sent to die? Where the wind keeps his sand for vengeance? Where the foolish meet immortality of a different kind? You trekked *through* it? Why would you do such a foolish thing?"

I sat frozen in place. The blood started to rise in my face and the heat of embarrassment started boiling over into a full-fledged blush. Ammar saw my discomfort and taking evil advantage of it he inflated the tale to new heights, taking some delight, I was sure, in making me squirm.

心爱的 **26** 啮爱心

CLAY

The damp morning crawled over the valley in clouds of mist and gray, a gentle rain on the crops during the night had stirred earthy smells of damp and vigor. We awoke to the rich farm smells and then a pleasant morning meal with hot tea brewing. Delicious aromas rose from the cook stove where Pingyang was busy preparing.

"Your smile brightens my whole day, Pingyang," Ammar said as we joined her. "The only thing better than a refreshing night's rest and home-cooked food is good friends."

"You are too kind," she said smiling. "Zun wants you outside after you eat."

With the bright sun drying the grounds and warming the air, we took courage to venture through the property until we found Zun in a large back building. He was directing two young workers with their wheeled carts and shovels.

"Ah, my friends!" he said, inhaling the morning mist like a ship taking wind to its sails. "As I told you I am on the most curious quest," he said. "A really strange quest that I want to tell you about—but honestly speaking, I hope it dies an early death."

With that, he waved the workers on their way and motioned us to follow him.

"It's paganism or self-aggrandizement, I haven't decided, probably both," he said as we crossed into a field and walked between the red-dirt furrows. "But edicts are commands, and for the sake of our lands and our families, we must obey. But still—we always hope an ending comes soon."

Zun walked us past animal pens and outbuildings, and over a pasture worn smooth with foot traffic. The upward slope took us quickly to the low hills. We could see from afar that earth and stone were scooped out to form shallow caves in the sides of the hills.

"I have only heard descriptions of your Rekeem and its magnificent dwellings carved in the rock," Zun said. "I can't claim any more artistry than simply mimicking your clever ways with these crude dwellings."

"People live here?" I asked.

"Not now, but long ago, yes," Zun said. "Today they are storage and workshops instead of homes. Let me show you."

The entrances were twice a man tall at the peak, and just as wide. There was no grass around their entrances. Zun led us to the center chamber and stepped inside. We followed into the dark. The walls were blackened with soot like the inside of an earthen oven.

"I have something to show you," he said, and stepped toward the back. When our eyes adjusted to the dark we could see facing us a lone figure standing still.

"Who is that?" I whispered to Ammar. He didn't reply.

Zun produced a slender strip of bamboo glowing at its tip and lit a torch. As the yellow flame burst to life it cast a dancing light that filled the room. Standing before us was no man of flesh but a full-sized man of clay—and not just any man. It was an image of Zun!

Zun watched our expressions and grinned. "Ha! I knew this would surprise you! Do you like the ghost of me in clay?" he asked, laughing aloud.

We stepped closer to examine. Toward the top of the statue the clay looked damp, even fresh. But toward the middle, his dress jacket and leggings all the way to his feet, it was powdery dry.

"What is this wonderful art?" Ammar asked. "It is exquisite work, my friend!"

Zun said nothing and let us discover the prowess of its details and dimensions.

"You like it?" he asked. "Yes, it is a statue of me!"

Ammar smiled. "An excellent reckoning. Excellent! Well done."

We circled the work slowly and methodically, each orbit revealing additional detail. The laces on his boots were meticulously detailed. The pores and patterns of his leather coat were clearly impressed. The collar of his shirt, the beard and pores of his face, his eyes oval and smiling, and his hair knotted atop his head exactly as he wore it today— all of it duplicated in meticulous detail and life-like. Even the folds in his jacket hung as if made of real cloth. His arms were molded forward as if to hold something. The knuckles of his hands and fingernails were perfectly mirrored in the clay. It was magnificent, I had never seen anything like it before.

"This work, this wonderful work," Ammar said, "leaves me speechless, I don't know what to make of it ...."

Zun held back like he was hiding a great secret.

"I know what you're thinking," he finally laughed and could not spread his grin any farther. "It's not what you think, no, not at all! Such vanity is reserved for the king of all vanities, or the king of all fears, whatever they be. But when Huángdi orders it, we must obey."

"We've been getting a riverside tour of his works for the past several weeks," Ammar said. "It's an enormous undertaking."

"And, it's a strange story," Zun said. "Everyone believes the man is mad. This expensive labor is all because of his madness. He fears for his afterlife and wants me to help him."

"Help him? And how is that supposed to go?" Ammar asked.

"He trusts on one—not those closest nor those he counts his friends. His years spent killing, hurting, dismembering, crushing, burning have come to haunt him. He worries that all these tens of thousands of souls he has killed await him in the afterlife. On the other side, they await his death to exact vengeance. And for *that* he fears for when he comes into their midst in the world of spirits in a more equal circumstance, he fears that they will get him."

"How does that involve you?" I asked.

Zun grinned and threw up his hands in surrender. "Well, it seems I have won the emperor's good favor. My labors with Abdali-ud-Din as a friend and a broker, and the great wealth you bring, and other trade I am able to arrange, Huángdi thinks highly of me for it."

"And he wants to honor you with this image?" I asked.

"Not exactly," Zun said. "He wants me in his grave."

"What?" Ammar said. "Now that *is* madness!"

"In his way of thinking," Zun said, "I am supposed to be present at his death and join thousands of others to negotiate with the angry spirits that he encounters, to leave his way free. But not just me," he said with a large wave of his hands. "There are tens of thousands with the same burden placed on their shoulders. Each of us is tasked with forging these replicas of ourselves. It's a chore he enforces with his soldiers who visit here regularly to check on the progress. And before he dies, Huángdi wants his ghost friends and ghost army placed around his tomb. Reliable sources tell me he is having whole armies created, men and horses of clay, and their bivouacs surrounding the great tomb to give protection. He is even burying suits of armor for those with no name who might be his friends—suits to don in his service when that time comes, to protect him."

The puzzled look on our faces was like food for Zun's soul. He relished in telling it as much as he relished guiding the artistry and embellishment in the clay that stood before us.

"Most of the army is being prepared in massive assembly houses closer to Chang'an proper, closer to his tomb complex. People like me have learned to do it at home, on our own. It's faster, too."

"Huángdi thinks he will be attacked after he dies?" I asked. "And these clay people will protect him?"

Zun nodded and shrugged his shoulders. "I don't know what they are eating up there at the palace, but it must be pretty rich to produce dreams like these."

"Why create it here?" Ammar asked. "It's a long ride to anywhere from this remote corner."

"Ah, the crux of my excellent idea," Zun said. "The clay must be baked and while others must move theirs to some place near the palace to be fired, I simply brick up my little cave and bake it right here, without moving it a hair. No damage while it is more fragile."

The blackened walls proved he had turned the chamber into a kiln many times before.

"It's the clay," he said. "Not far are the clay pits—red, just enough wet, just enough dry. My men cut it from the hillsides in blocks and we pound it on a rock until its parts are loosened and malleable. It is an exacting and precise project," Zun said. "We roll the blocks into thick coils and build from the bottom up."

"It looks heavy," I said, "why doesn't it crush the bottom layers?"

"Good question, excellent question, Bassam," he said. "That is precisely the problem, but I know how to do it. First, we build up the feet, thick walls of clay, hollow in the middle, and when we get it about knee-high, we allow it to begin to dry. With wooden slats we keep it from drooping. As it dries, my artisans carve the details into its skin—the shoes and lacings and clothing, their folds and creases, their patterns and markings. As the man grows, the artwork continues upward to the head."

It was amazing work. I admired the precision, it was no casual labor they performed—it was the work of master artisans.

"The head is last, and separate," Zun said. "It sits here on the body for finishing touches, but it comes right off—as do those who have fallen into Huángdi's disfavor!" he said laughing. "I would show you how my head may be so easily detached, but it's heavy and I don't want an evil omen whispering ideas into the emperor's ear!"

He showed us how the body being hollow let his men reach inside to thicken the interior before they fired it. Every wall had to be less than a thumb thick or it would crack in the kiln.

"That's your face, Zun!" Ammar said. "When do they finish?"

"Maybe a month," Zun said. "A different set of artisans will come for my sitting to finish and polish what they have started. I threaten them to make me handsome and young or I'll tell the emperor about their lazy work! It is a good start," he said, bending to examine his clay face from another vantage.

Zun explained it is the most important project for many people since Huángdi ordered it a few years earlier. Zun's image was being prepared to portray him with outstretched arms, and his hands open to hold a scroll or a bamboo book of negotiation. He explained that other clay statues made by his friends were designed to carry implements of their willingness to build Huángdi's empire—gardening tools, laboring tools, swords and halberds, scimitars and spears. Others were cultural in nature—dancers, singers, poets, philosophers, every manner of human expression for the glorification of Huángdi.

Zun told us how the clay is painted with special colors in hues that were approved by the emperor himself. The bright colors will give them enduring life, Huángdi commanded. The most magnificent color of all was C'ina purple, created from Egyptian blue, and made purple by C'ina's alchemists.

"At the end," Zun said, "they'll coat it with the blood of the wax tree. When it dries, the figure is glossy and rich, defined and real. An amazing process, don't you think?"

I had seen that wax before, on the railings and decks of the C'ina boats. The water beaded up and would not soak in, I knew it was something unusual.

"If you want to be a field laborer, Bassam," Zun said, "I will pay you well to harvest the wax! I pay *very* well! But you will work for it."

I smiled. "I can imagine you'd get me up before sunrise."

Zun laughed. "In the hot months you, Bassam, you must climb to the higher limbs before sun-up. The heat dries out the sap and she will not flow when you cut the bark. It is a hard job in the dark, torches show the way, but many of our wax trees have caught fire from careless torchbearers. Those workers no longer work for me."

We laughed with him. I decided Zun would be a good employer, a good man, a good manager. I could tell why Zafir chose him to be his steward at Chang'an.

"The wax is the last step," Zun said, "and then we are all prepared to serve Huángdi in the afterlife—but there's more. I can't speak it from my own eyes, but others tell me Huángdi is preparing a grand chamber for his tomb, a chamber so large you cannot shoot an arrow to its end. The grand ceiling is embedded with sapphires to mimic the constellations above, and it shields a massive map of his entire kingdom, true to size in miniature—complete with earthen mounds for mountains and hills, small models of the cities he has conquered and ruled, the roads connecting them and important places marked, and molten silver for rivers and lakes. An elaborate creation that is consuming the wealth and labor of millions."

I whistled softly at the enormity of the project. The Great Wall I had come to appreciate was only a portion of the man's expensive building. What else did he order to be built for his exhaustive labor in self worship?

"The emperor compels many to do his work," Zun said. "Some say 700,000, others say a million men conscripted for just this, his burial tomb."

"Such an investment," Ammar said shaking his head.

"His tomb is not far from here," Zun said, "I will show you if you have time for it."

"I want to see it!" I said.

"But alas, you are strangers in our land," Zun said, "and getting anywhere near it is sacrilege—and a man could be beheaded on the spot."

"Maybe not, then," Ammar answered.

"From afar you can see it safely," Zun said. "I know I can do that much, the rest depends on which of my friends is standing guard, that is what I was thinking about, getting you a closer look."

Zun went quiet a moment, and shook his head. "But none of us believe that all the architects and artists and servants involved in this project will be spared when the emperor does die. I am content to finish my contribution and then ship my guardian ghost to him in a bed of straw. Let the ox stand at the butcher's blade in my stead. They may place my effigy as they wish, but I am content to wait for word from here. Half a day away isn't enough but it's a start!"

We stepped out of the sculpture shop and into the sunshine.

"Ah, the sky!" Zun said, shielding his eyes from the bright sun and scanning the thinning clouds above. "Wait here a moment, I have something for Zafir."

He hurried to another of the chambers and disappeared inside for a few seconds. He returned carrying a small statue the length of his forearm.

"For Zafir," he said, handing it to Ammar. It was heavy and Ammar made a sound hefting it.

"What is this, Zun?" Ammar asked.

"We have long been burying these clay and stone escorts as protectors with our dead, but we usually use this smaller size. Much better! It's a tradition, many centuries old."

Ammar handed it off to me. I felt its weight and examined its workmanship. It wasn't as cleanly defined as the full-sized version.

"The firing does that, Bassam," Zun said. "The heat when it is not controlled will melt the finer points, and because of such flaws the more discerning buyers reject them. Only the best may go into the ground with the deceased."

"And this also is of you?" I asked.

"When I was younger, much younger," he said smiling.

On the underside, I saw the markings of a script. Zun explained it was the date of its creation and the name of the master sculptor who created it.

"We will treasure it," Ammar said. "Zafir will be so pleased. It will have a prominent place in his home."

"Or his grave," Zun said. "I don't care where he puts it, but let me abide the time with him by proxy through this small replica for when he passes—will you tell him?"

We agreed knowing full well that Zafir would have nothing to do with the pagan burial rites of this kind, but of cultural value he would be honored by this handsome gift. We expressed our gratitude, and carefully cradled the little statue back to Zun's house.

心爱的 **27** 咱爱小

BACK TO THE RIVER

Our return trip to Chang'an Harbor seemed faster. I didn't mind the oxcart that carried us, thinking perhaps it was made kinder by a cooler day and a healthier animal. Along the way I thought I could see Huángdi's grand tomb under construction in the distance. It appeared as a low hill, a great mound with a slow rise that stretched for thousands of cubits across from end to end. It stood above the tops of the houses with clusters of construction work near its peak—large blocks hauled about, tall poles for cranes. The whole mound was crawling with thousands of people moving like speckled mud flowing everywhere at once. I turned to Ammar to point it out but he had fallen asleep. As the activity disappeared behind us, the smells of the river front began to waft heavy as we neared Chang'an Harbor.

The river was as busy as we had left it. The traffic of commerce was thick and rude. It was then I realized that would I miss the quiet of the countryside, and frowned at the raucous activity that hurried past us to either side. Many of the harried made impatient gestures at our ox's slow gait, and with good reason. The pavement had changed from dirt to small bricks smoothed with wear. Deep ruts were worn on either side from ages of passage. After so many cramped hours we were feeling every jolt of every brick beneath the steel-clad rims of the cart's wheels. The barking, the shouting, the yelling, the smells, the bumps and jostles—alas, I was back in the anxious beating heart of Chang'an.

We found Zafir and Fawzi at a diner enjoying a midday meal. They were pleased to see us back safely, and glad for the miniature clay image of Zun.

"Very kind," Zafir said, hefting it gently before setting it on the table.

"What does it do?" Fawzi drawled, "Keep the servant girls away from your flirting ways, Bassam?"

"It's a work for hire, Fawzi," I replied. "We asked the artisans to capture the size of your intellect. They got it right, wouldn't you agree?"

Fawzi chewed his jaw, trying to concoct some rejoinder, and Ammar handed Zafir the leather message bag.

"Routine messages," he said as Zafir undid the lacings.

"Pingyang is doing well?" he asked.

"Oh yes," Ammar said. "Her energy is younger than her age, and we had a fine visit."

"Then she is healthy?" Zafir asked.

"Yes, and as gracious as a hostess could be, caught unawares by our surprise visit."

"Last time we were there she was deathly ill," Zafir said. "A tissue mass in her breast. Zun and the shamans predicted her death in just months."

"She seemed fine to us," Ammar said. "No complaints and no diminishing in her activity...."

"Then it must have worked," Zafir said.

"What?" I asked.

"It was tried before," he said, "cutting the mass from her, but it is not yet a science. I am glad for her, that is a good sign and good for Zun."

Zafir put his hand on the small statue and turned it about.

"I think Zun prefers he be so stricken than his wife, if he could *will it* that way," he said.

The captain stopped by our table with two of his mates and announced our departure soon if we were to clear the harbor traffic before dark. We adjourned to the dock, and Ammar let me carry the heavy statue.

"To earn your keep," he said.

It was good to be back on the river, I decided. If there were things to do, important things, worthwhile things, then I could get used to sea travel. Even so, I was impatient at the crowding of Chang'an proper. With this early midday start it took us several hours, most of the afternoon, to break from the hordes of boats and congestion and clear ourselves from Chang'an Harbor.

Farther downriver the traffic was not so entangled. Finding a docking place would be simpler here, and made me believe that if we planned it carefully, a good caravan could run a brisk business offering an alternative to the congestion at the great front gates to Chang'an.

I watched in silence as the majesty of Chang'an disappeared and a more humble countryside passed by during our ride downstream and away.

心爱的 **28** 咱爱小

INNOVATIVE

Night descended and the countryside came to life as we drifted for a dock. Sparkling with homes lit with lamps and cook fires helped guide our way. The docks put up torches along shore to light the way for late fishermen and travelers such as ourselves.

The men pulled in at a small village where we put up for the night. My legs were aching for dry land. I had endured my fill of that oxcart, and now this endless gray ribbon of water—I longed for the comfortable ride atop my Bakra stepping through the soft sands of home.

The captain pointed out a cozy diner that specialized in roasted chicken, and there we made our rest.

"Go for the fish," Fawzi intoned. "You can never get enough of it, fin face. It's a family reunion."

Over the last month I had eaten enough fish to last ten lifetimes. I wanted a change, and the delicious aroma of their roasted chicken wafted toward me with temptation. Every tasty variety was offered—it was hard to choose. Mine was a whole bird with shoyu and mee pok. I was almost convinced to order again—it would be a most worthwhile investment.

Our table was mostly silent as we sank deeper into thought, relishing each morsel of roasted meat dripping in one of a variety of specialty sauces.

"There are other inventions," Fawzi said, chewing on a bone.

"I suppose you have the list, right?" I asked.

"And discoveries, too," Ammar chimed in.

"That papyrus you've been writing on," Zafir said. "It's ancient, but the C'ina actually invented *paper*. We don't see much of it back home, but it's a much better product."

"Okay, I give up," I said. "What's paper?"

"They grind up old tree bark," Ammar said, "and shred the fibers from worn clothing and fish nets, and stir it into a pulp. They pound it out flat, squeeze out the water with rollers until it is thin and let it dry. Much easier, much cheaper, much better—paper!"

"You should write your journals on *that*," Fawzi said with a smirk. "Old clothing and fishnets, yes, perfect."

"Why did your mother not teach you to read, Fawzi?" I replied. He scowled.

"The list is long, Bassam," Zafir said. "Those little carts at the wall, with the wheel up front? Have you ever seen one before? Did you know about clapper-bells? They made them of clay long before anyone in the West had even thought of it."

"And coffins," Fawzi said, smiling at me with chicken in his teeth.

"Coffins?" I asked. "I thought the Egyptians ... for the pharaohs."

"Not the same," Ammar said. "The C'ina were the first to make them of wood, rectangular. Actually, it is the Egyptians who copied the C'ina. They made theirs larger and more decorative—wrappings, carved logs, clay, that sort of thing."

"The dagger axe, the drum," Zafir added, as if reciting from his own list of favorites. "Even the fork was invented here first."

"The fork?" I shook my head in disgust. "I just spent the last who knows how many months learning the sticks so I could fit in around here, to be part of the crowd—the refined and polite crowd, that is, not you, Fawzi. And now you say they invented the fork? How could they be so forgetful and leave that smart idea and turn to these sticks, they're just a lot of—"

"That's right," Ammar said, ignoring me. "Forks are as old as the land. They made them with small bones before they knew metalwork."

I took the knife and sliced into the roasted chicken, putting a tender piece into my mouth.

"Be polite, use the sticks, feather brain," Fawzi scolded.

"You mentioned that odd substance," Zafir said, "that smooth gloss on the planks of the boat that made the water bead up?"

"Oh, yes," I said. "Zun said they painted their clay statues with it."

"It's a liquid wax that dries to a nice finish," he said. "It colors and protects the wood. It's an ancient art to them. Many relics in holy places show amazing and delicate handiwork in the wax, work that you don't see much of anymore."

Ammar wasn't listening, he was pulling from his memory all the things he had learned about this amazing land and its inventive and creative people.

"Don't forget the oar for rowing and steering," he said. "They came up with that. And the triangle plow, you've seen such plows?"

I nodded.

"They also invented silk cloth, mee pok, and shoyu," Fawzi said, "and steamers for cooking instead of an open flame—all ideas from people smarter than you, Bassam."

Zafir chuckled and shook his head. "They made doors that open by themselves, paper money, a bellows for the fire, furnaces that melt metal, bore-hole drilling, toothbrushes made from bristles, cast iron, chain drives—"

"Chain drive?" I asked.

139

"Metal links in one large loop that turns wheels. That is how they opened and closed those massive doors we passed in Chang'an."

"And cuju," Fawzi said. "A great sport with a ball. They used to train their soldiers with it. I'll show you one day, but you might cry when I beat you."

"And your clothing, Bassam," Zafir said. "The C'ina invented the looms to make their exotic and fine fabrics. And gas for cooking and heat."

"Gas?" I asked.

"Oh yes," Ammar said. "They draw it from the ground and transport it through bamboo pipes. It burns hot to cook your food and keep you warm in the winter."

"Remember that bow that Tou' gave you?" Fawzi asked.

"Oh, yes, and excellent bow."

"They also invented a crossbow," he continued, holding up his hands as if sighting down the front of one and pulling the release. "It's a great tool. It holds an arrow ready to launch with the pull of a finger. I have one at home, I'll show you if you don't shoot yourself in the foot."

"And don't forget the horse collar and reins," Zafir added. "Also many foods and chemicals, ink and medicines. These many ideas were known to them long before we had them back in Rekeem."

"In math, they came up with the idea of negative numbers, Bassam," Ammar said. "You asked about them one time. These people used them first, a negative number to work a more complex math. And the umbrella to keep the rain off, deep drilling with ingenious bores that let their pipes go deep into the earth—"

"All right, enough, enough!" I said. "They came up with ideas everywhere. It's fantastic. So, why didn't these kinds of things get invented in the west? Why don't we *have* them in the west?"

My friends went quiet for a long moment and then Zafir folded his hands under his chin and rested his head, looking off into the distance. "I suppose," he said, "in a land where so much trade brings so many people from around the world, perhaps it became a landing place for ideas—new ideas. And when a people become so prosperous that they can afford to have many priests and artists and philosophers, maybe that is the fertile ground where new ideas can take root, and then better ideas come as fruit with seeds for more ideas."

Freedom, I thought. Freedom from hunting for food and preparing it, freedom from fighting for shelter and protection. That much freedom leaves a person time to think, time to create and risk failure with new ideas, to try again and again. *Freedom*. It was a principle embraced in the scrolls. I had never thought about it like this before. And when the elders or sheiks try to control too much of a man's private freedom, it kills the desire *and the opportunity* to explore an idea because—what's the point? No freedom means no time or reason to invent, no desire to create, and the result is no progress. For lack of freedom you are prevented from enjoying the fruits of your labors. Is this not what Huángdi was doing to his people? Crushing them into obeying his will and not releasing them to be inventive? Could that be why our Rekeem sits unaltered by the hands of despots and a land of peace and prosperity for these many dozens of centuries? Is that the real power of the scrolls, to show what freedom can bear given the chance? I must ask Zafir about that, I thought, the next time we can speak alone.

The days that followed flew by as quickly as did our little river boat. We sailed past several Xiongnu strongholds without incident, and even encountered some snow. But the river kept carrying us north, then east, and finally turned south toward the ocean.

I noticed one morning a salty scent in the air. I felt it in my lungs and on my skin, it was a different air altogether that revealed itself long before we arrived at the coast. It was the ocean at last, I could smell it before I could see it. No more river, no more little village stops, no more heavy hand of Huángdi. We had come to an end of his madness, and before us nothing but open ocean—*freedom!*

"Day 449—Dear Rasha, I was thinking of you these past few weeks. I saw Chang'an, it is all that we heard. I will bring you here one day and we will wander its streets and test its wares for a month—a year if you want it. Your father's leg is healing nicely. It has been almost two months and he can stand on it, but it remains sore. Shen told us he will need a year before it is whole again. I hope I find you doing well. We are at the east ocean. I am excited to see these great coastal waters that carry the world's enormous burden of trade and mystery and legend. —Bassam"

"Dear Bassam, Mother is doing much better, it was good to be with my sisters again. It is a long trip to Saba' and back, but I am safe, I have returned home. —Rasha"

心爱的 **29** 㑽爱小

ZHIGU

The harbor village of Zhigu smelled of ripe fish from one end to the other. The entrails and discarded waste from the shanty fisheries colored the water where they were cast, and gulls floated lazily overhead, already gorged from the steady diet.

Dozens of old wooden docks stuck out into the ocean like so many old men bent over with age, holding their burdens against the tide and storm-tossed seas. The planks were black from the unspeakable traffic of dead or dying sea creatures slaughtered and stowed away onto the carts of sloppy traffic that slipped away to the market places beyond. The salt-bleached moorings slouched in gray, weary repose, fixed to the platforms with frayed ropes whitened with time. Up and down the little harbor, the docks served as anchor to many dozens if not hundreds of boats—every size, every shape, some coming, others going. It was slower life here, nothing like Chang'an Harbor, and there was less anxiousness to it—many fishermen waiting on one who wouldn't move because he didn't feel like it, nor the other wishing to impose. Lazy.

But we had arrived at the sea! The river journey was now ended and the great ocean stretched out before us, our last long hurdle before home. I had seen the sea before, from Leuke Kome, and once from shore at the West Sea, but I had never traveled it for any significant distance. And now we stood at the beginning of a magnificent voyage that would take us probably three times the distance we had traveled on land, and perhaps as many months as well. Five months? Six months? More? Ammar said he and Zafir had taken this way twice but with trading stops along the way, a much longer voyage for them. So, the time at sea is hard to determine, Ammar said. "Plan on four months at least, if the winds are with you," he told me. "And if you sail during the storm time, expect a year." A year? "Oh yes," he had said. "And most of that time spent at some coastal village while you wait for the storms to pass by."

With the sun now rising hot and bright, the evening fishing vessels were already in line for off-loading, but their men growing impatient lest their labors become spoiled. They stood against masts and ropes waiting and wondering.

Across the walkways traders were already bartering, bargaining and shouting, while row upon row of the waiting boats bobbed gently on the rolling surf, patiently looking for their turn at dock, hoping to be bargaining and shouting for highest prices sometime before midday.

"Bassam, you stay with me," Zafir said. "Fawzi—you and Ammar find an ocean boat that is loading for the south and buy passage to

Kantoli, or anywhere near. We need good quarters, and ask about their foodstuffs and water. We will bring our own if we must. And bring back plenty of bread and drink—enough for three weeks. When you have a suitable boat, have men help you load the supplies and our luggage into my compartment."

"Don't get kidnapped," Fawzi said, kicking my foot as he and Ammar left for the shore.

"Don't scare the women with that face of yours," I yelled back. "We don't want another riot."

Fawzi picked up a small pebble and threw it toward my head, but missed. He pointed a finger and mouthed at me, "Next time, Bassam," as he walked away.

With the men swallowed into the busyness of the wharf, Zafir called me to his side.

"We have unfinished business with the scrolls," he said.

"Yes, I wondered about that," I said. "Did they survive the attack?"

"Yes, they're safe," he said.

"The ocean is a much different desert to do the reading," Zafir said.

I nodded and scanned the sparkling blue that turned various shades toward the misty horizons beyond.

"I don't expect the boat to stop each night unless it has business," Zafir said. "That will give us a good time to talk, perhaps on the deck and away from listening ears."

"Do they travel at night? Isn't that dangerous?" I asked.

"Yes and no. They have lanterns. By night the navigator steers a true path with the stars as his guide, and the lanterns alert the other boats."

"Do they have the south pointer to help them in the dark?" I asked.

"Not here, not that I've seen," Zafir said. "They stay close to the coast for the most part. If a storm kicks up, they don't always have time to reach shore. It's a much different life, Bassam. They get lost in the tempest on occasion, but once the stars are back, it's a quick trip to safety. If you want to test your south pointer, I want you to test it in the privacy of your compartment. See if you can chart the changes in direction as we proceed south along the coast."

I felt inside my coat for the little south pointer. I was curious how Ammar worked his—he still hadn't shown it yet.

"This last scroll," Zafir said. "It's somewhat different than the others, and I want you to prepare yourself to receive it, Bassam."

"Prepare? Yes, what do you need me to do?"

"The seventh scroll is the capstone of all the scrolls," he said, "the completion of understanding. It is the true test of your knowledge and your faith in virtues and principles. As you will see, it is the end of all teachings."

"The end?" I asked.

"Truth is the end of all teaching and the beginning of all learning—a lifetime of learning and new understanding. Grasp the lessons in the seventh scroll, memorize them, live them, watch for them, and the seventh scroll will finish the work that we started more than a year ago."

"Then I'll be ready to listen," I said.

I shuffled around a moment, wondering if Zafir wanted to say more. "Do you want to try me at a game of Weiqi?" I asked.

Zafir put on that old crafty smile of his and nodded *yes*.

An hour later, Fawzi and Ammar returned. They had rented space on a large boat and brought back six young men and carts to move our belongings. We helped Zafir hobble into one cart and packed our belongings into the other. The runners worked a path down the shoreline to the far end of the harbor.

"There it is," Fawzi said, pointing to a three-masted sea-going boat securely tied to the dock with six heavy ropes. "There's home for the next weeks or months."

As we neared, Ammar pointed out the characters painted all along the sides of the boat, just below the rails and across the planking. They dazzled with bright green and red paint, outlined in black, a scheme that shouted defiance at whatever forces its makers wanted to challenge.

"The C'ina call such images a djong," Ammar said. "The djong on our boat mean 'Flying Dragon,' and each call to the gods for protection and prosperity. The name of the boat is also called Flying Dragan to reflect that desire."

The large craft sat heavy at the dock, unmoved in the gently rolling sea. I counted 30 paces to the midpoint, and estimated another 15 paces breadth. It was the largest boat I had ever boarded.

There was a full castle bridge to the stern, an enclosure with windows and doors occupying the back third. It was ornately crafted with polished planks and rounded carved beams that kept the sleeping quarters protected and dry from the elements.

A door led to quarters above and another door to those below, while between the two forward masts was a floor hatch giving access to cargo. Zafir and Ammar were quartered down the steps to the stern—Fawzi and I were next to the crew quarters beneath the deck door.

I didn't like the stench below—it was acrid and noxious. Fawzi said such smells dissipate once we're at sea, and to stop complaining.

"Gutting her for new fittings is what this old boat needs," I said bravely. Deep inside I could feel the green nausea rumble but refused to let Fawzi see my growing distress.

The ladder was grimy and the planking below hid the sloshing foulness beneath it. The smell of rotted wood and decaying fish was partly masked by fish-oil lamps that gave a yellow glow to the long hallway. The lights hung by thin cords and swayed from creaking beams arching across each of the cramped rooms.

"We have the king's state room, how lucky are we," Fawzi said, dropping his things on a mattress stuffed with hard cotton batting. "And look, our own bunks—a straw bale for you, a straw bale for me, and rat-chewed blankets to sleep under."

"I suppose you'll be wanting to borrow my coat," I breathed. "But forget it."

"You keep rubbing my nose in Tou's betrayal of friendship, but I'll win it from you in a wrestle," Fawzi said.

"No deal," I said putting up my fists in defiance. "And if I catch you stealing it I'll give you a whopping from the broadside of the sword of Bassam."

"Watch your threats, fish tongue," he growled, "or you'll be wearing no coat at all, and Zafir will agree with me."

"Harrumph, then," I said.

Fawzi abruptly stopped his unpacking and looked over at me with bright-eyed astonishment.

"*Harrumph*?" he said. "Why Bassam, I think you've finally run out of words, *crab head*. It's a miracle! Perhaps there is some peace and quiet after all."

心爱的 30 的爱心

FISHING

THE sky cleared to crystal blue when our boat pulled away from the dock. The great sails strained at the masts, catching a steady cool breeze pushing us directly south. The *Flying Dragon* cut a frothy path away from shore and into the choppy seas that rolled out before us. I watched from the bow as wide, slow turns took us around other boats, steered us between tiny outcroppings of uninhabited islands, and then slid us farther south into the unobstructed and sun-sparkled rippling sea.

After just an hour we were distant enough from the coast to lose sight of the docks. More sail was added and our speed quickened. The vastness of the ocean finally opened, and we began our slow, rolling journey toward home.

The patterns of waves on the open sea reminded me of the endless stretch of dunes in the Taklamakan—except here there was a rhythmic, soothing harmony of motion and life. I loved the sound of waves slapping against the planks of the hull and the feel of the warming, humid breeze that accompanied them. It was still too cold to leave my coat below, but Fawzi was right—even on these waters I could feel the wintry cold losing his grip. The journey south made such heavy coats a blanket at best, and sometimes a burden.

"Good morning whale vomit," Fawzi said, climbing onto deck next to me. "I see you're ready for some fishing lessons today."

"Fishing?" I asked.

"What? Did you expect breakfast in bed, Your Lordship?"

"I thought those supplies we bought were …."

"Were for dinner. But for breakfast, you eat what you catch," he said, making a motion of catching a fish in one hand, dropping it in his mouth with the other.

"And if I don't catch anything?" I asked.

"Then you may join the crew at their table below, where blood and scales are wiped away so you may eat half-cooked mystery meat and drink a mug of silty grime that leaves you picking at your teeth long after you have swallowed it."

I frowned in disgust. "Fawzi—someday, I need to tell you how well you manage to spoil my appetite for food, for adventure, for curiosity. Why, you're—"

"I'm the best thing in your life, Bassam. Now stop wasting my time and go get a fishing pole from over there and I'll show you how it works." He pointed to a tall wooden box with an open door. I could see fishing sticks and lines, various weights, hooks, and wooden floating devices, all waiting for someone accustomed to fishing—unlike me.

Fawzi loved fishing and was long-winded in telling me about the art and skill of fishing, a pastime thousands of years old. Catching the fish was the job of a net, or so I had heard—nets were skillfully used to pull up many fish at once, or to herd them together in shallow waters where men threw them by hand onto the beach. But to catch a fish by hook? That was a much different science.

"You have to watch for your shadow. These fish are smart, they'll think you're a bird, and in your case, they'd be right," Fawzi said. "So let's get you set up."

I handed him the pole and a hook.

"There's an art to tying these hooks, Bassam. It's flaxen, so no ordinary knot will do. I'll tie this first. You watch and do the second yourself."

Fawzi carefully looped the line through the hole in the hook, wrapped it once and tied it through itself again. He pulled on the hook to test the strength of the knot, and then produced a small piece of fish as bait.

"Where did you get that?" I asked.

"The kitchen," he said, "on my way up. You've got to think about these things, Bassam. Knowing in advance what happens in that kitchen, need I say more?"

I looked across the waters and saw the small splashes and breaches of morning feeders, all kinds of various fish. "What fish live around here?" I asked

"Depends. There are red and white fish in these waters, I don't know if cachan swim this far north. The captain might. You would enjoy fighting a cachan—catch one and feed the crew for a week."

"That big?"

"At least, and they're fast. I've heard men brag about monsters longer than a man is tall and twice his weight."

"With this flimsy line?"

"They catch them with ropes, blubber brain," Fawzi said, pointing to a thick coil hanging from the railing. "Rope and a large hook. I don't know how they pull in a fish so large, but it should fetch a good price at the local market when they haul it to shore."

Fawzi led me to the stern.

"The secret is not to be seen," he said, peering over the edge.

"By the fish?"

"Who else, dorsal dunce?" Fawzi said. "*Certainly* the fish. I told you, they can see your shadow. You have to find a place where you don't make a shadow."

"And the pole? The cord?"

"Everything," he said. "In fact this brown cord may not work, something white is better, like silk. Harder to see."

"So, let me try this ..." I said, lowering the hook into the water. I let it drag just inside the frothy wake. "How far do I let it sink?"

"You're doing it fine, just where the fish will smell it," Fawzi said. "Hold it there a while and let's see what happens."

No sooner had the words left Fawzi's mouth than the pole almost yanked out of my hands. I gripped it hard in a quick panic, fighting a great weight that pulled and fought to yank the pole from my grip.

"Whoa! Look at this! Now what?" I yelled.

Fawzi was laughing. "You gotta hold it tighter than a girl, Bassam, hold tight, let out more twine."

I braced myself and doled out a cubit or two, and then a few more. After some moments, the fighting quieted but the pull on the rod remained.

"Is it still there? He's not fighting me like he was," I said.

"Oh, he's still there all right," Fawzi said. "He's just resting before he starts fighting you again. This time, slowly pull the cord toward you. This will make him grow tired, and when he is close enough, I'll catch him in the net."

I pulled carefully on the line using one hand, letting the excess pile up in loops on the deck. I took my sandal off and stood on the excess line for better control in case the fish wanted to run again.

For several minutes more I continued, keeping the tension in my direction until Fawzi reached over the railing with a small net. "I see it, Bassam, hold steady just a moment ... a moment more and breakfast is served."

Fawzi made a swoosh of the net into the water and pulled it out, dripping and whipping about. He stood with the net in the air and presented the morning's catch.

"It's a white fish all right, Bassam, but look."

I set down the pole to see my prize, but found that for all its fight, it could hardly be called a prize.

"What? This is no fish, it's hardly longer than my foot," I said. "This is a baby."

"A baby indeed," Fawzi laughed. "But what a fright he gave you, squid eyes. Should I throw him back to his mother?"

"Oh no, that's my breakfast. I'll find his brother tomorrow and his sister the next. I like catching my breakfast. Thank you, Fawzi!"

"You're the ruthless tyrant, aren't you, Bassam," Fawzi said, "going after the babies before they've had time to see the world. I'm glad I'm not hungry enough to find your hook!"

At the end of the first week our routine aboard the *Flying Dragon* was well set. There were about forty passengers, give or take some additions and subtractions each place we docked. We took turns with the chores, each of us rotating through the kitchen, the washing room, fishing for meals, scrubbing the deck. The crew kept the ship moving night and day, making more progress in a couple of hours than I had remembered the caravan making in a day.

"Tell me Ammar," I asked as we finished midday meal, "have you been following our progress with your charts?"

"I have indeed," he said. "I've been checking my readings with the stars after first watch, and we're right on schedule and right on track."

"How do they do it? I mean, without your charts?"

"They have a new type of kamal, it's made of brass and has no string, but it works just the same."

"But their direction?" I asked.

"I tried talking to the navigator about that," Ammar said. "He didn't know what I was talking about. He kept pointing to the coast. I gathered that so long as the coast is in sight, they consider it the right path and the right direction. I'm sure they use the stars at night, but perhaps not with the level of scientific accuracy that we strive for."

"I wonder how they manage it during a storm when no coast is visible—or stars," I said.

I looked at the distant green ribbon of the shoreline, and then squinted to the south. Nothing but open ocean led away to the horizon. I knew many new lands lay in that direction—so much to see, so many places to visit.

"Ammar, could you show me your south pointer?"

"Yes, I've neglected that, let's go below."

The cabins at the stern were better appointed than mine. Natural lighting kept them warm and inviting. Polished wood paneling led to each room. The narrow hallways had a few paintings and gold engravings, and small shelves with green statues tied to them with twine. Zafir and Ammar's room had two beds on legs, blankets and pillows, and a table with chairs. Several carpets of beautiful design covered the wooden floor.

"Have a seat, let me fetch the charts," Ammar said.

I pulled up a chair and noticed right away the bowl of fruit on a side table.

"What's this?" I asked. "The captain certainly knows how to reward a paying passenger's offering...."

"Oh? You don't have any of this? What are your rooms like?" Ammar asked.

"They'll do," I lied.

"So, let's look," Ammar said, rolling out his map across the table.

"Here is Zhigu, our last stop, and, let's see—according to the kamal, we have traveled about 1,500 stadia south." Ammar traced a route with his finger that cut through a peninsula jutting to the east. "Following the coastline I estimate we've traveled closer to 3,500 stadia, maybe 4,000."

"That's a long way to Kantoli," I said, pointing to the map. "At this rate it will take us a year!"

"Not that long, my impatient friend," Ammar said. "More like four or five weeks."

"A south pointer makes more sense. We'd get there faster, why not use it?" I wondered aloud.

"This is a trading ship. Following the coast is necessary—they deliver goods along the way. Also for safety. There are pirates around these waters and a lone ship far from shore is a nice target. But closer, where there's room to make a run for safety, it's better passage."

"So, let's see," I said, tracing a route with my finger. "If we oversaw this boat, we could go straight south and bear to the west and arrive at Kantoli in … I guessed two weeks."

"The winds are with us until about here," Ammar said, pointing to a place marked with arrows on the map. "And then we must work our way back and forth, that's what takes the time and patience."

"Time I have. But patience? What's that?" I said.

Ammar laughed. "Well said, my friend. Now, let me show you the south pointer Zafir gave me."

心爱的 **31** 啲嬰尐

THE TALK

I t was the start of the fifth week and a beautiful night on the ocean. The water was calm, the stars steady, sparkling and clean. On the sea, especially on the sea, the expanse of the night's star-lit sky radiated warmth that was so intense I could almost feel it. I held out my hand and closed my eyes, convinced that my palm warmed beneath its steady stare, even in this winter season.

I sat hunched on the damp wooden bench, alone on deck. Even without my kamal or charts I could read the stars to know the ship was pointed south-southwest. And that they glided through the dark at a speed that seemed reckless, though the breeze hardly filled the sails. *These men,* I thought, *risked wrecking on the shoals of who knows what out here in such pitch.* A lantern burned dimly on the bow in bleak warning, but a warning to whom I couldn't guess. The old seamen steering our boat wore the attitudes of long travel along these coasts. Here in the open sea I could trust such experience, provided the coast remained in view. Without it, I could trust my south pointer more.

The only noise breaking the calm came muffled talking and laughing from the people below deck. Their banter and friendships and joking was pleasant to the ear, but above decks, I had a more enticing accompaniment to my thoughts: the water. Its steady slapping the sides of the ship in sleepy, regular rhythms was calming and comforting. Toward the back the lookout talked quietly with the steersman as they idled away the hours—I was not alone.

Suddenly the door opened and a great yellow light broke my serenity with a blinding declaration of day.

"Bassam!" Zafir called. His silhouette cast a long shadow toward me.

"Let me help," I said, getting up to approach.

"Don't need it," Zafir said, "but if you'll carry these—" and held out the old leather sack of scrolls and the sleeping mats.

"Did you bring your lamp?" he asked.

"Yes, should I light it?"

"Yes, and let's move to the bow. The water is steady there, and we can be alone."

I found a light from the steersman's lantern and caught up with Zafir. He seated himself in the blackness.

"All right," Zafir said, working around the stiffness that remained in his leg. "Make some room. Let's just talk for a while."

I made a small circle of light with the lamp set close and the scroll bag lying flat between us, and sat down.

"So, you made a new friend in Kalila?" Zafir asked.

I gulped. I didn't expect that, and had nothing to say. "Well, in a way. We had good talks together," I stammered.

"You're of the age to think of a family, Bassam," Zafir said. "I'm sure your father has spoken to you. It's good that you made friends with Kalila. Has your father chosen you a wife?"

"A *wife*? Well, uh ... No, we haven't discussed it. I suppose he will."

"And what will you tell him of your friendship with Kalila?" he asked.

"I don't expect that to be a part of our discussion," I said truthfully.

"That's right," Zafir said. "It's a strange path all men make of their lives. Some seem destined toward one direction, and one day find themselves working toward another. You, Bassam, you will let your father choose for you because that is right, is it not?"

"Yes, I expect him to find me a wife," I said. "I just didn't think, well, I'm only 17 and not sure about it...."

"A wealthy man has many wives, Bassam," Zafir said, "but it's not always the blessing it seems. I love Rasheeda, she was my father's choice, and she is my first love. The others, they are honestly more work than help, but none of them has borne me a son. And you will have your first love, too. Be true to her and all else will follow in good order."

I wondered what Zafir was leading up to. We had never discussed romance or marriage at any time on the trip. Why now that we're headed home?

"I'm honestly not sure that having more than one wife is something for me," I said with a smile.

"And so it is for most men, and probably best," he said flatly.

"I don't see how you do it, Zafir. Too many women telling you what to do, isn't that what you complained about to my father?"

Zafir laughed and nodded his head.

"I love your father," Zafir said. "He and I have had wonderful times together, my boyhood friend, my best friend. But tonight, I want you to take this." He reached for his ring, slipped it off his finger and held it a moment in front of me. "This is the seal of my fathers, of the Abdali-ud-din," he said. "It carries their seal and the small crest of my family, difficult to see in this light, but it is most certainly the official ring. Can you see it?"

I studied it a moment, not sure if he wanted me to hold it or just look.

"Here, take it, hold it," he said, and put it into my hand. I turned it around. It was warm. I could see the crest of the Abdali-ud-din, an emblem I had seen many times before. And just below, as he said, Zafir's family crest.

Zafir sat up straight. "It is yours, Bassam. I give it to you," he said.

I made an audible gasp and searched his eyes. "What? Why?" I asked with perplexed bewilderment.

"When you return home, my boy," Zafir said, "your father will introduce you to your new bride. It was all arranged before we left Rekeem. We agreed it would be enough time for her to grow into a woman. This ring will validate my consent. It was the agreement."

My heart suddenly froze. I could hardly choke out her name. "*Rasha*?" I asked.

"With your father's blessing," he said, taking my hand in his and closing my fingers over the ring.

"It is the key to her dowry," Zafir said. "And to the treasures in Leuke Kome, at stops farther east, Kashgar, Chang'an, in every place we have visited and some we have not. You, Bassam, I want you and my Rasha to be the heir to my name and steward over my family legacy. Unless you have slept through the reading of the scrolls, you know the many treasures and properties of mine are not my true prosperity. That, my son, is my young Rasha. But the material accumulations are yours as a stewardship from many generations past and many generations forward—when you marry Rasha."

I gulped, speechless, a thousand thoughts exploding in my head all at once. I held the ring carefully, hesitantly, turning it around and around to make sure it was real, as if looking for something not already there. The lamp's light danced across the golden band and reflected the etchings and relief and emblems. It was worn and smoothed with age—the crisp etchings of the crest of Abdali-ud-din were softened from trial and use. In silence Zafir waited as I tried a few fingers, finding the pointer finger of my left hand to be fat enough to keep the ring from slipping off. I twisted it past the knuckle and closed my fist to embrace it.

"I cannot speak," I said quietly. "This is quite, I mean, I didn't expect, uh—" I stammered. "I didn't expect, that is, I mean sir, you have—it's a gift and, I certainly didn't expect this, but it's—it's an honor and a surprise and ...."

Zafir smiled with a new and pleased look in his eyes. A softer, trusting look, a side of him I had not seen.

My heart was pounding and my head was reeling. "These gifts of your hard work," I said, "I am not deserving. I mean, what I want more than anything is to prove my loyalty to you, to prove your trust in me, to be worthy of it. And to be worthy of one so beautiful and special and wonderful as your Rasha. She is my best friend—she means so much to me, she always has. I didn't know, I didn't realize what a strong spirit, what a beautiful person she is, and a strong companion to whoever she married. Yes, that is what I thought from afar, watching her at my mother's side, learning the ways of a home. She was so—so lovely and, well, we shared so many dreams growing up, I didn't think of it then, but my heart had become knitted to hers and has been for a long time, but I was reckless with her feelings, and—"

"She's forgotten that, Bassam, and forgiven too. Surely you know that by now?" Zafir said, waving his hand as if to brush all the past behind us. "But I will say this—a father's great secret, without asking from God a curse or a blessing, is that *your* boys will so torment you in the same ways before they come of age. You can plan on it!"

My boys, I thought. What about *that*? I couldn't fathom the possibility—I had never considered it. What if they *are* like me? I quickly vowed to never let it happen.

"And don't think you can make it otherwise," Zafir said as if reading my mind. "You are the harshest on your first son, trying to pattern in him something old out of something new, to fix your own flaws and deprivations through your first begotten. It won't work, and you will either drive your first child away from trying it, or learn soon enough that a new personality is as a clean stretch of desert sand, no steps of trespass and unmarred by experience. It is clean and new, and must be nurtured and encouraged to be what God has made him to be—not punished and forced into something he is not, into what you want him to be."

Zafir spoke of family, *my family*. The thought made me tense inside—too much too soon. I didn't want to be tied down, I wanted to go places, do things—a family would just, well, it would hold me back. That would mean a house—a grave for the living. And my Rasha? My boys? *Girls*? I had thought of it but not this soon, but only eventually, one day when I was ready. But now? I had too much life to live. All this marriage talk, it was an older man's talk, it was making me squirm with nervousness. And then came the distant memory of Rasha and our last goodbye—

"I sense your thoughts Bassam," Zafir said. The flickering light danced across his smiling face and kind eyes. "And don't worry about these new ideas. All good things will unfold at the right time and at the right place, and you will find in them great joy. You will find family to be your strongest foundation stone where upon you may start all new enterprises. Your family gives you strength, it gives you retreat, it gives you all things that you don't have at this moment. Never fall for the temptation to dismiss it for selfish reasons—that would be the most selfish of all to reject such a bright future. Don't let your impatience get the best of you. You will discover as you move a step at a time on the right path that you eventually will obtain the two great gifts of the deliberate life—*peace* and *prosperity*. But these are not all. To find the third gift, that gift that eludes all who live to forsake it, and rewards all who find it, is a companion. With Rasha you will find that third gift. You will find the peace, you will find the prosperity, and with Rasha you will find the *joy*."

The old boat creaked as the sea breeze ruffled the sails and the steersman turned to catch the wind. And just as suddenly, it went quiet again. I was left to ponder and think and try to absorb the revelations that had just been poured into my future—and unfolding of a new course in life, delivered in just moments, here, in the dark, under this sky, on these waters.

I could tell that Zafir had completed his goal for the evening and seemed ready to end it. I twisted the ring around on my finger several times, finding that it sat there comfortably, securely, as if crafted for my own hand.

"Don't think this scene hasn't played out before, my son," Zafir said. "I was 16 when my father sat me down on such a night as this, the sky above no different than now, and told me he had chosen Rasheeda, and gave me the same ring I have given you."

"This very ring?" I turned it about thinking of a time long ago, fifty, maybe sixty years, when a young Zafir received this ring from his father, and how it is replaying a role tonight, a pattern for living, a pattern between the generations, a pattern like the scrolls.

"And were you scared, too?" I asked.

"Oh, yes!" Zafir smiled. "These many decades later, I still remember it well. No amount of worldly treasure could win my complete allegiance to the idea of marriage, although my father tried his best, as I have with you tonight."

"And you knew? You knew it was right?"

"In my heart, Bassam, in my heart I knew it was right. I had loved Rasheeda for a long time, but it was not mine to decide. And the knowledge that my father wanted to share, that he wished me to carry on, and pick up the burdens of prosperity, to carry the family charge to bear the scrolls and strengthen the enterprise, that too was something I knew was coming but didn't expect so soon. Like you, I wasn't ready, I felt inadequate, I felt ill-prepared for my bride and for the business."

His eyes drifted to the blackness beyond, to the softness of memories and the happiness of joys gone by. It seemed to animate his countenance, transporting him to an earlier, joyful time.

"A man wiser than I might think you're bribing me, Zafir!" I said.

He laughed. "Yes, so did I, and accused my father of that same deception. And he laughed as well. Marriage is never so complicated as it is when it finally comes to *you*. The family legacy of wealth and economic influence requires two good people, Bassam. *You* to employ wisdom and knowledge so that the enterprises can grow and bless all involved. And *she*, a faithful companion who can hold your feet to the ground, give you strength. Your wife will give you correct bearings so you don't lose the most precious things in life to gain those things of least value in life."

"And Rasheeda, was she that for you?" I asked.

"Oh yes, and more. She has an insight into business dealings that has saved me from stepping into foolish arrangements. You must invite your bride into your whole life, Bassam. No secrets, no doubts, no judgments against her. She brings strength, her perspective is deeper and broader than you could imagine. It is important that you take counsel with her and never discount her ability to help you see things that she sees and that you don't. It is the great balance of life that God gives, a man and woman, warmly yoked together by their love for each other, and yet each independent in that sphere in which they were created. Marriage in the general sense makes a perfect match. Marriage in the specific sense is the grandest and most satisfying labor in life. You must never discount her or think you are master and she is anything less."

"I couldn't think of it," I said.

"But you will," Zafir said, pointing at my head. "And when you do, you will remember our talk this night. You will remember I told you that intimacy between husband and wife extends to all things—*all* things, Bassam. Together you share your worst and your best, openly within the boundaries of privacy within your marriage, and hand in hand. With like-mindedness, you will learn to build your own version of the perfect life. It will not be free of trials and difficulties and frustrations— perhaps anger and shouting, perhaps illness and death. But if you keep working at it with faithfulness and true love, singular to each other, it can become as perfect as your love is for each other—all along the way. Your mother and father are the best examples of that life-long love, the best example that I've ever seen. I envy them."

"You envy them?" I asked in surprise. "In what way could you envy them?"

"They're poor people in one way," he said, "but in another they have more than I could ever wish for. Their wealth is in their kind hearts and hardworking hands—even now. Kind hearts and devotion to their life's work, a rarity in the world no matter where I travel."

He was right. My parents did not have many coins or possessions. They were not able to provide much more than the essentials for our lives. But they were the kindest and most loyal and loving people I had ever known, always giving to others, always lending a hand or a smile.

"So, after your father told you of Rasheeda," I asked, "did you feel better about marriage, later?"

"Certainly so," Zafir said. "And you will too. But you must prepare for it and that is why I waited so long to let you know what waits you at home."

He stopped and studied me for a moment. I hardly noticed—I was lost, I was back home in Rekeem telling Rasha all that I had experienced, and she telling her experiences to me. And what of our plans, what of ...

"Bassam," Zafir announced, "I didn't think I would get your full attention tonight to discuss the scrolls. Let us meet here again tomorrow night." He drew his walking stick toward him and prepared to stand.

"No, I can stay longer," I said. "I want to learn."

He shook his head and waved me away with a smile. "Tomorrow, half before second watch. Here," he said, pointing to our little place near the bow. "We will meet right here. Get some rest," and he hobbled toward the door.

I nodded, gathered up our things and followed behind.

心爱的 **32** 咱爱小

THE SEVENTH SCROLL

The following night I had to excuse myself from a debate with Fawzi and Ammar. I was arguing in favor of adopting the processes of Roman sea trade to the overland processes of the great caravans. Ammar was arguing that the Roman monopoly on their eastern sea made that futile if not just impossible. Fawzi just argued for argument's sake and challenged us both. Seeing that we were going in useless circles, I made handy my excuse and pulled away to attend to my rendezvous with Zafir.

I went topside, standing in the darkness alone, and filled my lungs with a deep breath of salty sea air. Refreshing! I enjoyed these nocturnal escapes from the dank, foul air below decks—it was fresher here, cooler, and the sea air was so embracing.

I had the mats and lamp arranged when Zafir opened the cabin door. The burst of light and long shadow stretched across deck to my little station. Closing it to darkness again, he found his way and set down his walking stick. Testing his balance, he seated himself without the slightest greeting, neither review nor rehearsal. He drew the scroll bag to him and went right to work.

"This bag," Zafir began as he loosened the lacings, "was like unto my father's when he was a boy. In his old age, another was patterned after it, but it shows wear today. I want you to make a new one."

What? Did I hear that correctly? After six readings had these words finally changed? He wants me to make a new one?

And then it made sense—this was a rite of passage, the exchange from father to son, from one generation to the next. He was unburdening a stewardship into the hands of the next steward, handing the mantle to me. I could feel it—a ceremony, memorized, that was repeated for generations. The scroll bag as a symbol of a lifetime's care, and making a new one, is like making myself new, to carry the promises in my own way until that time when I, too, would pass them on.

Reaching into the sack Zafir carefully lifted out a long bundled scroll. It was smaller than the girth of the handle of my sword. It was tied in three places, but unlike the others it had no tassels dangling from the top—another curious difference. Shouldn't there be seven?

Zafir laid the scroll on the mat and carefully untied the cords. With the leather laid back he let the scroll rest untouched. Its yellowed parchment clung curled to itself, its visible edges worn from use. The two slender spindles were ornately carved in olive wood, no different than the others, their smooth artistry glowing with yellowed age.

I knew what words would follow.

"Most men," Zafir said, "hope to find in these scrolls some ancient and lost guide to riches, or the answer to all their troubles, or a treasure map that could lead them to wealth unimaginable. But these secrets are precisely the opposite. The wisdom of my fathers in these scrolls provide only the keys to such riches and a pathway through life for their attainment. But such a key is only for those who know what true riches are, and only for them will the words in these scrolls have meaning. You, Bassam, are wise in your young years, but you must learn for yourself the meaning of the words. And from them will come the most precious part of true riches. Most men cannot read these words because their hearts are not ready—they cannot understand them. I think your heart is ready, Bassam. Do you understand?"

"Yes, I do," I said.

"Then let us begin."

Zafir held the scroll at the base of the spindles and unrolled it carefully. I watched, eager to finally read the conclusion to the seven grand secrets he alluded to for all this past year.

And then—*what is this*? Zafir rolled it open wide. I was surprised then confused at what first appeared. Instead of columns of neatly inscribed words and phrases, instead of long texts of abstract philosophy and precepts, instead of a buildup to some great puzzle to be analyzed and dissected into natural laws of eternal importance, there was instead only one solitary line of text.

Zafir turned the scroll toward me. "You will do the reading, Bassam, and I will listen. If you have a question, you may ask me. But some things I will not tell you. It is part of the test."

Only one line? There was nothing more that I could see. I wondered aloud what magic awaited me this time.

I took the scroll as before, cleared my throat, and read aloud:

"My honor is my power."

That was it.

I read it again: "My honor is my power."

I rolled the scroll out to the end. The rest of the parchment was blank—no words, no riddle, nothing.

I lifted it carefully to examine the back side—nothing there either.

"Zafir," I said. "I don't understand."

He looked at me with blank, unassuming eyes, and spoke no words.

"Then I'll read it again," I said.

"*My honor is my power.*"

The brevity and simplicity of those five words stared at me like great blocks of stone laid out in front of me like a wall or a monument, something—something simple but something complex, a strange mystery. Or, was it?

My honor, how is that supposed to be my power? How does that work in a sword fight, or a barter, or to build a city, fend off bandits? Isn't real power in the sword and the gold and the warriors and ....

"Speak your thoughts, Bassam," Zafir said.

I couldn't, I didn't have any thoughts. What was I to think now? What could this mean? I had more questions than I had thoughts.

"I'm not sure what to say," I said. "I was expecting something different." I looked at Zafir and he just looked back blankly.

I read the words slowly, stopping at each to see if there was leverage to draw up some ideas for guiding my life that were profound or revealing.

Zafir sat looking. I waved my hands absently in front of me and shrugged and shook my head and took a wild stab at it: "My honor," I began, "is important because, well, because it needs to be preserved and respected, so I show loyalty to Al Murrah, honesty to others, respect to myself and to others ...." I had nothing. Zafir could see that I was shooting my bow without any arrows. "... I think that helps people trust you to do what is right...." I stopped and fell quiet.

"That's a beginning," Zafir finally said.

I was stumped. *My honor is important, but how is that* power?

The boat creaked and groaned deeply, a familiar sigh that reverberated gently from stem to stern. Its deck rolled quietly as a small wave passed by. The lines climbing the mast slapped twice and stopped, and all went quiet again. I looked up at the little flag on the highest mast, silhouetted against the starry sky, black against black, seeing no movement in the breeze.

Zafir cleared his throat.

"It didn't make a lot of sense to me either," he said. "So let me explain it to you as it was explained to me, and then it will become something powerful to you."

I suddenly felt encouraged.

"You will see young Bassam that the rest of the seventh scroll is right here," he said, pointing to my heart. "You will see. But I share it on this condition that you may not write it in your journal or anywhere except right there," and pointed to my head. "Only in your heart and in your mind, do you understand?"

"Yes," I said. "I can do that."

"Very well," Zafir said, shifting to ease the discomfort. "A long time ago," he began, "when I was young, perhaps not much older than you, I asked my father why so many men in his caravan followed him, obeyed him, loved him. He told me it was because they honored him. I asked, 'Why do they honor you, what does that mean?' In my way of thinking, as an inexperienced youth, their support must be something that my father purchased—they were loyal because he paid them to be loyal, he bought their honor with a wage."

"Yes," I said, "it only makes sense, the hireling performing a work, that's what I think."

Zafir nodded. "On the surface so it seems," he said. "My father told me that in truth the pay he gave them had nothing to do with money. He said there was something else at work, something much more important. Can you guess what that might be?"

"No, but I suppose it's something to do with honor," I said.

"It was honor, but that doesn't even touch the principle he was trying to teach me," Zafir said. "It had much to do with the previous scrolls. Indeed, it was everything the six other scrolls teach us. Can you rehearse them to me? In a single statement?"

I scratched at my chin and thought a moment. "I would say they teach a man to work on his personal refinement as preparation to serve others, to protect and give to them, to help," I said.

"That is close enough," Zafir said. "First, you must understand that honor begins from above. From God, from your parents, from your employer and associates, from me. It begins from above because that is where others lean on you to carry a burden, to receive from them an important stewardship. They consider you, measure you, deem you worthy of the burden simply according to the needs at hand. You receive a stewardship because they see you as responsible and capable. Do you understand me?"

"Yes, it seems clear enough," I said. "Such as working on the caravan?"

"Yes, that's one example," Zafir said. "You accept responsibility from an investor to carry goods, sell them, and return the profit. He wouldn't trust you with that responsibility unless he thought you capable. And by performing well, his trust in you grows."

I nodded. It was a different way of looking at work—that an employer was trusting me with a stewardship to perform.

"If you think about it," Zafir said, "you will begin to see this principle in nearly all things that you do. For example, when you pass a beggar in the street, do you ignore him? No, you give him a coin because the poor are stewardships for us all."

"I can see that, yes, but for the blessings from God, I would be in his same shoes."

"Indeed!" Zafir said. "And there are your parents who give you chores, your employer at the quarry who assigns you tasks. As a son to your father you carry his honorable family name. As a husband, you carry the trust of your wife to honor her trust in you. As a father, you carry the trust of a child to treat him with love and respect."

"Then honor is really about trust?" I asked.

Zafir smiled.

"Trust is the grand key of all keys for having honor," Zafir said. "You receive a stewardship from above because they can trust you, you are trustworthy. Think on it, Bassam, and you will see what I mean," he said. "And now that you see how important trust is, let us look at honor from the other side."

He pushed back to give more room to wave and gesture, and smiled as he spoke. "Tell me, how do you build trust with others?"

"Well, that's what we were talking about," I said.

"Yes, the virtues of trust, but how do you build it in the first place?" he asked.

I glanced around hunting for an answer when suddenly it all came rushing together—

"Ah! the *scrolls*!" I said aloud.

Zafir broke into a big smile.

"That's what you've been driving at," I said. "The scrolls help a natural man become an honorable man, who is trustworthy. To become truly trustworthy, I must *live* the scrolls!"

Zafir nodded and smiled. "If you are worldly, deceitful, dishonest, scheming, corrupted, lying, conspiring, undermining, and hurting others, people cannot trust you. Can such a person have honor?"

It made sense: if people can't trust you, you have no honor, and therefore you have no stewardship, no responsibility, no impact, no following, no power.

"Think on it," Zafir said. "If the Seventh Scroll is true, then the declaration that 'My honor is my power' is also saying 'My trust is my power.' If you can be trusted, you have more power than if you can't be trusted, it is as simple as that."

He was right. I had always known that but tonight was the first time it was ever put into words for me. I opened my mouth to ask a question but he suddenly straightened up and reached for his stick.

"Then I will see you here again tomorrow night," he said, quickly wrapping the scroll into its place in the bag. He set his walking stick upright and pulled to his feet.

"That's it?" I exclaimed. "I was going to ask you—"

"No, that's all for tonight," he said, cutting me off. "Tomorrow I will tell you about Mosheed and mercy. That, too, is about trust and honor. Don't be late."

心爱的 **33** 啲爱小

NARANJ

WE spent most of the next day on the deck of the Flying Dragon scrubbing it down with water and flat stones, tending to frayed lines, securing weakened planking, mending broken fishing nets and torn sails. The captain made good use of our time and strength, and Fawzi and Ammar were not shy about lecturing me on the finer points of every task undertaken. I accepted it patiently.

As the last evening meal was served, and with the others bunking down for the night, I went up on deck.

There was no moon again, and I found our place next to the railing and made the lamp to glow. I peered into the darkness, hanging onto a thick mast-line. The heavy rope strained taut and then relaxed as the breeze lightly filled the sail and let go her grip again. I gazed upward and estimated a new location according to the pole star. I wondered if the patterns of stars would show differently when the pole star finally sank into the northern horizon. As we journeyed south would we see new constellations, new planets, new sights?

I felt so small, so insignificant, almost drowning in the limitless shimmering heavens above. The expanse carried my thoughts to other places, other realms beyond reach. Then, back to my Rasha. Oh, that she could join me on deck this night and see these beautiful glimpses into eternity.

But tonight, I would have to be content with an experiment in eating. Earlier in the day Ammar had given me two small fruits. *Naranjs*, he called them. 'One is sour, the other sweet,' he said. 'Know the difference and you will become rich!'

I took them because Ammar was not one for pranking me like Fawzi. But still—one sour, the other sweet? How was I to tell the difference? "That's the test," he told me, smiling in a way that stirred my suspicions.

Zafir was not due on deck for a while longer so I decided our quest for learning about the seventh scroll wouldn't suffer for Ammar's experiment. I decided to pass the time by conducting Ammar's exploration into the skills of acute observation.

I took both naranjs from my pocket and held them side by side. They were the same size and shape, though one seemed to have a slightly different skin. I turned one of them over in my hand. Its bright orange skin looked almost black in the dim lamp light. "One of each," Ammar said, "and you'll know right away which is which."

"You won't tell me?" I had asked.

"There is a difference, but I will let you learn it on your own, Bassam. Knowing the sweet from the sour will save you some coins at the market the next time you buy—and you will thank your old teacher Ammar for showing you."

"But you're *not* showing me, Ammar," I had said. And his reply?

"Learn it for yourself," he said.

And so I would.

I arbitrarily chose one and dug my nail into the soft skin and began pulling away the thick covering. Small patches fell to the deck at my feet. A wonderful citrus smell broke upon the sea breeze and I brought the fruit to my nose. Its smell was fresh, biting, energizing.

"I like this," I said to no one there. "I could enjoy several of these at every meal for the rest of our trip," I decided.

I poked my finger into its core and broke it apart into a dozen segments.

"Okay, Ammar," I said aloud. "Here goes ......" and I shoved several slices into my mouth.

心爱的 **34** 的爱心

MERCY

Zafir finally appeared on deck. The only light to guide him was the shifting yellow flame of my small oil lamp. He found me seated on my mat and wiping my mouth with my sleeve.

"What's wrong with you?" Zafir asked as he took his place.

"I juth had my firth naranj," I confessed, my eyes squinting with sour.

"Ah!" he said with a smile. "That's Ammar, and he asked you to learn the difference between the sweet and the sour, didn't he?"

I scowled and spat some remains onto my sleeve and wiped it on my leg. "Yeth," was the best I could say.

Zafir smiled. "I see, and you have found the sour. There is no outward difference between the two," he said. "That's why you must try one whenever you buy them in quantity. Taste first, don't get a hundred stadia down the road before you discover you were cheated on a basket of sour when you thought it was sweet. It's the first scroll at work!"

The cool darkness surrounding us suddenly warmed. It felt as if we had passed through a curtain of changing climates, from cold to warm. It made me relax. I removed my yak coat and made a pillow to lean on. The bitterness in my mouth faded and my tongue started to work again.

"A great leader," Zafir began, "can direct thousands of camel soldiers into battle, or marshal thousands of workers to heft stones for a pyramid or a regal city, or more simply, call his family to join him for meal. And all men follow for one reason—"

"Because they honor him?" I asked.

"Think on it," Zafir said. "People say of him, 'my, what a powerful man, what a great leader, look at the many that follow him, look at the many works they do in his name, he is a great man!' But how can that be? He is but a man, and yet he can wield such power. Do you see that honor is what gives him power to do these things?"

It made sense. But evil men led thousands to battle, and evil men ordered tens of thousands to build cities, what is the difference?

"I thought honor was always a good force, a good virtue," I said, "but a wicked man also has followers. They too obey their leader."

"They do," he said, "but it is not honor that gives such bad men their power, it is something far more insidious. It is fear and *force*. He reaches into their weaknesses first, into their darkest desires, into those lusts that bring no lasting satisfaction or joy. He promises them their most pointless pursuits in exchange for their obedience.

There are many who will follow their greed in this way. Father Moses wrote of it, the selling of a birthright for a mess of pottage. That is how wages are used and wasted on others who obey for the wrong reasons."

"That does not sound like honor to me," I said.

"It most certainly is not," Zafir said. "True leaders who understand honor are resolute, unchanging, unyielding in their application of virtuous and correct principles. They must be consistent or they will not retain true honor."

"You tell me that, Zafir, and I believe it true," I said. "But what if such an honorable man must make an exception?" I asked. "That must happen, doesn't it?"

"All right," he said. "Let's go down this side road for a moment. Maybe this will help you understand how honor and power relate. For an example, suppose there is a man accused of a wrong. He is found guilty and he must suffer punishment, correct?"

"Yes, it is consistent," I said.

"Unless there are reasons otherwise," he said.

"Reasons?" I asked.

"If a man of honor will break one of his own laws, the reasons for holding such principles in abeyance must be *so* honest, *so* fair, *so* obvious to everyone that the exception is embraced by all people. Honor must be retained whenever such an exception is made."

I looked at him blankly, unsure of where he was heading. Zafir could read it in my eyes.

"What you are feeling inside of you, my son, is the need for mercy."

"Mercy?" I asked. "The fourth scroll?"

"Yes, mercy steps in at the strangest times," Zafir said. "And it happens all the time, with all of us, and you probably don't even realize it. Mercy is how an honorable man may violate his own rules of justice. Have you heard the story of Mosheed?"

I shook my head.

"Mosheed was a young man of Al Murrah. He was a rear guard and second watch. One night he fell asleep when he should be awake. Bandits came and attacked. Four of our men were killed. The rest of the camp awoke in time and fought back, killing a few of the marauders but the rest of them escaped into the night. It was difficult work fighting in the dark, but a moon gave enough light to keep us from killing ourselves. The following day, all the men were angry with Mosheed. They wanted him to pay for the crime of letting their four friends be killed just because he wanted to sleep on duty. My father was ready to execute judgment, to lop off his head with the man's own sword. But his brother came to my father's tent. The brother was profoundly sorrowful and expressed his great disappointment in Mosheed, and was sorry for the great loss of the four friends and the dishonor it brought on the whole family. He said that Mosheed felt terrible and expected to die for his lapse. The brother told my father that there was an important reason why Mosheed attached himself to this caravan, and wanted my father to hear it. Mosheed's sister-in-law lost her husband in an attack from the Tauri, leaving her a widow with five young children. Mosheed had five children himself. He took her and her children into his household as a sister, not as a wife, and worked to support the two families alone. Mosheed joined the four-month trek to earn sustenance. When my father heard this, he counseled with his elders and decided that for the sake of the children and their mothers, he would not make Mosheed pay with his life for his negligence. But this mercy wasn't for the sake of Mosheed, my father said. It was for the sake of the children. That was my father's decision, a difficult one. But when the others heard of it, and heard of the children and the women, they could see the wisdom of it. Every man supported him in it and he did not lose honor. Do you see it, Bassam? Do you see how mercy overcame the demand for justice, how a greater good was served even though a great tragedy stood at odds? My father was never criticized for handling it that way. It was a law for Moses, too, the law of mercy and the law of justice."

"What was that?" I asked.

"If a man killed," Zafir said, "Moses said the family of the dead were the first to cast the stones before anyone else, and execute him for his crime. But if the family chose to show mercy and withheld the stones, then neither could the rest of the host cast theirs. It was forgiveness, it was mercy. And, it was justice if they cast their stones. It was the law of Moses."

"So the exercise of justice was balanced with their sense of compassion," I said.

"And mercy," Zafir said. "Either way it was acceptable to the people. This law gave the people most severely hurt the chance to be the judge and decide the ending of the killer that was of greatest satisfaction. If it was a mistake made in anger they were inclined to be more merciful than if it was a planned killing for gain."

"What about Mosheed, was he a good man?" I asked.

"Yes he was, and a young man, too. He should have known better than to stretch his natural abilities beyond their endurance," Zafir said. "My father sent him home that next day with his earnings and told him the caravan was not the right pursuit for him, and to make his life some other way."

"May mercy always rob justice in this fashion?" I asked.

"You are missing the important lesson, Bassam," Zafir said. "Mercy may *never* rob justice. Mercy may satisfy justice, but never rob him. That is the great difference. Where a crime is from foolishness and weakness, and we can see in the perpetrator recognition of his mistake, great remorse, a sincere effort to rectify the breach, then are we more inclined to encircle him within the arms of mercy. But when he commits his crime in secret or conspiracy, and refuses to come forward to accept judgment, then must the laws of justice take him and mete out the punishment worthy of the crime. Mercy may satisfy justice—it may never rob it."

I recalled the misdeeds of several acquaintances who had become deeply remorseful, but only upon their discovery after the act, not before then.

"How would a judge measure the truly repentant from the fast-talking manipulator and pretender?" I asked.

"We must be careful with our judgments and mercy, Bassam," Zafir said. "It should take close examination and witnesses, if possible. Young Mosheed was a good man before that terrible night, and remained a good man after it. But inside he was crushed with sorrow and disappointment in himself. The truth was, he was overextended and underexperienced. He was not wise in the ways of Al Murrah. It would be foolishness to ignore the good man he was and refuse to let mercy have her say in that event."

"What became of him, then?" I asked. "Did he return to Rekeem?"

"Yes, and his guilt weighed so heavy that he took upon himself the upkeep and care of the families of those who died because of his neglect—and did so all the rest of his days. It revealed the integrity of the man. His remorse turned to resolute determination to undo, as best he could, the damage he wrought. It drove him to aggressively pursue the gold and coin, and he became wealthy."

"And that great wealth destroyed him?" I asked.

"No, not at all. He was above that temptation. I tell you that his wealth went secretly to those families who had indirectly suffered at his hand. An anonymous messenger delivered funds for years afterwards. None knew the truth of it until after Mosheed died. It was a long time ago," Zafir said.

"Keeping his guard always—Mosheed didn't," I said. "And tragedy happened. But he repaired as much as he could."

"It happens all the time, to all of us. It is the great common imperfection of all our lives. But it is never an excuse to stop trying. Mercy satisfies the demands of justice, so let us all be found worthy of her when those times come that we need mercy. The merciful are honorable. They retain their respect, their trust, their power."

Zafir let the silence embellish the darkness where such illumination glowed. I let the wonderful teaching of mercy take its place in my heart and mind. Mercy was a necessary part of honor and trust, I decided. These were no strict and straight laws. It was because of the application of human kindness in such balance that the better good was preserved alive.

Zafir watched me a moment and then reached for his staff. I stood to help and he brushed me away with a growl.

Day 459—Dear Rasha, We are at sea. Each night Zafir teaches me the Seventh Scroll. It reminds me of you, my Rasha, the laws of mercy, in so many ways that I may not write, but they are true just the same. I wear your father's family crest. Did you know of our fathers' arrangement? Is that why you veiled your face as one newly betrothed when we bid farewell, the last time I saw you?

The seas are calm, the food bearable. We eat a fresh fish every meal. The fish look different in each location, they tell us such fish are different, but to me they all taste the same. There is much boat traffic along these coasts so we stay farther from shore where it is faster and safer. The C'ina are very creative. Their manner of boat construction and rope weaving is good, very new. I will show you when I return. —Bassam

心爱的 **35** 的爱心

THE THIRD NIGHT

"I have wearied you with the scrolls these many nights, Bassam," Zafir said as he sat next to me in the dark. "We are nearing the end of the teachings of the scrolls. While there are yet a few things more, for tonight I will answer your questions as they come."

He looked at me and waited.

I was caught off guard. I had a thousand questions but I couldn't put them into words. It was generous of Zafir to let me ask, but I had not prepared.

"You talked about honor being power," I asked. "How then do both good and evil men have power? Does that not also mean that each has honor in the eyes of his followers?"

"A good question," Zafir said. "Can both good and evil men have honor? No. It is not possible because honor is filled with light. It is a positive word with positive attributes. Power is another positive word with positive attributes. Men obey a virtuous man from their own free choice, willingly, because they trust him to build the good and the positive—he has trust and honor. Evil men work conspiracies out of fear, and let murder resolve their difficulties. They don't trust. Their work is to destroy and to build the negative. The follower of such a man fears losing his place or his life, so he obeys out of fear. Obedience is compelled, it is not won, this is not trust or honor, this is darkness at work. It labors to kill so that it might gain power. The opposite of honor is force."

Zafir went quiet. The light of understanding was beginning to open in my heart. And then in a low and reverent voice he asked, "Bassam, do you trust God?"

I did, and nodded.

"Do you honor God?"

"Oh yes, more now than before," I said truthfully.

"Then can you say that you love God, this being you've never met or engaged with in any recognizable event?"

"Well, yes, yes I do," I said.

"Then consider this," Zafir said. "If God did anything to break that trust, that honor, would he still have power?"

My honor is my power .... Did not God have all power? Could he not do anything he pleased? Would he be pleased to do wickedly? If so, would that diminish his power?

"Do not answer it," Zafir said. "I only wanted you to think on it. If honor is power, then he with the greatest power must be him who is most honorable. He can be trusted to never violate our respect and love toward him, or break any law in the universe."

I had never even thought it before. It was a beautiful thought, a true thought.

"Consider your place on this earth, Bassam," he said. "Every day you are only *this far* from death, but you don't fear it, you continue with your life and your plans. All men have plans and hopes, and then one day, suddenly, it's over. They die. How many have died before today, no one knows. And how many will yet be born to die, no one knows. But every life that comes is different, unique, unusual, and carries talents that will bless the lives of others if they exercise them in the right way."

"Each life is a gift," I said. "I have always believed that."

"A pure gift," Zafir said, "that may either be treated with respect or destroyed as an afterthought. Consider the old legends that declare men who commit their evil acts are cursed by God. They also declare that blessings come from God because of their righteous acts."

"What do you think, Zafir?" I asked.

"I do not believe that mortal men could circumscribe anything about God with our puny intellects and weak frames, *not at all*," Zafir said. "But let me answer you in this way, my son. The honor we give God *must* rest upon the same principles. Do you think he forces us to obey him?"

"No, certainly not," I said. "When I escaped my kidnappers that night I was so afraid because I had no one who could help me—no one. And I *asked* God to help me, freely, filled with hope—I wasn't forced. He brought to my mind a thought about a coin that saved me. He helped me, I can't deny that."

"Your feelings toward God, what are they now, Bassam?" Zafir asked.

"Today they are alive," I said. "I feel I know something about God that I didn't know before. It brings comfort and joy."

"Is this love?" he asked.

Is this love? I had never considered it. Is this love?

"Yes," I said. "Yes, it must be ...it must be love."

"Do you see it, Bassam?" Zafir asked softly. "Do you see that he answered a desperate plea that you directed to him in the depth of your humility and abandonment? He helped you in a quiet, friendly, simple way. In just a fleeting moment his small gift of bringing to your mind a memory of a coin, that little act instantly resolved *every* worry, *every* collapse, *every* fear. It was *resolved for you.* Your work to make use of it was *not* taken from your shoulders—you still had to sort through your predicament, you still had to perform your own labor, you still had to find passage on a boat to escape your pursuers. The chore was not lifted from you, and you might have failed. But the means to achieve it was given to you because you found yourself dependent with no options that you could see, and so you sincerely asked for help. You had no other way that was honest and honorable. The tools for your own salvation were handed to you but you still were required to do your part, to perform the work."

Zafir's words rang true. The path to receiving that help was not arbitrary, just to be had for the asking. I had to be in a place and a time where ... where God was justified in helping me.

"Justified!" I suddenly said. "He helped me because I opened up to receive the help. Not selfishly, not casually, but with a desperate invitation and pleading. Like your father and Mosheed, your father was justified in what he did. Those hurt the most after a murder are justified. Yes, justification."

"For good or for evil?"

"That little help for me was for good," I said. "Moluch wanted to kill me, I had to escape to save my life."

"And was God's help an act of love?" Zafir said, his voice trailing off to a reverent whisper.

"It was for me, of the most sublime," I said. "Honor is love—this is a beautiful idea."

Zafir smiled and fell silent.

After a few moments, I had another question come to mind.

"Tell me about these things we call blessings and cursings," I said. "If honor is power, and honor is love, then why is this power not used to prevent death and suffering, darkness and hatred, war and accident? Why does God let that happen if he has power to prevent it?"

Zafir's countenance softened. He looked at me for a long moment as if measuring my ability to hear his words.

"There is so much we don't know," he said. "But I give you this assurance—the creator of all things does not act the part of magician or genie to grant us our every wish. Our lives are so short—it is foolishness to hitch our carts to theories that deny our most inner assurance that God is blessing our lives in so many ways."

I nodded and felt for Rasha's small veil tucked in my robe.

"And if God will do that," Zafir said, "so should we bless the lives of all those we can. What you need to see is that by whatever means all things came to be, and whatever God's role is in that, it must come from that same true principle of honor and power."

"No force," I said. "That's amazing, Zafir. No force. Certainly not. So, no matter how it works, God's power must be tied to honor?"

"I believe so," Zafir said. "At least in his dealings with us. How else could it work? If being 'good' is so important why doesn't he force us to be good, so that all men everywhere are acceptable to him and not be rejected?"

"No, that couldn't work," I said. "Forced charity is not charity from the heart. Forced love is not love from the soul. Forced goodness is not true goodness. It is all slavery."

Zafir stopped and looked at me, seeing that understanding was coming. He smiled and nodded. "Both good and bad that come to us are not forced on us," he said. "We are free agents to choose. By choosing our actions we also choose our consequences. Forcing either of these violates that basic law of free will."

"So God must stand by while terrible things happen in the world?" I asked. "And he can't stop them?" ——

"I believe he could stop anything," Zafir said. "He restrains himself for reasons we may never comprehend. But I believe it is because the gift of choice is what he allows to teach us wisdom and humility. To choose evil over good remains our gift, but when we make poor choices, we prove our unworthiness to benefit from his intervention and help, a consequence of our free will. And to choose good over evil is to live his will, a lesson all must eventually learn, for by this is order and harmony and love kept and maintained and enlarged."

I could see the wisdom of it. Horrible events are not the willful actions of an all-powerful God, they are the horrible calculations of evil people, or of nature, or of poor choices—but these could not be of God, not if the Seventh Scroll was a true principle.

"If a man of honor must intervene to exercise mercy," Zafir said, "it must be *purely* justified. And consider it, my son. This life is the great teacher for us all. If God labored to prevent every ill, every poor choice, every accident, every natural disaster, what lessons would be learned? Does a being of honor impose his own will in a world of corruption and failure when he is using these imperfections to teach his creations all the rich and lasting the benefits of making right choices? Personal choice and experience *is* the teacher, even if it leads to misery, difficulties, or death. From such trials come new efforts to stop the suffering—the needles to stop pain, the cutting of a mass to save a dear friend's wife, the invention of a marvelous bow to protect the innocent, the risks of a long caravan trip to build business relationships—all these steps forward come because someone somewhere made good or bad choices, and others dealt with the consequences—because of agency."

Zafir looked pained. His shoulders were tight and he sat as though suffering from his leg. He held his peace about it, and waited on me.

"The last question, then," I said. "For honor to be a man's power, for honor to be trust and love, all men must be free, am I right?"

"Yes," he said. "That is why freedom is so precious to us. Free will to follow a path of honor, both to honor and to be honored. There is no other way."

The simplicity of it started to construct itself inside of me. Self-control was freedom from vices, temptations and addictions. Learning was freedom from ignorance. Rejecting the imperfections of the soul was freedom. Drawing others to me based on trust and love and respect, that was freedom. And if I was true to their trust, I had power, power to lead them, to ask of them, to serve them, to become one with them. I could see it clearly—my honor is my power. I must remain honorable.

Suddenly an idea hit me. I sat up in startled surprise, my eyes wide, my mouth hanging open, staring into the blackness of the night, my palms up as if to receive.

"I think I know something now—it just came to me, just now," I said.

"Will you share it?" Zafir asked.

"From the riddles in the scrolls: 'Embrace the virtues, thou Prince of Peace,' I think I understand what this means," I said.

"Yes?" Zafir smiled.

"I think the virtues are those attributes of the man who has conquered himself and changed himself into another being—a new man. He has turned good ideas into real virtues, personal virtues. He *is* those virtues. He is a man of virtue."

The lamp light flickered on Zafir's face. He was smiling as if anticipating my understanding. "Go on," he said, nodding.

"And that part of the riddle, that part about 'embrace the virtues'—that's not a command to the man to adopt these ideals. No, this is a plea, *his* plea, an urgent and humble begging plea, it is a prayer!"

"A prayer to whom?"

"Why, it's a prayer to the Prince of Peace, *to God*," I said, almost too breathless to get out all the thoughts at once.

Zafir nodded.

"It's a prayer to God," I continued, "a plea to please accept me *not* for what I was, but for what I have now become. It's a prayer to God to embrace the part of me I have made acceptable, to embrace *me* for my virtues. That's it, isn't it? 'Embrace the virtues, thou Prince of Peace'? I ask it of him because I have become honorable?"

Zafir smiled and watched my animation. Almost whispering he replied, "Yes, my young son, it's a prayer. A prayer to Him to receive you, the new man of virtue—honor from above, power from below."

"It is asking for his love ...." I said.

I sat there churning a hundred thoughts through my head at once, a thousand questions. The scrolls—suddenly they melted together into one beautiful whole: the whole man refined, prepared, perfected, ready for ... *ready for what?*—ready for anything.

"And think of it, Bassam," Zafir said, "is that plea for acceptance any different than what you could ask for between you and me? Can you accept the friendship of a virtuous man?"

"Yes, I could," I said. "I could trust him."

"Trust! Do you see it?" Zafir said smiling. "Virtue begets trust, trust begets honor, honor begets love, and love can then be exchanged between people to work together toward anything, anything at all. It is true living power—*My honor is my power.*"

I was so excited I could not sit, and stood up and walked toward the bow of the ship and closed my eyes and inhaled. I felt the fresh ocean breeze blow past my face and through my hair. Exhilarating, refreshing, awakening. The stars above now shone a new completeness to their existence. All things seemed to resonate with a kinder existence, a rational place in the heavens.

I returned to my place in silence and sat down quietly. I found myself in a reverent, almost sacred, place. My whole being was illuminated in ways that words would not let me describe.

Zafir held his peace a few moments longer. "It is a great misunderstanding, my son," he said softly. "Some religious philosophers declare that obedience is the foremost law of heaven. But now you can see this cannot be. The first law of heaven must be free will, the freedom to choose."

It fit like a great puzzle, a puzzle of broken lessons in life that were coming together to become a mosaic of beautiful perfection.

"It's the most amazing ... no, it's the most important truth I've ever heard, Zafir," I said. "All men working together, free and honorable, it could be a perfect world, Zafir. *It would be perfect.*"

"It is the world of the seven scrolls, Bassam. That world is already here for some people living them right now," he said. "And with that, I leave you this one last question."

"Yes?"

"If God so loves us that he seeks our joy and prosperity, to create a partnership with us that will benefit all his children, what of the stone tablets Moses brought down out of the mountain in Sinai?"

"The ten covenants of God?" I asked.

"Yes," Zafir said. "Are these commandments ten demands that God makes of all men, or could they be something more sincere?"

I hadn't thought of it. "They sound like demands to me," I said. "Good demands, but still ...."

Zafir smiled at me. "Think on this, my son. Could they instead be something far more valuable and important? Could they be, instead, ten amazing secrets, ten pathways, ten keys, ten right ways to live, to love, and to exist? Instead of being ten chains or restrictions or impositions on our free will, could they be sign posts to keep us on the best path forward in this life? Are the ten commandments in truth ten beautiful blessings? Ten actions within reach of all his creations to achieve honor?"

The question froze me in place. I looked at Zafir with unblinking eyes. *Ten actions to achieve honor?*

The ramifications of this profound understanding were so far-reaching that it left me speechless. All I could do was stare at Zafir, unblinking, struggling to process an idea that suddenly and profoundly changed everything. *Not ten commandments to stifle my free choice, but ten blessings, ten secrets that lead to joy, to lift me from my blinded state of the natural man to a realm of bright clarity, where I could see the beautiful foundations of true honor, to become my finest self?*

The oil lamp was flickering—not from a passing breeze, but a wick that needed trimming. In silence Zafir drew out his knife and tended to the chore, and the flame burned brighter.

心爱的 **36** 的爱心

NIGHT FLIGHT

The lesson was ended, and on Zafir's signal I got to my feet. I brushed at my clothing and offered my hand to help. Suddenly, there rose from out across the black waters the strangest whistling, flittering noise—like a loud insect. We both turned to listen. And then the water started to churn, frothy, disturbed, as if a thousand fish were leaping at once. I looked out into the noisy darkness, not knowing its source but then heard the whistling come right toward me, from behind, a flapping noise. It grew nearer and suddenly, *thud*! I was struck hard in the back by something invisible.

I jumped forward, staggering to retain my footing. "Yeow!" I shouted, "What was that?" And turned looking for the invisible hand that almost knocked me to the deck. Zafir's eyes darted to mine and he started to stand. Just then, another, and then more, an invisible something, came rushing past me in a breezy rush of high-pitched fury, the whistling, flittering noise growing loud. I fell to my knees thinking to take cover as the sound grew louder and seemed to envelop us from all sides. The swarm roared past us in a great wind of mysterious wings working from the dark to race by and then just as quickly, it disappeared. *What were birds doing on the ocean at night?* The distant splashing and rush of air faded into the dark.

I was crouched low, rubbing the bruise on my back. "What was that?" I called to Zafir. He remained at his place, turned to the sea.

"Are you all right?" he called back.

"I don't know!" I said. "Something struck me in the back, three times, and ... wait a minute, what is that?" I said pointing at several strange flopping squirming things, twisting around on the deck. I crawled away from them and hurried to my feet. "Look at that! Did those baby dragons attack me?"

Zafir stood by me and called over the crew. "It may not be as evil as you think," and said, and grabbed the lamp to investigate. "Let's get a closer look," and walked near to cast a yellow glow on the creatures.

"*Don't get close*? They tried to kill me!" I was already backing up, pointing.

Zafir held the light just so and bent over for a closer look.

"Bassam," he said, "go get Ammar, he'll enjoy this."

Whatever it was, they squirmed and rolled about, ugly little creatures. In the light, I could see they were as long as my forearm, slender, and their fins were almost as long as their bodies, partially flayed open, pulling at the deck.

A crewman arrived and seeing what lay on the deck, went to pick one of them up.

"No, don't!" I started forward, and the man just looked at me and smiled, grabbing the creature in both hands and wrestling it tight.

"What is it?" I asked, taking a step toward him.

The man showed his crooked yellow teeth and spoke several words the rest of us could not understand. He gestured with the creature, holding it up and jabbering more. He smiled again and spread out one of its fins showing it was webbed like a duck's foot, then jabbered some more and gestured toward the ocean.

Just then Ammar emerged from his quarters.

"What's all the running around up here?" he asked. "Don't you two know we're trying to sleep?"

"Ammar," Zafir said. "Look at these," and pointed toward the little man holding the fish.

"It tried to kill me!" I said, stabbing my finger at the scaly perversion. "I was talking and then *wham*, they attacked me, charged me right in the back. They attacked!"

Ammar came closer to see by torch light.

"Oh my goodness," he said, shaking his head. "Never in all my days have I seen so much fuss over something so silly!" and reached out to touch its fin.

"They're a lot larger in these waters," Zafir said as they studied the specimen.

"Larger?" I asked but no one was listening.

Ammar turned the little beast over in his hands and extended the webbed fin.

"Bassam, you know our ship, the *Flying Dragon*?" he asked.

I nodded.

"What attacked you, Bassam, is no flying dragon, it's only a little flying fish," he said. "Well, not little, but innocent enough. No teeth here," he said, opening its mouth to see.

Zafir smiled and nodded. "Look at the size of him," he said. "We heard the rush of an entire school of them skipping and skimming across the water."

"It's a baby," Ammar said. "Look at these fins, they're enormous, quite unusual."

"So what's he doing attacking me at night?" I asked.

"They were most likely chased by a predator," Ammar said. "And if not that, it was probably the light," and gestured toward the lantern hanging over the bow. "And your little oil lamp didn't hurt either. They like the light, that's how we catch them."

"Catch them? You mean you've seen these before?" I asked. I remained behind Ammar, peering over his shoulder, lest the little dragon try to attack me again.

"Naturally," he said. "We see these all the time in warmer waters, usually far to the south. I've never seen one this large so far north. Very strange." He turned the fish side to side, looking at its underside and pulling back the other fin to measure it with his hand.

"I can think of only one answer," he said. "The currents in the ocean must be pushing warm water north. These fish must have followed."

"I thought you just said it was a baby," I said.

Ammar smiled. "Just teasing. It's good-sized for a flying fish, probably make for a man a whole meal."

I wrinkled my nose in disgust. "You eat them?" I asked.

"Oh yes," Ammar said. "The flying fish make a fine meal."

"They do indeed," Zafir echoed. "Very tasty."

"So what's a flying fish? Fish can't fly," I said.

"That's correct," Ammar said, "but they propel themselves from the water and manage to flap their fins like a bird. They can travel quite a distance, Bassam, maybe 10, 20 paces, I've seen it with my own eyes. They splash back a moment and propel themselves again.

Never any higher than maybe the height of a man, but you'd think it was a bird."

"So what are they doing on the boat? That seems the wrong place for a fish out of water," I said.

Ammar handed the fish back to the crew member and turned to go back to his room. "The lantern, Bassam," he said as he closed the door behind him.

Zafir motioned to the crewman and pointed to the lantern and the fish. The crewman nodded his head enthusiastically and chattered away as if he knew exactly what we were talking about. He spread out his arms as if to point out a vast number of fish, and gestured to the deck and mimicked scooping them up into a pot. He rubbed his tummy and smiled.

"You want to eat this?" Zafir asked.

The little man nodded and put out his hands.

"Anybody mind?" he asked.

"Not me, that's the most disgusting thing I've ever seen," I said.

"Wait till you taste it," Zafir said. "I think it will change your mind."

I wrinkled my nose again as the little man took the fish, and holding it firmly in front of him, stepped across the shadows to the door, picking up others from the deck and placing them into a basket. He disappeared through the door, joining his fellows in the kitchen below.

"Thank you, Bassam," Zafir said. "That was an unusual way to end our talk tonight."

"Are we finished?" I asked.

"For tonight, anyway," Zafir said. "Flying fish isn't exactly what I had in mind to close out the night, but maybe I can fit it into the lesson somehow. Let's meet here again tomorrow night after first watch, and we'll talk more."

心爱的 **37** 饱受心

THE TOKEN

Aheavy rain blew in the following day and kept us pinned inside our cabins the whole time. It rumbled and growled, flashing its fury with lightning and sheets of water that poured across the deck. The seas were choppy, but no big waves crashed across our bow. I thought the men would bring our boat to shore. The captain explained there was a belt of calm along the coastline, a barrier that broke the large waves before they reached the coast. His men fought the winds and waves to bring us to that safety zone where we were far enough from the rocks and heavier waves for safety, but kept us within the storm's path—and drenched. The rain didn't abate all that day, that night, and the next.

Despite the rolling motion of the boat, we managed five good games of Weiqi, and I won the last against Ammar.

The third day broke open sunny and bright. Against blue sky, shreds of storm-vented clouds clung to the coast but soon vanished. It was a beautiful day. I shed my yak coat and the wet that soaked the ship for two days seemed to steam right out of the wood itself.

The passengers and crew were in the sunshine most of the day, breathing the fresh air, and otherwise tending to the boat.

After dinner concluded, the night fell in the usual way—the black canopy was crisp and clear, the stars shown bright. There was a new warmth in the air. In my quarters, I paced around until first watch and then there came the knock on our door.

It was Ammar. "Zafir said it is time to see him topside," he said.

"See you later, fish feathers," Fawzi said. "Ammar! Come on in, let's talk about Bassam behind his back while he's gone."

I excused myself and hurried through the passage to the ladder and climbed on deck. Zafir was already seated at the bow, a single lamp beside him and the scroll bag at his side.

"We are almost finished with the seventh scroll, Bassam," he said.

"Yes," I nodded, finding my place next to him. "I'm ready."

"Very good," Zafir said. "I will take your questions now."

I pondered a moment, thinking I had gained an understanding of the Seventh Scroll and its simple yet complex message.

"The other six scrolls," I began, "they are really meant to prepare a man to have honor, and that is his power?"

Zafir nodded. "That is the purpose of the other scrolls, to build virtues into the core and fabric of your life whereby you become an instrument of good. If you corrupt yourself, you lose power, you lose your honor."

"Then it is a lifetime of effort," I offered, "a lifetime of fighting the daily battle and working to build good things in the world instead of merely existing."

He nodded and looked at me for the next query.

"I understand enough," I finally said. "Now I must prove myself worthy of the words, and that is the journey of my life, is it so?"

"A life-long journey," he said. "Never let down your guard. There is both safety and power in your honor, my son."

It was enough for me. I wanted to go back and study the scrolls on my own now. But a single question remained.

"Zafir, I was just curious," I said. "Maybe it is not significant."

"Yes?"

"There are other men of the scrolls, I couldn't guess how many," I said. "How do you communicate your common bond? How do you work together and combine your labors in a common cause? Do the scrolls create such bonds with foreigners and sojourners along the way?"

"I'll tell you," Zafir said, "if you tell me about the seven tassels of the seventh scroll."

"The tassels?" I said with raised eyebrows. "There are none. I noticed it when you first removed it from the scroll bag. They're hanging from all the other scrolls, from the second handle of each. But this last, it has none."

"None?"

"No, see, nothing here," I said, lifting the seventh from the scroll bag, as if he had never noticed before.

Zafir didn't even look but studied my face for a long moment. "Bassam, I will give you this last token of the seven scrolls that you must hold sacred all of your life and not share it with anyone except your heir to whom you will give these scrolls. Do I have your promise?"

"You have my promise," I said.

"Then I direct your attention to my bakra," he said.

"Your bakra? What do you mean?"

"My bakra," he said again. "The gāmāl you've seen me ride these many months past."

"From Rekeem?"

"Yes, that one."

"All right, I remember her—" I said. "What about her?"

"Describe her for me," he said.

"Describe her? Well, all right, she was white with a shaggy neck, mottled hair, tall like a war camel, beautifully dressed with her saddle and adornments, well bred, sacred stock, strong, tame."

"Tell me of the adornments," he said.

"Well, as I remember, you had a beautiful saddle with bells, and leather reins and a stick in her nose."

"Anything else?"

"No, nothing else that I remember. Why?"

"These scrolls are ancient," Zafir said, pulling the bag from me and drawing the cord tight to close at its top. "They are known among few people, but I assure you, they are known among *a few people*. Those who receive them treat them for what they are—precious and sacred words, wisdom that leads to peace, to joy and prosperity, to wealth. And you know what I mean by wealth, I know you do."

"Yes," I replied.

"When men of the Seven Scrolls come upon each other, we acknowledge our faithfulness to our covenant by so signifying the token of the seventh scroll."

"Token?" I asked.

"To identify ourselves," Zafir said. "And even if we're not sure if another has made a covenant to the scrolls, we can still identify them."

"I don't understand."

"Do you know my saddle?" he asked.

"Well, yes, very much so, it is beautifully made."

"How many large tassels hang from my saddle?" Zafir asked.

"Well, there were … Oh, I see! Yes!" I said. "There were three on each side, six in all … Six! Is that it?"

"What do you think?"

"Well, six is not seven," I said.

"Bassam, you asked me to tell you how you can build a love that lives with God," Zafir said. "To build honor in yourself, to build it among others, even among strangers. The answer is in the seventh scroll. The saddles of the men of the scroll always carry six tassels that they ride upon as a constant reminder."

"But I see thousands with such hangings," I said.

"Most certainly," he said. "But too few are men of the scrolls. You might wonder if you can test them to see if they are carriers of the great secrets."

"I could ask, I suppose."

"No, you would never ask," Zafir said. "A price rests upon the head of the man who knows the great secrets of the Abdali-ud-din. A holder

194

of the secrets would never confess to them—it is their burden for life, and a requirement for death. They will never tell."

"Then I watch for virtuous actions?" I asked.

"Many men not of the scrolls are also virtuous, it is in their souls, good people from the start. Your test is simpler than that," he said. "And so I ask you, 'Is your praise of God in the seventh?'"

"I'm not sure what you're asking," I said.

"'Is your praise of God in the seventh?'" he asked again.

"I suppose so," I said. "Yes, it is."

"Most certainly," he said. "It is in our humility before God. It is in our great respect for his eternal honor, his great glory, his endless power, his strong justice and his divine mercy. It is in our gratitude for the endless benevolence of this great giver of life—life and its abundance that is enough for *all*, everywhere—that we bow down before him with our deepest love, in all things. Therein, Bassam, is the seventh revealed. Men of the scrolls carry the six tassels, invisible in plain sight as they ride their camels across the lands. But the seventh? For that you may ask me."

"Ask you?" I replied.

"Yes, ask me—test me if I am a man of the scrolls," he said.

"All right, I will. Zafir, 'Is your praise of God in the seventh?'"

"By my oath, it is in the seventh," he said. And with that, Zafir bowed his head toward me, as if in reverent and humble worship. In the flickering, yellow light of the oil lamp, I could see neatly wrapped around Zafir's headdress, holding the bindings secure, a clean band of golden silken threads exquisitely woven and bearing at the crown, a simple, solitary, single tassel.

"The seventh?" I breathed.

Zafir lifted his head and looked me squarely in the eyes. "The seventh," he said.

心爱的 **38** 咱爱小

THE BROWN MEN

After so many months traveling across deserts, mountains and now on a boat, I decided that sailing through the open sea wasn't much different than riding across the sands. Every few days the *Flying Dragon* stopped at the coast to discharge trade items and people, and take on new passengers or goods. With each docking, new fees were extracted by a village magistrate or owner of the dock—not fees so much as they were bribes to keep the pirates at bay. But even that did not guarantee safety.

The trip moved along at a scheduled pace until seven weeks out of Zhigu.

In the dim light of an early morning, the watch suddenly began shouting and rang his bell. Fawzi and I were asleep below and both of us sat up at the same time in alarm.

"What?" I asked, rubbing my eyes.

"Grab your things," Fawzi said, "follow me."

"Things? What things?"

"Tou's bow, your sword. Now!" and he raced into the hallway and hurried up the ladder.

I was only seconds behind him, almost tripping as I slipped on my other sandal. I could hear shouting and the pounding of many feet on deck. Clamoring up the ladder I poked my head through the opening and found myself in the heat of a frantic, bloody battle. Small brown men in loin cloths and bearing swords and knives shouted as they leapt over the railings onto the deck and slashed at our defenders. The captain and his crew were fully engaged, swinging their swords at the attack while sleepy passengers staggered topside to learn of the noise.

The work of death was well under way when I arrived. Fawzi's sword was deployed, taking quickly one man and felling another in the same swipe. Dozens more were climbing ropes thrown to the railings with hooks, and poured into the mayhem, teeth gnashing, swords gleaming in the musky gray light, and shouting their terror in one great roar.

I threw the quiver over my shoulder, pulled an arrow and nocked it steady. From the deck opening I stood long enough to spot a target, aim, release, and a man fell backwards into the sea. I drew another, nocked, aimed, and let fly, finding its mark through the neck of a swordsman who instantly fell, dropping his sword. I drew another and then another until all the arrows were spent. And then I pulled my sword to join the fray.

The deck was slippery with blood. Screaming men limped for mercy, begging the brown swords to restrain, but the blades were cruel. I slashed and clashed, finding the pirates in their legs and arms, their backs and necks. A blade grazed across my shoulder, searing pain followed, and I turned to see another who was determined to stop me. I twisted my body in time to miss the follow-up and struck at the man's loins. He crumpled, screaming as I turned just in time to stop a downward slash from another. We exchanged three quick strikes before I ran him through.

The fighting continued in heated exchange for several minutes more until I found myself backed against the wood-works of the captain's quarters. Fawzi was at my side, with a dozen swords suddenly raised against us but didn't strike. They had pinned us back.

I was breathless with panic. "Do we die fighting or do we negotiate?" I called over to Fawzi.

"Negotiate," he said. "Look at them. They could strike us down but they don't. Their leader wants to talk."

Another brown man with a loose red shirt and laced leather boots that climbed halfway up his lower legs, approached us, parting his men and sheathing his sword. With a gruff frown, he pointed angrily to the deck, shouting a threat. We dropped our swords.

"You western, no?" he demanded.

"Yes, Nafud, Syria, Rekeem," Fawzi said.

"You here trade?"

"Yes, long time," Fawzi replied.

"Stay. No go," he commanded.

I swallowed hard. The swords pressed against us were smeared with crimson evidence of that morning's work. I shuddered to think whose blood it might be.

The red shirt turned about and ordered two other men, shouting instructions in a tongue none of us understood. They flagged six others to follow, and with swords they leapt down the deck door. Footsteps followed, kicking noises, crashing, throwing things, but no shouts. More footsteps and then the men emerged again, climbing onto the deck with personal belongings from the passengers. One held up two black leather satchels, Zafir's satchels of coins, and with a twisted smile speckled with yellow spittle he opened his mouth wide in a big toothless grin, "Ah!" he said.

The red shirt stepped proudly to the messenger and threw a stiff arm around his shoulders. With his other arm, he took the offering of the prize, holding it high. "Ah!' he said, and the other men cheered back, stomping the deck with their feet.

The red shirt looped the satchels over his shoulders and parted the guards to come again and speak to Fawzi.

"You go, western man," he grinned. "You go west, bring back more. We find you. Come back, western man, come back!" He turned and raised his arms in victory and all his men cheered.

He shouted another order and the brown men lowered their swords, stepped over the bodies of their dead comrades, and hurried to the side of the ship and slipped over.

With the last man overboard, Fawzi and I bent down to pick up our swords.

"Be careful!" Fawzi said suddenly.

"What?"

"That arrow, over your shoulder, in the wall, don't touch it," he warned.

I turned cautiously and looked. A short black arrow with black feathers had stabbed the beam I stood against. It was poking out of the breastwork at shoulder height, one of many dozens that skewered the upper quarters—their tips and stems wet with a brown paste that glistened.

"Poison," Fawzi said. "I've heard of these—that is a lethal poison. While it is wet, it can kill. Doesn't have to break the skin. Be careful, don't touch it, Bassam."

I backed away cautiously, scanning my footsteps for more of the errant arrows.

We both crouched low as if expecting the pirates to suddenly appear again, and stepped over bodies, hurrying to the railing. A distant bank of fog was rolling back to sea and was taking with it the stiffly blossomed sails of seven small fishing vessels that hurried away into obscurity.

"Bassam, come! We must find Ammar and Zafir," Fawzi shouted, looking about suddenly. "Go below, I'll check here," and hurried to the captain's quarters.

I found the rooms below deck thoroughly ransacked, my journal supplies dumped and scattered, my south pointer underfoot with other bags and baskets dumped everywhere. And then Fawzi called from above. "Bassam, here, hurry!"

I raced topside and toward the captain's quarters. There I found them in the hallway just outside the door to his compartment. Zafir was leaned up against a wooden chest, breathing short, shallow breaths. His face was ashen and his legs and arms trembled. Fawzi ripped away the seam of Zafir's shirt to expose a bleeding puncture wound in the flesh of his shoulder. Immediately above him, stuck into the wall, was a short black arrow.

I looked with terror into Fawzi's eyes. He was hovering over Zafir, exposing the wound, pushing blood onto a shred of torn clothing. Zafir's eyes were closed.

I knelt closer. "Zafir, it's me, we're safe, they're gone," I said.

The old man could hardly speak. "My boy, my boy," he gasped, and raised a limp arm towards me. I took him by the hand and held it.

Fawzi pressed harder into the shoulder muscle, working it like an olive press, massaging it deeply to force out the poison.

"You—you will love my Rasha?" Zafir mumbled.

"Oh yes, I do already, I love her very much," I said.

"Many children, that is the way, many ..."

"A dozen, and many grandchildren, I promise," I said. "We'll visit you every day, and ..."

Just then Ammar arrived with a bucket of sea water. "Out of the way, Bassam! NOW!" he ordered, and dumped the bucket over Zafir's wound. They pulled Zafir away from the wall and laid him on his back and continued the work, forcing blood to ooze out of the wound. Zafir tightened in grimace and moaned.

"It must wash itself out," Ammar said. "Bassam, more water, quickly."

Dark blood swelled into a small puddle and then overflowed in a steady trickle down Zafir's arm and onto the floor.

I took the empty bucket and jumped out to the deck and bounded over to the railing, reaching for water. Hurrying back, I poured it over Zafir's shoulder while Ammar and Fawzi continued to massage the muscle and press the blood outwards. I ran for more water.

"That's it, Fawzi," Ammar said. "Exactly like that. Keep massaging. Deeper. We must get the blood that's pooling in the wound, get it out if we possibly can. More water Bassam."

I made another trip to the rail and when I returned, Zafir was mumbling something.

"Zafir," I called out. "Do you hear me?"

The old man went silent.

心爱的 **39** 的爱心

SEVENTH

Fawzi and Ammar carried Zafir to the captain's bed. I stood at the door growing sick to my stomach. Zafir's arms hung limply, he was pale, the very visage of the dead. But the two men refused to accept it and continued to work his shoulder.

I could stand it no longer and backed out of the door to find a dark corner at the far end of the corridor, I slumped down to the floor and pulled up my knees to bury my head. "Oh God," I murmured, "please help Zafir, please?" That same acid knot of horror and loss started swelling in my stomach. *No, not again, not again,* I mumbled aloud, shaking my head. Could it be happening all over again? Zafir told me himself that the caravan would always continue, that it never carries around the memories of the dead. *But what of him, the great living legend, this mighty leader whose honor and name is known with love and respect from the pyramids to the far east of Chang'an. This great man has endured so much, and now this?*

I remained for a time, I don't know how long, numb and lost and sick. I watched through blurry eyes at the shadows moving back and forth under the door at the far end of the corridor. I wanted to enter but it was still too soon, I couldn't watch.

What about Rasha, what would I tell her?

Finally, the moving shadows stopped. I waited anxiously for a long time. The door opened. Ammar walked out wiping his hands on a towel, looking to find me. Spotting me pressed away in the shadows at the end of the hall, he called.

"Bassam, I think he'll make it," he said.

My heart started beating again. "He will?" I stammered.

"I think so," he said. "I think we're over the worst of it. He's still unconscious but his heart beat is stronger. If we can walk him some more and get more grape wine into him, I think he'll come to. Will you run to the captain, tell him we need grape wine, red grape wine?"

My eyes grew big and I jumped to my feet. "Certainly," I said.

"Yes, we think the worst is passed," he said.

I broke into a full run and rushed to the captain and explained with gestures our need for an antidote.

Cradling in my arms a full corked bottle, I returned to Zafir. He moaned and reached out with his right arm to nothing there, and turned his head side to side. His forehead glistened with beads of sweat, his breath shallow and quick. Ammar and Fawzi made him start sipping the wine.

"He's coming to?" I asked Fawzi.

"Slowly," he said. "We need to get him on his feet, we need to flush him with wine and water, a lot of liquids, will you help?"

The three of us pulled him from the bed and despite his complaints, walked him down the hallway and out to the deck.

Zafir felt the fresh breeze on his face and squinted his eyes open. He mumbled to anyone listening, "Where am I?"

"You were poisoned," Ammar said. "We think we've got most of it out of you. Can you drink?"

"Can I what?" he scowled.

"Can you drink some water?"

"You goat heads, we're surrounded by water."

While Ammar and Fawzi kept Zafir moving and drinking, I followed behind. Then seeing that I was doing little to help, I joined the crew and passengers to clean up the mess.

Under the captain's orders, we dragged the dead to the railings and threw them overboard: nineteen of the brown men, and eight crew and passengers. They were weighted, bound for burial at sea. That much excitement drew a crowd of seagulls that squawked in frenzied competition for a sample of the discards.

The captain had cautioned the others about the arrows, and we took special care to remove them. They protruded from the walls and the floor, beams and shutters. Those too were bound and weighted, then cast overboard—swords, knives, and the horrid bits and pieces of flesh that always remain from such panicked melees. The captain suggested we keep one arrow to show a medicine man who might help Zafir more fully recover. The rest of the cleanup was hard and gruesome work for all of us.

By mid-afternoon Zafir appeared much improved. He was returned to his bed and promptly fell into a heavy sleep. We breathed a collective sigh of relief and hoped for a quick landing so we could get more help.

Near sundown, Zafir was awake and asking the same questions he had asked twice before. We answered them again, and he lapsed back to sleep until the boat made a bumpy stop at a village dock. It was the village of the Lower Gate, the nearest hope for recovery.

By mutual consent the crew and passengers agreed to keep silent about the attack. Ammar told me that such news as pirates and death always played havoc on local superstitions. The people must believe we bring good fortune, he said. And sure enough, when the villagers saw our late arrival they were indeed pleased with the good fortune of new sellers and new buyers. They didn't know that we were all of us much lighter after our loss to the brown men. They were eager to barter.

Our first action, though, was to hurry Zafir to a local medicine man. We gained directions to an old artisan on the other side of the village, a trip made shorter thanks to a wagon and donkey.

Stopping in front of a small adobe home, we found a thin, elderly man tending to something foul-smelling that boiled in a black pot over a smoky fire. We startled him with our approach, but he was polite, recognizing that strangers needed his help.

Fawzi and Ammar helped Zafir walk from the wagon, his arms draped about their shoulders. Seeing Zafir's obvious distress the old man waved us to the doorway and pointed to a daybed where they laid Zafir on his back.

Fawzi showed the wound, produced the arrow with its poison that he had carefully preserved in a thick leather wrap, and tried his best to describe what events had transpired. The old man was already ahead of us and shushed us out the door waving his hands and arguing something in a high, squeaky voice. Then he shut the door and disappeared.

We stood on the road looking at each other with concern and doubt, feeling helpless with our charge out of view. Should we should stay or go?

"I know," Fawzi said, and turned in the direction of a delicious smell that was drifting toward us from the market, and followed it.

"How can you possibly think of *that* at a time like this?" I called after him. "I'm not going."

"Suit yourself, barnacle bottom," Fawzi said. "We'll eat your portion for you."

"Better come, Bassam," Ammar said. "Fawzi is right, the old man will take care of Zafir. I think he is out of danger, but we can't do anything waiting around here. Would you prefer doing that on an empty stomach?"

I didn't feel like eating much, but followed them anyway.

Seated at a diner, a young waiter served us fresh broiled fish with rice and greens. None of us were talkative. In fact, it seemed the weariness of the travail had seeped deeply into our bones. We were contemplative, anxious, tired and concerned.

"How's that wound, Bassam?" Fawzi finally asked, disturbing the conversations that raged inside each of our heads.

"I'm okay, nothing deep. I bound it up."

"You'll have another story to tell," he said, reaching into his mouth to pull out a small bone. "Cheap food," he said, dropping it to the floor.

"It's another mark, a memorial to fighting," I said.

"If we can't get this boat cleaned up we'll have to buy passage on another," Fawzi said. "One to carry us through the straits."

"Buy?" I said. "They took Zafir's gold—his satchels."

"Bassam, Bassam," Fawzi said shaking his head. "Don't you ever pay attention, flounder face?" And with that he grabbed his lapel and shook his coat like a bag of coins.

"Oh, yes. Never mind," I said, casting an empty gaze in the direction of Zafir and his attendant.

"A boat to the straits," Ammar said. "That's not for another eight weeks by my reckoning—*if* any are built for that long haul, and we don't want to be stopping at every village and dock."

"Will such a boat be found in such a small village?" I asked, looking beyond them at the sparse businesses still open for food and drink.

"I think if we ask around," Ammar said, "especially among the Indus people. I see many in these parts. We'll find somebody anxious to return to their blue waters—"

"Hey, snail feet," Fawzi said pointing to my plate. "What's taking you so long, is your brain working as fast as your mouth again? Wrap it up," he said, "Zafir must be starving, we'll give him yours. And when he asks what took us so long, I'll say it was you and the servant girls again."

"Yeah, right," I said, "I'm done eating," and pushed away from the table.

Upon our return, we found Zafir pleasantly relaxing on a cushioned chair under an ornate tree in front of the medicine man's little house. He was wrapped in a blanket and talking while the little man stirred that foul-smelling pot.

"Zafir!" Ammar called as we neared. "Are you all right?"

"What took you so long?" he smiled. "I'm hungry. Let's go eat."

For a man already so terribly beaten-up on the trail, and now recovering from the poison arrow, Zafir seemed energized and able to defy death. The medicine man made it clear that Zafir was fortunate that the arrow passed clean through his shoulder and didn't lodge inside, or his troubles would certainly be worse. I wondered if that was why the poison was so slow to act on him.

We stopped to feed Zafir and then returned to our inn. Zafir went straight to his bed for a poultice change. The medicine man gave Ammar enough supplies to change the dressing for three more days when Zafir should be out of danger. Ammar stepped in to do the work. Zafir rolled to his right side and closed his eyes.

An hour later, we had run out of things to do except keep an eye on our snoring patient. Fawzi busied himself by sharpening his knife and sword. Ammar was seated under the oil lamp poring over his charts.

As for me, I was bored. So bored I began pacing for something to do. I fumbled around with Zafir's clothing, his head covering, his robe, straightened his belongings. I couldn't sleep, I didn't want to sleep. I couldn't write, I didn't want to write. I didn't feel safe. Was the door secure? Were the windows secure? Should I strap on my sword to be ready? The day was too full and I couldn't let it loose.

"Bassam!" Fawzi barked, looking my way, perturbed. He held up his knife as if to fling at me. "Can't you sit still, hoof-head?"

"No," I said.

"Then go see the beach," he barked. "Get some air."

Good idea.

There was no moon to light my way, only brilliant stars above. They helped me find the shoreline easily enough—a short stroll through some broad empty streets that led away from the thinning lights and fading activity of the drowsy marketplace.

I soon stood on the compacted wet sand of the black-shadowed shore and looked toward the horizon. Its straight line where sky fell to ocean was pleasantly joined like the carpenter's edge, with jeweled reflections of stars dancing restlessly across the black void of empty sea.

The night air was cool, salty and fresh. The sea washed politely over wide stretches of beach in a calming steady rhythm. Its white foaming crests collapsed into racing ponds of salty mirrors that rolled toward me in silence, then disappeared into the sands with a sleepy hush, just in time for the next drowsy front to come rolling at me with diminishing strength.

I closed my eyes and let the sea breeze sift my thoughts and my worries, letting loose the anger and fear. It was a pleasant escape to stand quietly still for a moment and breath in the delicious renewal of the tides. I felt the eons of time joining me on this beach, their rhythmic voices speaking no differently to the ancient times than they did to me tonight. The stars knew the language, and stood stationary to speak it aloud in their familiar formations. Their constellations and patterns brought a deeply settling comfort, like the anticipated visit of an old friend returning with gifts. I recognized precisely where I was by their standing in that shimmering sky—I didn't even need my string.

I was not alone on that midnight beach. Occasional laughter and distant excitement rose above the muffled crush of waves on shore. I counted half a dozen fires spread up and down the beach, their bright flames danced with the breeze. Small groups huddled about them in the glowing embrace of others, most of them young like me, carefree, laughing, eating, teasing.

It made me smile. Life goes on no matter what else, I thought. With the suffering of one just a stone's throw away, the others are oblivious to its harsh lessons, yet life must go on. The beginning and the ending, the cycles repeat, but oh! So quickly do they pass from view and then from memory. Nights such as these are the mortar that binds the bricks of experiences that make a well-lived life, experiences from this wonderful world—but not all at once, not in one great gulp, but piecemeal, some here, some there, as it should be.

I let my mind reconstruct the hard events of the past year, the lands we saw, the lessons learned, the laughing and the mourning, so much of life packed into a long series of months that suddenly seemed so short across those paths of heat and cold, dry and wet.

I heard a baby cry from a nearby fire and then some laughter and loving words from others. The sounds of new life made me smile—at this late hour, the child must be hungry for those same delicious smells that drifted seductively toward me. I was truly tempted to introduce myself on the hope they might share, but decided just to watch. Their joyful exchanges caused me to reflect on the clean start in mortality that each soul is given, a miraculous chance to start this journey with innocence and purity—but also born with the power of kings and queens within them—omnipotent, omniscient, it is their choice or their happenstance. But each new human comes filled with the vigor and enthusiasm for the promises of a new life, a new day, a new chance, such as that little one held in arms that love her. And then the vicissitudes of experiences that unfold in so many ways to mature that early hope into lessons etched into the clean slate by experiences. Most will choose to build on their limitations, while others will choose fight and aggression, hate and pushing, deception and theft. *Why is that*? I wondered aloud. So much anger and bloodshed by a few whose choices make the great whole of us suffer for their selfishness. Is this the inescapable destiny for mankind on earth, a constant and unending array of man standing against man in the bitter conflicts of struggle and tyranny, murder and war? Or is there a better way?

I took another deep breath to implant forever in my mind the feeling of this quiet time on the beach. I realized just then, by accident, that I had in my hand the answer to these ponderings about life and fate. I opened it to full view under the stars and the distant flickering lights of the fires. There lay the lacy strings of Zafir's seventh tassel, neatly curled in my palm, absently taken during my nervous taunt back at the inn.

"Oh yes," I spoke softly to the night, stirring the strings with my finger. "There *is a better way*."

"Day 469—Dear Rasha, I have new life in me now, I'm determined to finish this journey no matter the trial or treasure. We almost lost your father to treachery by bandits. They stole his gold and nearly his life. Through the worst of it he remained strong, stronger than all of us combined. He

has promised you to me, you are my greatest treasure and I come to find you as quickly as God will blow his winds to bring us together. I pray his benevolent hand to preserve and protect you until we meet again. — Bassam"

心爱的 **40** 咱耍小

WIND AND TIME

Seven days rolled past like the gentle waves of the sea beneath our majestic *Flying Dragon*. The captain had refitted his boat before leaving the dock at The Lower Gate with a different configuration of sails and more goods in the hull, sparing us the bother of finding another boat. It had traversed the straits many times, and we hoped it had yet one more crossing left in her. The captain was pleased we chose to stay and finish the journey on the *Flying Dragon*. And so, we continued with the winds and current that carried us onward south. The ship and its crew seemed up to the job, and had stocked supplies to spare.

On this beautiful morning Zafir was on the deck with the rest of us, enjoying the healing strength of the warming sun and sea breeze in our faces. The ship skipped along under the power of a strong wind. Everything about her felt ready for what they told us would be a difficult journey ahead.

"Sixty stadia an hour?" I exclaimed. "That's 600 a day—or more. I didn't know this boat could move so fast."

Ammar wasn't impressed. Perhaps it was too early in the morning for him, I couldn't tell. Already we were at full sails and the sun wasn't even high enough to burn off the ocean mists.

"The farther south we go, the less help we get from the wind," he said. "Sixty an hour is good, but that's with *favorable* winds. We'll find good hard winds when we near Kantoli, but in the wrong direction. It's the wrong time of year to be headed west."

"So, we'll tack, we'll drive into the wind, back and forth, right?" I asked. "Like you showed me?"

"But don't expect miracles," he said. "We can waste a lot of time on the ocean trying to do just that—tack here and there, day in and day out. When we hit those doldrums, it is faster to take an oar and row our way south than wait."

"You'd be good at that, blister butt," Fawzi said.

The port stops down the C'ina coast were few. We saw hundreds of fishing villages but found few cities to make a stop. It was difficult to find places where the larger boats could safely tie up and unload.

After three more days of good wind, we finally pulled in at Ye. This was a busy little village, happy for the business but too crowded to accommodate us. Fishing boats took the available berths and we had to wait till mid-day to tie up.

We took on supplies, off-loaded some passengers, and the crew worked to repair one of the smaller sails. And then for reasons not made clear, the captain told us we had to spend the night in Ye, something about barnacles and grasses on our keel. He invited us to sleep on board in our compartments, or find an inn. Either way, the boat was in for the day and would not leave until morning. Zafir opted for the inn and we all followed.

Our old friend was hobbling better now and refused to make us slow for him. "There's a simple solution for the barnacles," he said as we headed toward the market square. "I offered it but they didn't believe me."

"Don't you have to dry dock and scrap at them?" I asked.

"Yes and no," Ammar said. "You just have to go into fresh water."

"Fresh water?" I said. "What difference does that make?"

"They live in sea water," Zafir said. "The fresh water kills them and they stop growing. You still must scrape and chisel, but the new arrivals will just let go and fall off, and then your trip is made that much quicker."

"Then how do you get it into fresh water?" I asked.

"A river, bait breath," Fawzi drawled, rolling his eyes.

"Such as the Ganga," said Zafir. "We've got a stop planned for Tamralipta, a large trading city that's right at the mouth."

"Must we go far?" I asked.

"Not far," Ammar said. "Maybe a day up and back. It's enough time in the water."

"We'll check for messages," Zafir added, "and be quickly on our way."

"Messages?" I wondered.

Ammar lowered his voice. "*Al Kalimat*, Bassam," he said.

"What?"

"*The Words*, Bassam, remember?"

"Oh. Yes. Al Kalimat, I remember," I said, and lowered my voice. "Ammar, how do the messengers know where to send their pouches? How can they know where Zafir is going?"

Ammar leaned over and explained. "During his travels Zafir always dispatches messages through his stewards with his anticipated routes and stops. The pouches travel faster than the caravans, they help when plans change, just like now. One time a few years ago he summoned an army of swords to meet him at Kashgar, and they came together within a week of each other, surprisingly efficient."

The power and expense of stewards along the trade routes suddenly made sense. It was so practical—I didn't dream he was so organized, and this, across the continent, it was amazing. And there where the river met the ocean was another perfect location. Zafir's regular caravan route was supposed to pass right along the mouth of the Ganga, an ideal place for a messenger coming by sea. I wondered what other contact places Zafir had pre-arranged—he seemed so adept at protecting himself for every possible emergency and need.

Entering the market square, we found ourselves surrounded by booths and tables laden with fruits and greens. The aroma of roasted nuts and meats filled the air. It made me hungry. The loud confusion sounded just the same as any other stop. Different language and place, it was the same, melding into the same cacophony of calling and arguing, laughing and telling, selling and scoffing, inviting and rejecting. All I wanted was some peace and quiet, and a good hot meal.

To the far side we saw the inns. Zafir chose one that offered the best view—not for the pleasure of the scenery, he said, but for safety from the streets. We followed behind when suddenly Zafir veered off to the side, hobbling down a narrow lane crowded with little shops.

"Zafir! Where are you ...." I asked.

"Follow me Bassam," he said, and led us right to a shop that sold leather and pre-made leather goods.

We were greeted by a short, thin man in a straight, silver-silk robe with sagging sleeves. He stood as we entered and bowed politely, his hands clasped in front of him. His pinched face was framed with a neatly trimmed white beard that hung to his chest blending as one with his long, white moustache. His tired eyes twinkled as we approached.

Zafir made gestures indicating his intent, and picked out a large skin of thick pliable leather. He also bought supplies—two spools of thin cord and a dozen bone needles.

I watched in curiosity as Zafir picked from the offers with the deftness of an experienced worker of textiles. His shopping complete, he offered the required silvers.

"What's this all about?" I asked him. "Are you making a project or something?"

Zafir received the old man's thanks with a slight bow, and then rolled the leather for me to carry and put the thread and needles into his pocket.

He turned to me as we left the shop. "Have you forgotten so soon, my son?"

"Forgotten what?"

"The scroll bag," Zafir said, and hobbled toward the nearest inn, not even looking to see if I followed.

心爱的 **41** 咖翠小

WARMER CLIMES

That next morning we left before daybreak in the dark. The captain said we had a busy schedule to keep and hurried as if trying to catch up to something we could not fathom. The plan was a non-stop day and night sail to reach our next docking place.

They steered us farther from the coast where a better wind sent us toward a port they called P'anyu'. After four days at sea and a lot of anticipation, the captain decided at the last moment to continue south, and didn't even slow the boat long enough for us to wave. We watched with disappointment as P'anyu' and all of her exotic colors, sights, and crowded harbor passed by with hardly a glance from the crew.

It was difficult remaining entertained on the long stretch. Boredom returned at the worst possible times. We passed the hours with just about anything we could invent. Even the ritual of cleaning the boat brought welcomed distraction. We scoured its top, bottom, inside, outside, leaning so far out from the railing to reach the planking with a brush that one slip would certainly be a soggy one.

Using sea water for soap, and arms and backs for encouragement, we scrubbed hard to pull up as much neglect and filth as we could—the deck, railings, forecastle, bilge, cargo, sleeping quarters, lookout, storage, and anywhere else we could reach—and then we started it all over again the next day.

Ammar and Fawzi waved away my offer to play Weiqi. "You're too good at it now," they said. "Try your tricks on Zafir, you might surprise him."

It was just an excuse, and not good for that because we all knew Zafir rarely took time from his reading to do anything other than, perhaps, to meditate.

That's when Ammar and Fawzi turned their attention to a board game of different sorts. They called it Naquala, a word I finally understood, meaning to move. Ammar was packing it around for a couple of weeks and decided times were desperate enough to bring it up on deck.

The game board was two palms long and half a palm wide, with two rows of holes or depressions: six on each side. I gathered from watching them play that the object was to drop or "sow" the hole with little stones, somehow capturing your opponent's stones. It seemed interesting enough, although they made many excuses to exclude me.

Zafir finally pulled me away for a more important task—the new scroll bag. I joined him under his awning amidships, supplies in hand, to learn another of his rituals.

"It's an ancient pattern," he said. "First, carefully, take apart the old scroll bag. You will use it for a guide."

I used my knife to cut the seams neatly and carefully. It was tedious work, but eventually I separated all the threads and could lay the leather out. A lifetime of habit in the old shape had molded the leather into bends and folds that I had to tug and pull until it was a flat shape that I could trace. It bore the wear of many years' travel, blackened with marks from fires and large water stains, all giving proof it had endured an entire life of adventure, hardship, and trial. Zafir said nothing and watched quietly as I worked.

As the bag began to unfold I suddenly realized I was undoing something he himself had prepared long ago, when he was my age—the undoing of a bag his father made, to make this bag of his own. I realized this was not a routine exercise but a tender time for Zafir, and I went about my work with greater respect, saying nothing.

With the leather finally flattened and laid out, I was surprised to discover it was cut of one piece. I centered it on the new leather and used an awl to trace its outline, careful to make it the same as the old.

Zafir examined the work for perfection, stopping me at each step of the way. "It's the same process I followed as a boy," Zafir said. "I don't know how far back this pattern dates, but my father told me it was always the same."

"Then that is what I will tell my son," I said.

Zafir smiled.

The pattern created a double layer for the bottom, and two flaps that folded inside and outside the top, an ingenious design to keep out the wet and mishaps.

Loops with cords kept it closed, leaving the scrolls well contained and secure inside.

It took a good part of the afternoon to cut the new leather to Zafir's exacting specifications. He showed me how to score and crease the leather to give structure and rigidity to its form.

Just when my hands were too tired to hold my knife any longer, Zafir declared it was enough, and started me on the first stitches.

The actual stitching was the most tedious chore of all. Part of the trial was enduring Zafir's insistence that I do it *just so*, including a triple stitch at every seam. He showed me some techniques to make the task easier—grease on the needle, an awl to make holes in the tough places, a way to hold it against a board to make the work easier. And, a chant to keep a rhythm of conformity and uniformity. The entire process was inscribed indelibly in my mind, a memory sure to last me till my own time came to repeat the exercise.

At the end of that first day my fingers were raw and sore with blisters. My back ached from leaning over, and I had broken two of the needles. I was glad he bought a large supply of them. At the rate I was breaking them I suspected we might need to get more.

On the second day things went better. I started to get into a rhythm to match the chanting. My stitches became closer, tighter, neater. I didn't realize it until then that Zafir knew this step-by-step learning procession was natural, and he had planned for it. He made me start stitching the inside layers first, the least important part of the project, where my sloppiest work would not weaken the final product.

"You learn with practice," he said, "and rather than learn by error and sloppiness where it counts the most, I give you practice where it doesn't count. When you reach the outer part where strength and neatness means more, you will have become an expert trained for the task. So, did my father teach me, so I teach you. It is a metaphor for life, Bassam, the pattern of patterns."

He was right. The repetition and coaching had changed me into a modestly meticulous workman of the leather.

"Keep up the work," Zafir said, "and listen to what I have to say. This is a good time to speak because it has been on my mind for some time. I may not have another chance to tell it."

"Tell me what?"

"The great scrolls we have studied, they have opposites, you know."

I looked at him, confused. "Opposites? What do you mean? Is there another set of scrolls?" I asked.

"You pay attention to your work," he said, "and I will tell you."

I obeyed and focused on pushing the needle into the stiff leather and pulling through the heavy threads. "Yes, I'm listening," I said.

"There is opposition in all things, my son. Everything has its opposite."

"Everything?" I asked.

"Everything. Good and bad, right and wrong, life and death, cold and hot, sweet and sour, righteousness and evil, forward and backward. Opposites."

"This sounds like the fourth scroll," I said, glancing up. I saw Zafir casting his empty gaze out across the ocean. I didn't respond but kept my fingers moving the thread—into the leather and out again, careful, tight, neat—letting patience lead me to make gentle motions.

"Those brown men who attacked us," he said after several moments, "the C'ina emperor, Kahn and Habib, the bandits, the broken and confused among my men, the beggars at the wayside in the villages we pass through, the thieves, the many darknesses you have witnessed, these are all opposites to the teachings of the scrolls."

That much I understood. I dismissed them as people caught in the actions of the natural man living natural lives near its most raw level of survival. Enduring without the illuminating benefits of proven values and ideas—the secrets—to better steer themselves to better paths.

"These opposites have a name," he said. "We call them the *seven deadly forces*. There are seven perfect opposites to the scrolls, and they *are* opposite. They are not written but you may put them in your journal if you wish. Knowing them helps you see the eternal nature of the scrolls, how to apply them in the real day-to-day living of your years on the earth, to build your family, your life, to build and sustain a great nation."

"Then I want to learn them," I said.

Just then an energizing sea breeze blew past, lifting the canopy over us and popping the sails to full bloom. It enveloped the boat in a cool, cleansing softness that refreshed and seemed to calmly set things right. High above I heard the squawking of birds that had come with the wind, floating above, their wings outstretched, unmoving, spying for scraps. It was a sure sign that land was near.

心爱的 **42** 啪耍小

DEADLY FORCES

"There are seven deadly forces," Zafir said. "Find the deepest meaning of each scroll and there you will find its opposite. Learn them, my son, and you will see them forming in dark corners of conspiracy and contempt for the lives and welfare of others. The wise will take steps to prevent such establishments, though they often stand alone in such a cause. The *seven deadly forces* are the starting places for the ruin of all men, for all nations."

"You make it sound like they afflict the whole world," I said.

"They do," Zafir said. "They are as old as the principles in the scrolls. Let me show you. The first scroll, *Govern Thyself*, what would you say is the opposite, the opposite of exercising self-control and self-starting each day?"

The opposite ... I let the query linger on the tip of my tongue, suddenly remembering back to that dark night when Zafir unfolded the first scroll and its meaning. It was a starlit magical time in that dry, flat desert. Was it now more than a year ago? With my attention wandering, I poked my thumb and a red drop quickly formed. I pressed it against my robe. Other such spots in the fabric already bore witness to my clumsiness.

"Lack of self-control," I offered. "Isn't that the opposite?" By his look I knew it wasn't, and so I listened.

THE FIRST FORCE

"The real opposite of self-government is governing others," Zafir said. "Do you see it? Controlling yourself or controlling others—imposing yourself on others is the ultimate act of selfishness. Ruling by force, governing against the will of your subordinates, for your own benefit—it is pure selfishness."

The idea struck home with such clarity, I stopped sewing. What does a man do when he can't control himself? He goes around ordering and bossing and forcing others to obey his own accumulation of lusts and vices and selfish demands. Governing others is the opposite of governing yourself—it clarified as a new idea in my mind.

"Tyrants such as Huángdi and that leader of the Brown Men," he said, "such men are beholden to no one—no law, no governing body, no court, no other but himself and his selfish pursuits—a tyrant. That is the opposite of the first scroll, the dark opposite of self-governance. We name this first deadly force *The Ruler*."

THE SECOND FORCE

I started a list in my head, the seven ruinous parallels to the seven scrolls. "The first force is the all-powerful *ruler.*"

"The selfish ruler is the beginning of decay in a nation," Zafir said. "Now you will better see the opposite of the second scroll, *Humble Thyself*. A man who is not humble does not want new knowledge lest it awaken him to his awful ways, to his error. He knows if he were humble to new knowledge he would have to make positive change."

"Why not?" I asked. "Why not want to be better? Who wouldn't?"

"The first scroll, Bassam," Zafir said. "They think 'better' is power over others. Most rulers are pleased to govern others but not themselves. With that they always build a caste system. Look about you, the tyrants always have structure in their oppression—at the top are his friends who are happy to relay his orders. In the middle are those who are happy to enforce the orders in hopes of some reward or honor from those above. At the bottom are the masses who unhappily must obey or die."

"The emperor's spies," I said, "they were his enforcers, making the people to believe his superstitions, or die."

"Yes, even the tyrannical have structure," he said. "Remember the second deadly force is the *caste system*. It is a sad truth, but a people divided is a people weak. Such nations divided within themselves, divided into castes, must fall. Watch for it in C'ina, among the Xiongnu, the bandit cities. It is an eternal law that corruption must collapse, no matter how long it takes, it is a law that must be obeyed."

Just then a massive green slick of floating debris appeared directly in our path. The *Flying Dragon* did not pause or divert. Its keel cut forward, pushing aside the large mass. For where I sat it looked like a carpet of moss, twigs and seaweed, sticks and flotsam. An old rotted smell accompanied the slick, and then the air was fresh again as it passed behind us.

"You expect it to sew itself?" Zafir said glaring at me with a frown. I quickly resumed my work.

THE THIRD FORCE

"The third scroll teaches *Give of Thyself*," Zafir said. "Its opposite is to force others to give, compel them against their will. Look at all the rulers you have studied. They always promise to take from the rich and give to the poor. 'All things in common,' they say. It is a powerful promise to win the support of the vast masses who are not rich and never will be. Many fall for that lie."

"But giving to help," I said, "to help the poor and hungry, is that so bad?"

"No, helping the needy is a good and necessary thing," Zafir said, "but forcing people to do it, that is where the trouble begins. Charity must be voluntary or it will destroy a nation. The Rulers appeal to compassion in their people, to curry their favor to help the downtrodden. Once the people agree, because we are all loving and compassionate of our fellows, the Rulers start taxing and taking. The receivers stop struggling because, suddenly, living has become easier. This draws more people to beg for help, so taxes must go up to support them, and the cycle spirals out of control. You know for yourself, Bassam, that the people do not like the fruit of their hard work taken by force and given to those who have not earned it. Encourage the people to give voluntarily and they will give forever. Try to force them to give and they will forever search to avoid the tax and not pay it. And who suffers? The needy. And all this grinds away, year after year, while the rulers build their power and control. They sit at the top living in comfort and vice off the labors of the masses, hardly lifting a finger to support themselves. It is the opposite of giving. Remember the third deadly force is promising *all things in common.* It is an enticing lure that enslaves millions, and few are there that understand why."

THE FOURTH FORCE

The fourth scroll was one of my favorites. Seeking the golden mean between extremes—*Balance thy Judgment*—was a challenge. I worked on it during the many idle hours riding my bakra or pacing the deck of our many boats.

"Do you recall our discussion about gluttony?" Zafir asked.

I nodded.

"Then you remember that when a man is hungry, he may choose to eat too much or not eat enough and still be hungry. The best choice is to eat adequately and not fall for the extremes."

"I didn't do that well in C'ina," I said, patting my stomach, "thanks to a few bouts of nasty personal experience."

Zafir gave me the look, and I returned to my sewing.

"The opposite of that balanced center is the human vice of greed," he said. "Greed has no place in our lives, it always destroys. Let me teach it with this parable I learned as a youth."

THE PARABLE OF THE GOLDEN SWAN

"There once was a woman whose husband died. In her grief, she petitioned God to restore him to her. The prayer was granted, and the husband could return to her once every year as a swan with 100 golden feathers. Each spring he could offer her a single feather from his wing so she could buy food and sustain herself. One day, in fear and greed, she plucked off all the feathers at once. With all the feathers gone, the swan died. It didn't take long for her to squander all her gold, and she too died hungry, cold and alone. Her greed cost her the blessings of a miracle. So is it with those who fail to balance their judgement, to see the future from the past. So is it with those who let greed cause them to step freely into rash and extreme choices."

I had seen it a thousand times on our trek. Greed that consumed the best of intentions and left behind nothing but carnage and death.

"This is the fourth deadly force, the *Force of Greed*," Zafir said. "Greed also plays a dark role in learning wisdom as taught in the Fifth Scroll. Let me teach that to you."

THE FIFTH FORCE

The fifth scroll taught *Be Thou Wise*.

"The opposite of learning from mistakes," Zafir said, "is to be forced to do what is right at all times."

"That's like violating the First Scroll," I offered. "If you can't govern yourself, others will govern you by force."

"Yes," Zafir said. "The lessons of our past should teach us to be wise. My father taught me that the possession of true wisdom comes from a life-time of making foolish choices."

That made me laugh. "If that's the case, then I should be wiser than you, Zafir!"

He smiled. "Don't be so quick, Bassam, you don't know me well. But so is it with all of us. We believe our lapses and mistakes are unique failings committed only by ourselves. They're not. We are all flawed. And from those flaws we learn to repair our lives and choose better next time. So grows our wisdom, a mistake at a time. What could be the opposite of wisdom? It is simply this: force. Forcing people to do what is right, forcing their decisions, forcing their pathway through life, forcing their choices. You can't learn from mistakes if you aren't allowed to make any. You miss out on learning true wisdom. Force is the opposite of learning from mistakes. Let this parable teach it better—"

THE PARABLE OF THE FREE BREAD

"There was in a faraway land a man who wanted to be king. 'Choose me to rule,' he said, 'and I will put free bread on every table.'

"The people put him on the throne and awaited his promises to be answered.

"In due time the Ruler took his escort and rode to the fields. He said to the farmer, 'You will sell your wheat a silver for a ten-weight, no more.' The farmer could not feed his family on such an income but he was forced to obey.

"Then the Ruler rode to the stables and told the wagon master, 'You will transport the wheat a silver for a hundred-weight, no more.' The wagon master could not feed his family on such an income but he was forced to obey.

"Then the Ruler went to the pressman, 'You will press your oil a silver for a thousand-weight, no more.' The pressman could not feed his family on such an income but he was forced to obey.

"Then the Ruler went to the miller, 'You will grind the wheat a silver for a ten-thousand-weight, no more.' The miller could not feed his family on such an income but he was forced to obey.

"The Ruler went to the baker, 'You will give your bread to the people for free, and I will give you a silver for each ten-thousand weight, no more.' The baker could not feed his family on such an income but he was forced to obey.

"The Ruler returned to his throne and forced the people to pay a tax for this service, 'To run the kingdom,' he said, 'so I may fulfill my promises to you.'

"For this first harvest, every man had bread on his table and was joyous. The Ruler was praised and adored.

"Then came the season for planting. The farmer sold his land because he had nothing left over to buy seed. The wagon master sold his ox because he had nothing left over to buy feed. The pressman sold his press because he had nothing left over to pay his pressmen. The miller sold his stones because he could not grind a profit. And the baker closed his store because he had nothing left over to pay himself a wage.

"The starving people ran to the Ruler. 'Have I not fulfilled my promise?' he said. 'This calamity is the greed of the farmer, the wagon master, the miller, the pressman, and the baker. Give me power to take their fields and ox and press and mill and bakery and you will eat again!" And the people did.

"And that," Zafir said, "is how a ruler works his way to gain complete control, by forcing people to do what he believes is right. Remember this my son, a tyrant will choose an outcome, not a process. That is his great folly. Teach the people correct laws and they will eventually learn from their mistakes how to properly govern themselves. The opposite of learning wisdom from mistakes is being forced to do what is right, and thereby learning nothing at all. It is *Force*."

THE SIXTH FORCE

The sixth scroll taught *Live to Teach*. Zafir showed me the opposite of sharing truth and information is to control information. Control what is learned, control what is taught, control what motivates, control the basis for decisions by all others. This is how a ruler controls information, it is the opposite of the true teacher, it is propaganda.

"Sometimes he destroys books to control the information, just like Huángdi," Zafir said. "Leading the people to believe a lie and live in ignorance."

He said people naturally follow leaders, and even if what a leader says isn't true, they tend to follow anyway, sometimes when they know he is lying or is evil.

"It is our sad experience," Zafir said, "that people will endure the hardships of bad rulers so long as they have their basic needs met. The ruler will tell great lies to keep his people weak so he may more easily control them. And people will put up with that, they will endure it if they believe this is the best there is, no matter the hardships facing them."

The man who teaches truth can keep his sons strong. But the ruler must prevent the truth from becoming known, at any cost, because the people will discover he is weak and break free from him.

"The sixth deadly force is the opposite of spreading true information," Zafir said, "it is *Control of Information*."

THE SEVENTH FORCE

The seventh scroll, the most precious of all, teaches that honor is power. To win honor, to deserve it, to earn it, a man must be respectful of others. This is how he earns their respect, and likewise, achieves power to do more good in the lives of those who trust him.

"Its opposite," Zafir said, "is pure force—no honor, no respect, no transparency, no integrity, simply pure force to put down one to lift up another. This is the smothering of ethical rights, the rights given to all men by God. In destroying such rights the destroyer has no honor, and therefore, no power—do you see it Bassam?"

I did see it. A ruler imposing on his subordinates in this fashion did not build trust and love, respect and honor, only the worst kinds of fear.

"The seventh deadly force," Zafir said, "is to deny natural rights, human rights, rights given from the Creator"

This idea was new. It opened my mind to see other people in a different light. No longer were they well capacitated or gifted or advantaged over others just because of where they were born or their race or nationality. Suddenly they all became the same to me. All men in a different light, not as superior or greater, but as equals in their rights to pursue life in their own way, with varying skills, talents, desires, ethics and goals. No one, therefore, has any innate rights to abuse another, and instead of using persuasion to encourage voluntary change as taught in the

Seventh Scroll, those seeking power over others must use force, which is the opposite of free will and free choice. It is worse than deadly force, it is deadly *moral* force.

"Day 532—My Dearest Rasha, Our journey takes us through a land I've not heard of. Your father is healed of an attack on our boat, and his leg is much stronger. His mind keen and alert. He teaches me the science of government and now I see that the government of myself must be no different than the government of a village or of a nation. It is all the same. Leaders have no more powers and rights than do those they lead. That is the great secret to freedom.

"We eat the fish we catch each day. They are dark and not tasty in these waters. Ammar says they are scavengers, bottom dwellers. He tells me we will find better fish in the other ocean. Our boat drags moss and seaweed caught on the barnacles. We loosen it with sticks but it is not enough, more must drag beneath. Zafir speaks with urgency now. He senses something. I have grown to love your father like my own, he is a wonderful man who reared a beautiful and brave daughter. I miss you. —Bassam"

心爱的 **43** 啪燮小

BROKEN NEEDLES

The ideas planted in my mind by these *seven deadly forces* kept my brain churning during my hours at the needle. I remembered scenes of the seven forces growing in all the places we had visited. I had not properly understood the dark powers that were at work, but the more I reflected on it the more their presence became dangerously clear.

I started to see the seven forces in almost every enterprise about which I had knowledge. I decided to ask Zafir about a government that is correctly built upon the seven scrolls. Was such a government even possible?

Our sail to the next stop took eight days, to a place named Ka Van. The days were not as difficult and went by faster thanks to Zafir's explanations while I did the sewing. These were pleasant distractions.

I became quite adept at stitching. The quality of my work made Zafir smile, he was pleased.

After Ka Van, we sailed yet one more week for Kauthara. It was at that same time, just as the men steered the boat into the harbor to an open dock, that I finished the last knotting of the last row.

I called to Zafir and announced it, holding up the scroll bag for him to examine. He seemed pleased.

"And how many needles?" he asked.

"Ten" I said. "With two to spare."

"You've done well, Bassam," he said. "When I was a boy, I used up all twelve and my father had to buy six more before I was finished."

"Perhaps the leather was thicker—more difficult to work," I offered.

"No, it was the same," he said flatly, handing the bag back to me. "You work well with your hands," he said. "With such gifts and hard work, my son, you will never be without things to do, and gold for your labors."

That night Zafir showed me how to place the scrolls so they do not scrape and scar during the rough and tumble of the caravan. Together we placed the scrolls into my new bag. They fit snugly and the bag held them securely. A feeling of connection swept over me as I finished yet one more ritual with Zafir, the replacing of the old scroll bag with one that is new. Noticing the tenderness in my fingertips, it became clear why part of his ceremony always began with a telling about the bag being made under the tutelage of his father, and was so cherished. I realized right then I could share a similar story with my own son when that time came, with passion and affection.

"What will you do with the old leather?" I asked.

"The same thing my father did," he said. "This draw-cord becomes a tassel for your head covering, I'll show you how to make it—*the seventh,* as we talked. You will wear it always. And the leather becomes a belt for you—a token of passage and a protection for you, from my generation to yours. It is your constant reminder to make all your choices within the embrace of the scrolls, as you are embraced with the belt. Do you see it?" he asked. Then he pulled aside his robe for me to see a wide leather belt around his own waist. I had seen it before but gave it no thought. Suddenly it became important, a part of his garment that tied him to his father and their fathers for centuries. "For the rest of your life, Bassam."

"And your belt," I asked, pointing. "What becomes of that?"

Zafir smiled with a hearty laugh. "You'll bury me with it," he said. "You'll have your own, you won't need two unless you continue eating like I saw you eat at every diner and kitchen we visited in C'ina."

I smiled and picked up the creased leather—old and worn from who knows how many adventures—and turned it over for the best place to cut.

"Finish this soon," Zafir said. "The Straits of Kantoli are just a day away, and you will want to take my word for this," he said with a cautionary smile. "When we get there, you won't have time to sit."

心爱的 **44** 咱愛小

ROCKY SHOALS

The Straits of Kantoli was the violent meeting place where the eastern ocean crashed into the western ocean. We were still a long way away from the straits when our sailor friends pointed out the tell-tale signs that we were getting close. Far ahead was a great bank of mist, almost a cloud, lying low on the horizon. It was rolling and churning to mark a place unlike any in all the oceans of the world. To our west the brown line of land ended where the great mist rose, a clear ending of rocky shoals and the start of a watery violence unlike the great cataracts of the world. Ammar said it is a great mirage, inviting travelers to assume it remains smooth ocean sailing. But once within its relentless grip, sure death comes in a violent way to those unprepared. Could such tales of terror hold true on a crystal blue day as today with such a warm sun sparkling off the sea around us?

It took many hours to approach the straits, giving us plenty of time to turn around if we changed our minds. Coming into better view, we could see where the ocean was compelled to funnel itself between two large land masses. The great mountain-sized slabs stood to either side like two crumbling canyon walls forcing the sea against its normal currents. In that passageway, the waters crushed together in massive white rapids that churned and boiled, slammed and crashed into the crumbling crust of granite to either side. The rushing winds lifted the mists high into the air, stretching the violence for the entire length of the shoreline before disappearing into the distant horizon.

The long peninsula of southern Kantoli was home to a greedy people. Twice during our approach, they sent small boats with swordsmen to board us and extract a heavy tax. Fawzi suggested they wanted the money before we were ripped to shreds on the rocks and our treasures forever lost to the sea. Zafir said the real reason was their greed.

"They tax us here because there is no shorter way to the oceans west," he said. "Traveling farther south is more costly and dangerous, and most people will not risk it. But crossing the straits from the other side is a much different story. The Indus people are not so desperate. They are an old culture, long industrious in their land. They encourage the visitor to visit, to trade. They oppose the pilfering activities of their greedy neighbors. By boarding us these tax collectors reveal the poverty and greed that abounds in their people. It is sad."

When the Kantoli pirates boarded us the first time, it was gold from every passenger. The penalty for not paying was capture and arrest to the mainland.

They could see in us that we carried no valuables or commodities, and viewed Zafir as a liability in whom some mercy should be granted. What they didn't know was Zafir's mastery at the wordless negotiation. He indicated with his hands and facial expressions that we were impoverished sailors separated from our band, searching for a way home, having lost all to the bloody attack by the brown men.

While his attempt produced no complete pardon, they did allow us to continue for the discounted payment of a silver each.

"A silver," Ammar said afterwards, "the going rate for paupers in these waters."

As we neared the straits the sea became choppier and the pitching deck made it difficult to stand. I was looking over Ammar's shoulder at his map when a sudden swell pushed the boat sideways. It almost knocked both of us off balance. When the ship settled right again he neatly penned onto his parchment the name that the locals had given the straits. For some people the name held honor and prestige, especially if they had survived the passage. For others, it was not so easily considered, in particular the faint of heart. For us, Ammar wrote the name used by the survivors of this dangerous journey—"The Devil's Throat."

Setting sail directly toward the center path through the straits, the wind immediately pulled us into her grip and jerked our boat forward. At first the wind came at us from behind, then suddenly grew stronger and violent, popping out the sails and pushing us ahead with such intensity I was surprised the sails did not split at the seams. Our boat left behind a wide foamy wake and soon the sea's calm was heaved to white caps of heavy ocean mountains that started crashing over the sides with spectacular spray. We began to heavily pitch to and fro.

I shouted above the noise. "Zafir! We've never gone this fast, have we?"

The old man just held tight to a wooden post toward the back of the boat with a reflective smile of exhilaration. Sporadic spray glistened his face. He received it with zest, as if remembering a similar ride many years before.

Ammar answered me, shouting over the wind and crashing waves. "They should lose some sail," he said, but his words quickly whisked away in the deafening roar.

Just then a mighty wave exploded across the bow, throwing foaming cold spray across all of us, instantly drenching us to our skin. I tasted the cold salt in my mouth and it stung my eyes. Overhead the sun and sky disappeared behind a shroud of rising mist—in mere moments it became as dark as dusk.

The bow suddenly dropped and slammed hard, lurching all of us forward. A few others on deck lost their footing and were thrown down. Others crawled their way to the hatch for safety below. The boat pitched hard to one side and then the other, slamming against the sea. The spray washed over us again and again, and with each mountain of water that lifted us atop its crest, it dropped us rudely to a trough below. We slammed hard. Heavy spray stung against our skin, ripping at us with icy claws. The jolting and jarring sent us crawling for safety, to grab a post or railing, as had Zafir. He remained with his pleasant smile—alert but calm while the rest of us were hanging on for dear life.

The captain yelled to his men, shouting orders. The spray poured over us repeatedly and the crew scampered about, fighting the rolling deck but quickly responding to his every command—working the rigging, fighting the halyards, raising sails, lowering sails, working the sheets, giving slack, pulling the yardarms this way and that, tying them off, securing lines, loosening again. And all the while, the boat pitched and slammed across crests and troughs, throwing mist and waves across deck and through. The violence knocked the standing to their knees and the kneeling to their faces, and didn't slow its vicious assault.

I watched in pure fright as a mountain of gray water directly in front of us rose ominously high above our heads, and seemed to look down with swirling black envy, ready to slam us into oblivion, but collapsed just as quickly. Our little boat was suddenly lofted high on the shoulders of another wave and dropped with a stomach-jolting slam.

The men quickly brought down the main sail, and the wind took it immediately, wrapping it around the mast, soaked and clinging. The smaller sails were kept deployed for steering while the ship leaned far to one side, taking two more waves, then three, then another, and leaned the other way and violently jolted back again—then dropped the bow, slamming the water with another jarring jolt that made our teeth loosen in our mouths.

"The boat can't take this," I yelled to Fawzi.

"Hang on!" he yelled back.

The foremast holding sail suddenly cracked half way up with a loud snapping noise and then broke through, and for a moment shadowed over us like a massive flapping bird, then crashed to the deck. The fabric flattened across the mess of tangled ropes and pulleys and splintered remains. Another giant wave crashed over the bow, and then a side shot of four waves in rapid succession tipped us dangerously the other way. The bow slammed to the sea again and the boat teetered on its other side.

My soaked skin was freezing in the blasting fury and my head pounded from the nonstop beating of the sea. Wave after wave crashed into the boat pouring across the deck, nearly drowning us with each hit—first this side, then the other, bobbling us to the top of a large wave, and thrusting us to the trough, only to be lifted and dropped again, with nonstop pounding of seawater fury.

I saw the captain standing atop the castle works, hanging on for dear life as the angry torrents exploded over him, then bravely getting up again to direct against what I couldn't see from below. The crew did their best, staggering about with hands out for balance to grab something lest they be washed overboard. Just then the captain ordered the main sail up again. Six men scurried to the center mast and strained to hoist the heavy soaked fabric, but with no success. Fawzi and I jumped up to help. Our frozen hands were weakened against the taut icy lines, but together we managed to raise it in place and the wind grabbed it immediately, popping it into shape and the boat jolted forward again.

Ordering his men on the aft mast to reign in the yardarm, the boat turned and ran parallel to the largest wave groups and picked up speed. There was still no horizon, as if we were in a canyon of water rising on all sides, with ocean spraying over us again and again, pushing the deck from beneath our feet and slamming us down.

"Like Moses and his children through the Red Sea!" Zafir shouted at me with a smile. *How could he think of that now*, I wondered?

At that moment, a rope came loose and the pulley at its end bounded into the air, jerking madly across the deck like a big fish fighting a hook. We all shouted a warning, but words went nowhere in the nonstop scream of wind and rage. The pulley went swinging in a high arc out over the railing, and suddenly came rushing back hard and fast, right across the deck, smashing directly into two men struggling with some rigging. One was knocked over the railing and the other thrown limply to the planks, red gushing from his head. In seconds, more sheets of water washed the red clear but his body remained without moving.

Fawzi and I jumped to help the man and were thrown to our hands and knees. We crawled as best we could across the pitching deck and took two more heavy hits from waves as we worked our way to the injured man. He was alive but a severe gash on his head left him unconscious. We dragged him across the slippery deck to aft and watched the loose pulley dance in the air, swinging in every direction, causing others to duck to escape its lethal throes. A moment later it caught a yardarm and wrapped around it several times fast and tight before snapping to a stop. And then the water opened beneath us again and we slammed into the bottom of a trough and an enormous wave crashed over us, washing the broken mast overboard. It hung by ropes and rigging and started banging against the planking.

"Will it punch through?" Fawzi yelled to the captain, pointing to the side.

The little man made a cutting motion and Fawzi crawled quickly to the railing. Another wave suddenly pitched the boat to the left and threw Fawzi right at the railing. My heart froze and I tried to stand to help but Ammar grabbed my slippery ankle and held tight.

"NO!" he yelled and then I saw Fawzi pull his knife and start cutting at the ropes. With all but two lines cut free, another wave lifted the boat the other direction and crashed over us in a drenching, smothering submersion that left us coughing and sputtering for air. When my eyes cleared again, I saw Fawzi gripping the railing with all his might, and the broken mast severed away with the frayed ends of ragged ropes left in the running sheets of water.

The deck rolled violently to the right again and the bow slammed hard. Fawzi pinned himself against the railing while more waves pounded us. I heard another cracking noise but nothing that I could see, and then we pounded down again, and again. How could this old boat take such a beating? Part of the railing opposite Fawzi was gone, and the bowsprit and jib were gone, snapped clean off—perhaps being dragged beneath us from the rigging.

Two more slamming waves across the deck and one mighty jarring hit into another trough, and suddenly, quite suddenly, just like that, it stopped.

The roaring waves washed past us and an abrupt calm replaced the roaring wind with a gentle breeze. The heaving and pitching dampened out and the deck rose to level like a cork balanced in water, riding steady again as if nothing had just transpired.

I waited with cold water dripping from my chin and elbows, looking about for another watery assault, wondering if it was over. The deck shed its wet sheen and reached dead center once more. I could tell from the sound that the roar of the straits had passed behind us and a peaceful calm quickly settled on everything.

None of us trusted the peace we felt, and hardly noticed the sky above that was thinning from dark mists to white fog, and then from diluted gray to shallow blue then deep blue. The sun finally crested over the edge of the great misty cloud and the sparkling sheets of water running off the deck reflected the inviting warmth of its hot rays. Almost immediately the warm decks started expelling the water in wafting clouds that rose curling dissipation. Warmth filled the air.

I didn't dare break the calm. "Is it over?" I asked Ammar.

He looked up at the captain, squinting. "I think so," he said.

I turned my head to see the shorelines this side of the straits slowly drifting away, fading behind us into a thin brown line of coast. Somewhere back on those shores were rocky shoals that might have chews us to pieces had we drifted close enough. Though too far away to hear it, I watched with new respect the pounding they received from the sea's nonstop frothy assault with breakers and crashing waves. No ship could possible survive an encounter with those enormous chunks of sharp and ragged rocks.

Those on deck sat looking at the water dripping off the man next to him or the sloshing pool that had filled the resting place of another—and we all smiled. *We had done it.*

I staggered to my feet. It was good to feel a steady deck beneath me. Others did the same. The hatch opened and heads poked out, everyone checking for lost belongings or the safety of their companions.

The captain remained at his high place, soaked, exhausted but alert, and barked new orders. The crew rallied to new tasks and began repairs and securing the sails.

The congeniality of the collective relief put smiles on all our faces as the reality of the moment started to sink in. Somebody shouted praise of the captain and gestured to him. The others started clapping and echoing the sentiments. Though we didn't know the words we certainly understood their meaning, and joined in the clapping for our captain. He smiled back, acknowledging the praise with a toothless grin that stretched ear to ear. Shining in his eyes I could see gratitude that he himself was alive, that his crew was alive, that the ship was intact and the rest of us had survived. But behind his gratitude I could also see the etching of pained sorrow for a lost man and another injured who would not survive the morning. All of us were grateful that he had brought us through. There was a confidence in his posture and an attitude that required no translation: it was clear that for his children and their children's children afterwards, he could always brag with perfect justification that he had taken upon himself the worst possible battle of any sea captain in these parts, or perhaps any parts. He and his men had traveled the Devil's Throat—and won.

心爱的 **45** 啪爱小

SERENITY

The Bay of Bangla was a perfectly beautiful welcome after the foaming terror of the Kantoli traits. Bangla's turquoise tropical waters were warm beneath the high sun. The hues of blue changed from crystal clear immediately beneath our boat to deepening blues farther away. We could plainly see below us great white fields of beautiful sunken coral reefs with slowly-waving grasses growing from white grainy sands. Assorted fish of bright colors schooled through the troughs and peaks of their undersea world, casting shadows on the submerged sandy dunes. The pleasant mirror across the top of the sea glistened toward the lush green landscape far to the east, and to our west, deep blue all the way to the horizon. The water remained clear all that morning, revealing slender orange fish sporting a leopard-spotted covering that swam in a teeming swarm alongside us, curious about the grasses entangled in our ship's encrusted barnacles.

"They want your hook, Gill Face," Fawzi said, chewing on a dried piece of hard bread. "Look at them, they can hardly wait."

"And I'll be happy to oblige them," I said. "I'll get a small one for you while I'm at it." Fawzi flicked a piece of crust at me that missed and fell over the railing into the water. A sudden rush of golden frenzy churned the water for a moment until all the pieces were claimed.

Watching the little fish play alongside the planking of this old boat made me appreciate the ship's integrity. The pounding it was built to endure was a credit to the creative people who built it. Its name, the *Flying Dragon*—for flying it truly was, with her able crew—was a name honorably won. Those men had managed to bring us through the straits safely, although the wickedness of the stormy passage cost them the faithfulness of two crewmen.

I inhaled the sweet ocean air. It felt right in my lungs, energizing and refreshing. It made the peaceful calm that spread in front of us that much more magnificent.

But there was work to be done.

"Let's go," Zafir said, rising stiffly on his sore leg. "We've got a mess to clean and the crew could use our help." He hobbled around to pick up the broken shards of wood and rope that littered the deck. The three of us joined him.

Finding Ammar on the far side, I asked about the masts.

"How do you suppose we'll continue with two of them broken?" I asked.

"They'll repair them," Ammar said.

"Right here? On the sea?"

"They're good at it," Ammar said. "I saw the replacement pieces in the hold. In fact, let me ask and maybe we can help them make the repair."

With that he went to the captain, and with gestures indicated we could get the parts from below and bring them here on deck and participate in the repairs. The captain agreed and nodded his appreciation. Before long we were pulling from below several large, heavy sections of replacement masts and handing them through the hold to the crew on deck.

"Interesting problem, Bassam," Ammar said. "The only real power for these boats is the wind, so being without a means to capture it after losing a mast or sail is shortsighted."

I had not given it any thought, though it made good sense. I wondered how many spare masts they could carry. Were not coastal waystations abundant along these coasts?

"These sections attach with an iron cuff," Ammar explained, pointing out the crude engineering. "It's not much, but it's strong and it works."

The crew removed the broken stump of the foremast and put in the new base. To this they lifted the second section, slipping it into place in another iron cuff, and lashed it securely. Two men clinging to the growing tower helped fit the additional sections, pulling rigging to the top of each as others stiffened the lines to secure it from below. The last sections went up in no time.

"What about the sail line?" I asked. "How do they hoist the sail?"

"Watch," Ammar said, "I think they're handling that now."

Everyone stopped to watch in amazement as a short wiry man with the end of a rope tied to his waist took to the tall mast and worked his way to its top. Barefooted he went hand-over-hand right up its total height.

"I'd like to see you do that," Fawzi said.

"Show me the way and I'll be right behind you," I answered.

The man clung to the slender mast thirty cubits high, stepping on rigging, walking the ropes, right to the top.

Holding tight in the broad sway that was made that more pronounced so high up, he quickly fed a hoist line through a loop for the sail, dropping it to his fellows below. Finished, he scampered down faster than he climbed, to join his fellows to tighten the ropes while others attached the canvas. No sooner did they hoist that large, ribbed sail into place than the wind billowed it out to fullness. It floated before us like a great white cloud against the pleasant blue sky. I felt our boat lunge forward and pick up speed.

The bowsprit was a smaller piece and less complicated. The spare was also below decks, but it was in one piece. We fished it out of the hold while the crew repaired the socket that held it. The most difficult part was securing the lines for the little jib. This was critical for steering so they had to be taut and secure. In just an hour the repairs were completed and we were again plying the sparkling gentle waves northwards.

"Day 541—My Dearest Rasha, Today's brush with death hatched some new ideas in my head. I appreciate your father's reticence about sea trade but I must seriously wonder. Could it get much worse than what we've experienced? We know what pirates can do, we know what the wind and sea can do, and down all the coast nearly every village is close enough to see us pass by, and beckons our trade. We must discuss it when I get back. I hope you are safe. During our struggle in the straits my worst nightmare became the real possibility that I might not ever get to hold you in my arms again. —Bassam"

I stood at the railing and looked out at the blue ocean, chewing a crust of bread in contemplation, and anchoring my gaze at no place on the horizon. I had to admit that during these three months of life on a boat, I had come to love the ocean and the grand expanse of the open sea. *There might be something I could do about this,* I thought.

And then I felt the breeze cooling me uncomfortably despite the hot sun shining on my shoulders. I sought out a place outside the shadows and laid down on the deck. With my arms at my side, my toes pointed up, and my eyes closed, I waited for the hot rays of the warm sun to finish drying me out.

心爱的 **46** 咱爱小

JUST LIKE FISH

"Why Pegu?" I asked.

Ammar turned his map to find the little alcove. "The captain said it would be only one night. Pegu is the largest trading stop on the west coast. Did you see what they have down below?"

"In the hold?" I asked.

"Yes, it's amazing," Ammar said. "They have several tons of silk, it's an important cargo."

"*Tons* of silk?" I asked. "Did it stay dry?"

"I think so," Ammar said. "I went down there after the straits. Everything seemed well bagged and protected—he's got planking down there to keep it out of the wet. In fact," he added, "it was probably *that* tonnage that kept us upright."

"From tipping over?" I said, turning over my hand like a fish.

"Our heavy keel was lifesaving," he said. "Even in strong winds, a good ballast keeps a boat moving hard forward without going to its side. The little *dhows* back home don't have deep keels. That explains their many accidents."

"I'd change the design if it were me," I said.

"Agreed," Ammar replied. "But I suspect they're too busy making treasure to worry about a lost boat here or there."

The trip to Pegu took us six days. On the way, I learned how to catch fish with no line, no hook, and just a net. It was particularly challenging because the fish had to get close to the boat—and I had to get close to the fish.

One bright day with only a soft breeze and the warm current to push us along, I was enjoying the beautiful scene of ocean waters resting still with silky smooth calm, troubled only from the occasional long, gentle swells. I decided it was a good time to employ my new-found skill and try catching my lunch with a small net. I was alone at the railing with the others sitting in the shade watching me.

After half an hour and a dozen near misses I spied a large brown fish lazily flicking a fin in my direction just an arm's reach below the water's surface. He was coming by to take a closer look, probably curious about the little fish that scurried around the hull. His little companions were nibbling at the grasses and barnacles growing in the cracks of the planking just beneath the waterline. It was an ideal fishing place for someone like me with a net to catch him unawares.

I saw he was coming within range and held my breath hoping he'd close the gap just a little bit more.

As I leaned out to position myself, I had the net just over him and was about ready to spring my trap when suddenly I lost my slippery grip and fell right into the water with a big wet splash.

I suppose it was a sight, me going head over heels, because when Fawzi and a crewman threw me a rope, they were laughing so hard they could hardly pull me back. But I did climb aboard with the net still in my hand, and a fish—not the brown one I was aiming for, but a fish nonetheless that had become caught in the strings. They fetched me a blanket and had nothing to say—they were laughing too hard to take further advantage of my embarrassment.

My little fish wasn't so little after all, and made a fine meal. I was happy to share it with those who pulled me from the water, even Fawzi who took obvious opportunity to advance his incessant mockery. His favorite nickname was *moss mouth*, although *fin face*, *gill face* and *bait brains* tied for second.

It was evening when we pulled into the harbor at Pegu. The dim of dusk didn't stop the captain from his duty, and he began unloading immediately. As decided before, there was to be no sleeping on board. There were dozens of men emptying the boat long into second watch, and others loading it up again into fourth watch—a constant stream of footsteps across the deck, up the ladders and back again.

As for us, we were bothered by none of it because we were sound asleep at an inn in the village some distance away, slumbering with stomachs filled on new spices and delectable dishes that were deliciously unique.

That night a dream came to me that I was caught in a net that pulled me down into the brilliant colored world of the shallow sea—tall columns of bright-green plants stood around me like a sun-drenched forest of thin trees growing to the top, gently waving side to side in the rhythmic crystal current. Long shafts of warm yellow sunshine streamed through the water, spotlighting the colorful shells and plant life that littered the soft gentle billows of the sandy sea bottom. Around me hovered dozens of large, ballooning fish that were yellow with black spots, orange and brown and red with stripes. They looked at me with surprised eyes, all of us wondering who had caught whom.

心爱的 **47** 咁愛小

CONQUERING

Ammar calculated the trip to Tamralipta would take us about fifteen days if the winds didn't fail. He was especially busy with his charts these days, measuring and calculating and writing everything he could about this region.

It was the close of the third day out of Pegu that Zafir asked me to meet him on the deck at the start of first watch.

To pass time I finished some last-minute notes in my journal until the appointed hour. When the crew changed at first watch I went topside into the quiet darkness of another perfect night.

Zafir was waiting at the front of the boat. I saw him in the shadows, awash in the flickering glow of a single oil lamp, reclined on a mat and resting his back against the railing. He was wrapped in a brown blanket for warmth and held a short stick in his hand—limply, without purpose. To his side was a metal plate with an unfinished crust of bread, a fruit, and his large clay flask of drink. He seemed meditative—looking off into the darkness at the glistening starry display cascading down to a sudden stop at the black horizon beyond.

"Hello!" I said waving in the dark.

He looked up and smiled.

"Come," he said. "Sit right here. Thank you for surrendering another night for me. I know we lose a lot of sleep over these scrolls."

I found the mat and took my place.

"I caught another of those fat brown fish," I said, crossing my legs and resting my sword next to me. "Did you get a taste of it?"

"Oh, yes," Zafir said. "Very delicious, very tasty. So, that was one you caught, was it?"

"I think it's the same fish that escaped me yesterday," I said. "He came back to mock me and to test my little net."

"But you showed *him*," Zafir said smiling and looked away again.

"Oh yes," I replied. "I showed him."

Zafir seemed contented and at peace.

"Bassam, we've had a wonderful adventure together," he began.

I nodded. "Much more than I ever could have dreamed," I said.

"And yet, not once have you asked me about my treasures and riches, my network of stewards, their responsibilities, the most coveted portions of my enterprise," he said.

It was true, I had never asked although the thought had crossed my mind—several times, in fact. Even so, I was happy to be on the caravan and learning all that I was. I twisted the ring a few times around my finger, wondering what Zafir had yet to say.

"For this evening," Zafir said, "I want to pull together for you the teachings of the scrolls and the seven deadly forces. Just this one last time, until you come to me with questions. Can you spare one more night here on the deck?"

"I would enjoy that," I said.

"This is not for your journals, Bassam," he said. "These ideas are for your head, your heart, and your understanding, just like the Seventh Scroll. Do you know what I'm saying?"

"Yes," I nodded. "For me only."

He turned again to look off into the darkness. The black swells rolled past us in slow, smooth silence, hardly disturbing the steadiness of the deck. It was a lulling, soothing motion that probably had already rocked those below decks into a fast and nice slumber. Topside, the new watch sat on the upper deck at the stern, keeping an eye on things and talking softly among themselves in the glow of a single lantern that hung above them.

"I've been thinking about our discussion on the scrolls and the questions you've been asking," Zafir began. "I want you to see these scrolls as I see them, here at the ending part of my life."

"I hope *not* an ending for a long time," I said.

Zafir didn't smile and looked at me as if I had interrupted. I held my silence.

"Peace, true peace, lasting peace cannot be counterfeited, Bassam," he said. "We all look for peace in so many places. And when the end of our life comes, too few of us realize that peace was with us from the start. The reason we don't recognize it is because of the war we're always fighting inside. And so we go looking to spend the precious hours of every day working for things we believe will bring us peace: an estate larger and more luxurious than our neighbor's, or more gold and horses, slaves and holdings. Some of us seek influence among our peers or the village. Or to gain power to change the course of great enterprises with the mere wave of a hand. Others want attention. They adorn themselves to be elegant, different, unique—to draw praise to their extravagance or to the vanity of their simplicity. Some want intellectual prowess. They must win a battle of wits and words with whomever they encounter. And the few who obtain these positions of superiority or power can't help but parade around their accomplishments for others to see. Have you seen it, Bassam? Have you seen this vanity?"

I knew it was rhetorical, but I nodded. Yes, I had seen it all the time.

"From these various vain and desperate endeavors, we always find ourselves at the end of time surrounded with all kinds of *things*—nice things, expensive things, many things, of gold and glass and brass, large and small, and nearly all of it just sitting for show, useless, cold, dead and meaningless. And yet we think such things bring us an easy life, that by parading them in front of others we are admired and adored. We treat them as trophies or proof of our many achievements. But to be lacking in this vanity, always lacking, is the settled glow of true and lasting inner peace. I don't disparage such worldly gain, or such high and lofty pursuits, or such men who must obtain them. There is power in the pursuit of vanity, both good and bad. I only observe that while these elements of wealth and power serve roles in our world, their accumulations by themselves *do not* and *cannot* bring true peace. Only in here," he said, pointing to his heart, "only in here can true peace be found," and he pointed to mine. "There is no counterfeit for true peace. I want you to remember this important truth, my son: a truth that makes God the fair teacher and creator that he is. There is no greater treasure than peace, and true inner peace requires *no* money, *no* position and *no* authority to obtain. It is ours for the having if we choose to be worthy of it. That is what the scrolls teach you, Bassam."

Zafir stopped to take a sip of water from his flask. He offered me a drink, I declined. "I'm not the one talking," I said.

He smiled and continued.

"Most of humanity worries itself to the grave trying to compete with his neighbor. If you look at how far we have come in our little Rekeem, you will see something fantastic. The shops and carts and foods and water and clothing, all things you enjoy today were not there a century ago. A century ago it took a king's treasure to obtain many of those necessities. And the poor in those days? The poor lived horribly, many died early, nearly all squandered their best talents for the obligation imposed on them to simply *find their next meal.* Today, the average man lives the life of the kings of old. Even the poor among us have the basics of life unlike those before. Back then it took a fortune to buy the things that we enjoy as common place today. This is because Abdali-ud-din has built marketplaces to give the world a place to trade. This exchange has so improved our lives that the pauper and common man of today live like the kings of yesteryear. And in another century, those elements of the wealthy lifestyle will always become commonplace so long as there is freedom to develop it. And that, my son, brings me to the point I wanted to discuss with you tonight."

"Point?" I asked.

"Yes," Zafir said. "It is this: Weak people make weak nations. We are only as strong as the one man's integrity, the one couple's marriage, the one village's support of law, and the one nation's resilience to fend off usurpers and thieves who worm their way into the highest realms of power for personal gain. Do not be a weak man, and do not support weak leaders. Short of reading the scrolls, all men should learn at least that much—don't be weak, retain the virtues of strength and self-governance."

He looked back and me and smiled.

"That all for now," he said, and drew up his legs as if he had reached the end of what he wanted to say. "Help me to my feet, could you Bassam?"

I stood and helped on one side while his sturdy walking stick helped on the other.

"I need to retire. It is late and we have many such nights ahead of us," he said. "But tonight as you sleep, I want you to chisel some important words in your mind and into your heart."

"Certainly," I said. "Tell me."

Zafir put an arm on my shoulder and spoke directly.

"These words come from the first scroll and you must not forget them, Bassam. The greatest nations rise on the strength of the individual man and woman. Nations are no stronger and no weaker than the best and worst of its people. And so, my son, I want you to always remember: A man is not conquered from without until he first destroys himself from within. I'll say it again: *A man is not conquered from without until he first destroys himself from within.* You say it."

"A man is not conquered from without," I repeated, letting the words sink into my memory, "until he first destroys himself from within."

"That is right," Zafir said. "*The first scroll.* Stop working so hard to destroy yourself from within, and you will be strong. And then you will learn for yourself the opposite of those words: A man is not conquered from without who first *conquers himself within.* That is the secret, Bassam. Have you conquered yourself within? Think on that, it has a lot to do with that elusive prize called true inner peace. Now, let us retire, I'm tired tonight."

And with that, he hobbled across the deck to his quarters, leaving me standing there alone in the dark—suddenly quiet, to myself, introspective—and astonished.

心爱的 **48** 咁受小

TWO EQUALS ONE

Afew days later when I was on deck, I saw Ammar scale the center mast all by himself. I had never seen him so agile or athletic. He climbed it like he was an old sea dog reared and raised on the rigging of a ship. Up he scooted, not as frisky as the crew could do it, but surprising to me considering his age. He worked his way up one section, hand over hand up the ropes, then the next, until he was at the top.

"Ammar!" I yelled to him. "What are you doing? Did you drop something back there?"

He didn't react, probably didn't even hear me. But I could see him hang on for dear life as the ship rolled gently from side to side, dipping the top of the mast a long way out over the water and a long way back. It was a beautiful day and the seas were steady, but that tall place magnified what was merely gentle rocking where I stood.

He stayed up for half an hour and then worked his way down to find me sitting with Fawzi under the shade of the foresail.

"What was that all about?" I asked.

"Just checking," Ammar said, breathless from the exertion. He curled himself into a seated position close to us and reached for his leather bag next to Fawzi. "There's an old rule of thumb around these coastlines," he said.

"Like 'don't climb thirty cubits over a pitching deck'?" I asked.

Fawzi reached over with his foot and mashed it onto mine, making me yelp and pull my foot away. "Listen up *mast mouth*, he's going to teach you something," Fawzi said.

"That's right," Ammar said, not paying attention to the mild assault. "This rule of thumb helps coastal people protect their waters."

"Protect what? Are these vast oceans not enough for one nation?" I asked. "Stretching for months in all directions?"

"It's the fishing," Ammar said, fumbling around in his bag, "and the security."

He pulled out his knife, a pen, a small ink pot and some squares of papyrus.

Ammar cut a new tip on his pen and dipped the ink. "The old men say that if you can see a boat, it is trespassing in your waters."

"If you can see it?" I asked. "Isn't that selfish way out here?"

"Not really," Ammar continued. "You've seen the tall masts of boats sink from view as they travel beyond the horizon?"

"Yes, below the curve," I said.

"Hey *moss breath*," Fawzi cut in. "Do you have the least little clue what Ammar is trying to say?"

"Well .... not yet," I said. "Tell me the rest."

"I was watching for land," Ammar said. "Up on the mast, I was watching. According to my map, we are traveling north along the coast, about 100 stadia away. I couldn't see it from up there for a while, but when it came to view, I had to rework my numbers to see how far out we are. If I know how tall the mast is, I can figure out how far out we are from shore."

"Did you figure it?" I asked. "Can you tell how far from shore we are by those calculations?"

"I estimate we're about 120 stadia away," Ammar said. "That's enough for the captain, he likes to stay safely out of view because of pirates, but close enough just in case."

"Here? More pirates?" I complained.

"I knew it," Fawzi said. "You're more than a *fin face*, you're a *fish spine*."

"Day 565—My Dearest Rasha, we are in the seas of the Indus people, and a beautiful place this is. We see their boats, a different construction of boat with a tight curved nose to its bow, single arms for sails. They patrol

the coasts not for us but to fish or to travel. Their sails are decorated to honor the benevolent gods who dwell in these waters. No one has come to demand a tax of us, and anyone close enough to hail us is kind and smiling. They wave us on to shore, to trade, to stay, to live. This is a good place, it feels different, the people have good hearts. Your father is walking so much stronger now, I might ask him if we should reconsider our plan to return home. The caravan is due in these parts at any time soon, if not already, and we could join back with them. —Bassam"

心爱的 **49** 啪爱小

TAMRALIPTA

Ammar's map showed the Ganga with many mouths discharging its rushing drainage directly into the ocean. As we approached the northern coastline I could see only one mouth: a wide expanse that looked more like a bay than a river. For much of the afternoon we sailed through the river's gray wash that was slow to dilute into the blue of their sea.

"This is the place," Ammar said. "The captain will steer us through that entrance and we should arrive at Tamralipta by sun down. We'll spend the night there."

"Bassam!" Fawzi said, kicking my foot. "Zafir's *message*."

"Oh yes! What will you say, Zafir?" I asked. "Will you send any dispatches back to Rekeem? Maybe my journals to ...."

Zafir was silent a moment as though lost in another world. "Message? Quite right, the message," he said. "I'll leave a report for the caravan about our journey to this place, and leave word when I expect us to arrive back in Rekeem. If they're on schedule, they should pass through in a few weeks. I don't see a need to dispatch any messages back home, we'll arrive there soon enough. I'll let my stewards know of our whereabouts. More importantly we must resupply ourselves with gold and buy passage on other boats headed west. And yes, we must leave word for Ziyad and Sofian and the others that all is well."

"And tell them about our near catastrophe in the straits and the attack of the brown men?" I added.

"Certainly," he said. "I'll tell them the four of us made it through those events safely." And then as an afterthought, "But not your journals, Bassam, I wouldn't try to return them to Rekeem. They are safer with you than with my couriers, you keep them."

A s the boat entered the river proper, I could discern only a slight change in color of the water, from chalky gray to a milky brown. The current was against us, but a nice steady wind blew us northwards upriver.

"It's the rainy season in the highlands," Ammar said. "The finest soils wash down and deposit in the flood plains, a rich gift each year that feeds millions."

Millions. How can so many people live in one place? I wondered.

The land was flat but green—no mountains broke the horizon. On either side of the river, bushy trees stood many paces apart, alone, solitary. Yellowed grasses grew from the shallow shores, poking their bushy heads from the water as if caught by surprise in some gently-rising flood. Like a breathing carpet of changing hues and color, the grasses farther up the banks had turned dark green and lush. Their tops waved gently in the breeze. Dirt pathways that followed the distant banks were a rusty red, trodden flat by dark-colored men in loincloths with white lumpy turbans. Others lounged on fallen logs or near vacated shacks to watch from the shadows as our boat worked its way upriver.

The sky was overcast and the air had a nice earthy perfume to it— the smell of waters purifying the land, cleansing it of old decay and washing it out to sea.

After another hour of sailing there were few signs of civilization. The villages were not close to the river's edge. Ammar told me the flooding keeps them back from the worst of it. In the far distance I spotted several tiny twisting threads of gray smoke leaning into the sky, evidence of habitation and cooking somewhere beyond our view.

As we neared Tamralipta proper, some signs of civilization began to show. The coastal life was not heavily concentrated, but the river traffic was modestly busy. Small sail boats with long oars steered past us. Their tenders were usually four or five young-looking dark men in loincloths and turbans, squinting at us in wonder—perhaps weighing our intentions and wondering: do *they* come to sell or to buy?

I watched them from the railing, smiling and waving to those who sent us a greeting. They chattered at us in a strange tongue that was a delight to hear though I understood nothing. I had no idea by their gestures or words what their communications were, but there was nothing hostile in their actions.

The shoreline of Tamralipta was nothing like the fantastic trading centers in C'ina. Standing beneath the shade of tall, bushy trees were dozens of ancient, gray, cut-stone buildings, artistically carved, ornate and statuesque, just barely taller than two men. Some were just wide enough for a family, others much longer, 150 paces or more. Old-growth vines with dark green leaves and small pink blossoms clawed up the sides of the gray walls, messengers of neglect that reached around corners and columns for a stranglehold against time. In the limbs above, curious birds talked their alarm while a pair of small monkeys blinked at us from a low-hanging vine.

"Look, Bassam," Fawzi said, pointing out the little tree monkeys. "Your lost brother and sister, at last! Run to them, *run!*"

I ignored him. I was mesmerized from staring and wondering about the dark empty openings in the stone buildings, openings that once had doors and windows and mercantilism and life.

"It is the end of a great empire," Ammar said, coming to my side to watch the passing specter of abandoned glory. "A local hero of theirs, named Maurya, settled here with his teacher many centuries ago, and founded one of the greatest empires in the world. He was the first of their many kings."

I couldn't stop looking at the lifeless hollows of the stone buildings that seemed to watch us like great black eyes. It looked more the home for bats and hungry night creatures than a center of exchange.

"Those are the remains of their enormous shipping businesses that once thrived here—warehouses to store things and places to trade."

They looked long-ago abandoned. The masonry was streaked with black stains that painted their lines over eroded carvings and caplets, columns and buttresses, the runoff of who knows how many centuries of rain.

"There isn't a lot left," I said.

"At their peak they ruled the whole land," Ammar said. "They were the keepers of Lord Siva's gifts of water. One day you will see the great mountains yourself, the spring of this mighty flow."

As we continued northward I observed the fresh water runoff had combined to create this tremendous river that remained busy, constantly washing the land into the ocean.

"The water travels a month to reach these outlets," Ammar said. "And farther west is the Khyber passage that carries Zafir's trade through this region west. The Mauryans guard it for all the caravans moving north and south. It is another great intersection of trade."

But not around here at Tamralipta, I observed. A few people with carts drove their donkeys in front of the stone facades, carrying loads to somewhere. And little children, half naked, chased and laughed through the abandoned structures, racing in and out of the neglected hollows as if it was a playground built just for them.

The Indus people lived a slower pace. I felt a pleasant trust in the rhythms of life and season, a peaceful calm that permeated all living things right into the soul of their land, an existence regulated according to the steadiness of a shared common heartbeat. I liked it.

Approaching the dock, the crew steered us between other boats already tied, their fishing nets hung from tall poles to dry. The nearness of the land let us hear the chattering and singing voices of the jungle, mingled with the voices of nearby men as they hurried about the dock, off-loading that morning's catch.

The smell of rotten fish was in the air, mixed with a dampness of moss and washed rocks. I couldn't help but notice the same tangles of seagulls drifting overhead as always, squawking their selfish displeasure at our arrival, and swooping in close to steal a forgotten morsel, a test of our patience before darting away again.

Somewhere beyond this barren coastline was the city we were sailing toward these past two months. With the boat tied and the ramp secured, I followed Zafir's careful hobbling to land. I looked around and wondered, was there news from the caravan awaiting us here?

心爱的 **50** 咱愛小

THE MESSAGE

Zafir's steward in Tamralipta was a man named Arja. They were friends since his first visit some four years earlier. They built a fast cooperative of trade between Chang'an and Arja's connections farther south into the peninsula. Zafir told me that four years was not enough time to prove the integrity of the usual business dealing, but Arja was a good man. He had ten children all grown, and 30 grandchildren with two on the way. He had become a fast friend. Arja had a place of business along the river, but his home was reached by passage through the village. It was nestled in the green foothills that stood guard against the jungle that lay farther beyond.

The little streets in Tamralipta were paved with cut stone. To either side were curbs tightly joined to direct the runoff, and ruts worn by centuries of passing wagons. The stone pavement produced a whimsical clip-clop sound as animals and moving carts hurried here and there, a noise of activity that was almost lost beneath the chattering and calling of men and women who scurried about with their shouldered loads, or driving loaded animals, crowding against us as we followed Zafir through the village. It was the first time I had ever seen a water buffalo with their thick horns curving inwards above their heads, and with black hides almost blue. A woman and her daughter walked one of them with only a thin rope looped around its horns, and were leading it through the square like he was their pet.

The congestion of people and animals became so severe that we lost Zafir in the maze of turbans and great sacks atop so many hundreds of heads. We found him again waiting for us on the stoop of a shop, wondering why we couldn't keep up with his hobbling.

With a determination born of familiarity, he led us through the noise and smells of the crowded marketplace. We emerged out the other side to a quiet, shaded street where birds chirped overhead and the sounds of commerce quickly faded behind.

"I love this place," Zafir said, inhaling the smells of leaves and blooms and trees and vines. A bee buzzed past, and two colorful birds fluttered away from a puddle they were pecking at. Shafts of yellow sun danced across the pavers from the shifting leaves and branches high above, spotlighting the fronts of the little painted houses that lined both sides of the small street. Except for two women sweeping water away from their stoops, it was pleasantly quiet and empty.

"The people pay for their paradise," Zafir said. "They pay for it by enduring the flooding storms and killer winds that pound this little cove and sometimes sweep homes and families into the river beneath a mudslide or torrent. Every time I come, I can't help but think the seasonal punishment is worth the cost to spend a life in this peaceful place."

We continued without talking, consuming the delights that lulled our senses away into an opulence of natural beauty. Zafir led us up the street to a corner, then down a heavily shaded, tree-lined dirt pathway. Each of us was smiling at the delicious cool of the air and the varied sweet smells that announced a perpetual spring blossom of this one sort or another. The blooms were in great quantities and bunches, growing wild and prolific, and too beautiful to attempt description.

We finally emerged from the trees into the full blaze of sunshine. The sky was crystal blue with massive clouds billowing up from the horizon. In front of us, a quaint little house of cut stone welcomed us with a wide pebble walkway. Thick grape vines clung to the walls, and a small tended garden with many flowers—yellow, orange, some purple and red—guarded the walls beneath bright windows. Near one window opening, a large green parrot clung to a vine, carefully scraping with his beak at something between his claws.

Beyond the house we could see a large, fenced vegetable garden green with newness. Its produce was neatly arrayed in straight rows, and was in the fullness of growth with yellow blossoms both large and small. The red dirt was clean and free of weeds.

Toward the back a man and a woman were hunched over, wearing broad woven hats, working the dirt to keep the stragglers at bay.

"Arja!" Zafir called out.

The two figures suddenly stood and looked.

"Master Zafir?" the man called back. "Is that you, my friend?" He dropped his small tool and took off his hat.

"It is us indeed! We have come for a surprise visit," Zafir called.

The woman remained, brushing the dirt from her hands. Arja lifted his skirts and hurried down a furrow directly to us.

His appearance was typical of those we had seen already—thin with short, gray hair, a round, smiling face, hunched shoulders, a brown skin to match the river. His eyes were dark brown and his teeth white. Throwing his hat as he came up to us, he extended a wiry hand to Zafir's.

"This is the most pleasant of surprises," he said, shaking Zafir's hand vigorously. "I am so glad to have you here. It is a great surprise to me! Welcome to all of you, welcome to my home! Will you come in, won't you? Will you come inside, all of you?"

"You must meet my associates," Zafir said, introducing each of us. "Fawzi and Ammar, you remember them from last time."

Arja smiled with his two hands pressed in front of him, and made a polite bow. "Welcome to you my old friends. I am so glad to see you again and in such good health you are."

"And this is my young heir, Bassam," he said, putting an arm around my shoulders. "He is the son of my dearest friends."

"And welcome to you, my young prince," Arja said. And then turning a sly look to Zafir. "You teach him the ways of the caravan?"

"Indeed."

"And he is a good student?"

"He is an excellent student, my friend," Zafir said. "He will lead my caravan the next time we pass through."

Arja took my hand in his and held it, looking deeply into my eyes. All I could see was sincerity, warmth, and kindness.

"Then you are welcome when you come, young Bassam," he said. "My home is yours, my family is yours, you always will have a safe place here to come and to rest."

"Thank you," was all I could say. He let go my hand.

This man, I thought, is indeed worthy of Zafir's trust in him as a good steward, as a good friend. I watched Arja brighten up as he conversed with Zafir. The old chieftain is well loved in many places, I decided.

"Please, all of you, please come in," he said, gesturing to the great room inside his front door. A dozen cushioned wicker chairs in a large circle awaited us in the cool shadows.

"Your home is *just* beautiful," Zafir said. "As before! And that garden—you've enlarged it since the last time, haven't you?"

"Many mouths take much food, but for *that* we go to market," Arja said smiling. "But this garden," he said, almost whispering, "this keeps my wife happy with our children gone. A full house is fast emptied, and once busy hands now resting are soon anxious hands, they need work, and work I give them. Shush, don't tell her our secret," he said smiling.

"Oh yes," Zafir said, laughing at the tease. "I know exactly what you mean."

"Please, sit. May I get you anything? It is time for our dinner, will you join us? There is plenty, you must eat."

"Once again I find myself imposing on your kind hospitality," Zafir said. "It would be our honor to dine with you, if you will let us help your good wife prepare it."

"Nonsense! She is a jealous guard over her secrets *and* her kitchen! You will sit here and we will talk and she will bring us a tea."

And with that he hurried to the back of the house where his wife had just arrived, giving instructions for the care of the surprise visitors.

"You'll love Maghi," Zafir said. "She is a gracious and beautiful mother of their children. She is the true strength in this home, you will see."

"Watch out, *monkey cousin*," Fawzi said, leaning over to me out of earshot of the others. "She might kidnap you and make you a slave, it's happened before."

I just shook my head.

Arja returned breathless. "She is preparing it. Now, sit, all of you, and let us talk."

We found the cushions deliciously comfortable, especially after our long walk to reach this place.

"Before I forget, Arja," Zafir said, "I need to leave some instructions, a message for Ziyad when he comes through. I expect he should be here in another five or six weeks."

Arja suddenly sat up straight, the smile gone from his face and panic in his tone. "Message! Oh, Zafir, I had forgotten—I had forgotten until you said it just now."

"Forgotten?" Zafir said.

"A message. It came for you. Urgent."

"A message?"

I furrowed my brow, puzzled at the alarm. And then—and then, I understood: *Al Kalimat.*

心爱的 **51** 的爱心

THE SMALL VEIL

Arja jumped to his feet and hurried from the room. "I have it, I have it, one moment please," he called back, disappearing down a hallway.

We turned to Zafir.

"A message?" Ammar said. "That could only mean that—"

"Yes, I know," Zafir replied. His face turned ashen, his smile dissolved.

Zafir stood up impatiently, followed by Fawzi and then Ammar. They paced with clasped hands behind backs, fidgeting with this or that, waiting.

A moment later, Arja came rushing back, fumbling with a worn and tattered leather pouch.

"I am not sure," Arja puzzled, "—not sure if this is authenticated," he said, pulling at the knotted strings.

"Authenticated?" I asked.

"Validated," Fawzi said. "Secure, proven, tested. Some form of proof it came through *Al Kalimat* true and unchanged. Men have tried to trick us into a trap with such messages. We need proof it comes to us pure. *Validation*, Bassam. Very important."

"How could you know?" I asked. Nobody answered—all eyes focused on Arja's struggle to open the pouch.

"How long?" Zafir asked.

"Four weeks ago," Arja panted. "Maybe five—"

Ammar looked up as if making a calculation. "That's two months, Zafir," he said with worry in his voice. "That's two months and four or five weeks, at least."

Zafir stood silent, his jaw tightening.

"Here, let me," Fawzi said, taking the pouch from Arja, and with his knife he quickly cut the strings and handed it to Zafir.

The old man took it in his hands and quickly pulled it open, removing a small scrap of parchment. It was a corner torn from a larger sheet, obviously taken in haste.

Turning it over to read, his eyes darted across the message— paused—and he read them again. His lips moved with the words.

"What is it?" Ammar asked.

Zafir frowned, handed the note to Ammar, then turned his back to us and walked to one of the large window openings. He folded his arms and stood in silence, his head bowed in thought. Ammar took the note and read it aloud.

"Father —
Rekeem sacked.
Army of Tauri. Many dead.
They're taking me away.
Come quickly.
My love to you and B.
The small veil."

260

"Attacked—is it possible?" Ammar breathed in disbelief. He handed the note over to Fawzi.

"The *Tauri*?" Fawzi puzzled. "I thought they were disbanded. Dead. Gone."

"What's this *small veil*," Ammar asked. "What does that mean?"

"It must be a trick," Fawzi said. "It makes no sense. Who sent this, Arja? Who brought this to you?"

"Just a messenger," Arja stammered. "Someone local who received it from another and another and ...."

The men looked at each other and shrugged, and then looked at me.

I was twisting Zafir's ring around my finger, not listening anymore— their words were falling on me like rain but I was not hearing them. My head was buzzing with panic, distraught confusion, frustration.

Sacked—dead—taking me—my love ....

Her desperate plea burned through my brain and down to my feet like fire. I couldn't move, my pounding heart climbed into my throat, crushing my breath. With trembling hands, I reached into my shirt and felt about for her gift. I pulled it into the light and held it up for all to see.

"*This* is the validation," I whispered, searching their eyes. "*This* is the small veil. It is from Rasha."

Zafir turned, and seeing the veil he lifted it quickly for closer examination.

"Yes, the small veil," he said, spreading it flat across his palm. "Her gift to Bassam," he said. "That note *is* from Rasha, this is the validation," he said, handing it back.

"Arja!" he commanded in a sharpened voice, "Show this note to Ziyad when he arrives, and tell him, tell him this ... do you have an ink and papyrus?"

Arja hurried away and returned with an ink pot, a slender writing scrawl and some curled sheets of papyrus. Zafir hurried through a message and folded it into the leather pouch. "Tell Ziyad when he comes that he must obey its every word. Will you do it?" he asked, pushing the pouch back at Arja, who nodded.

The old chieftain hobbled to the door and stood there a moment, letting his eyes fall on each of us for a brief painful moment. His countenance had changed to one that only the father of a daughter could possibly understand.

"We must go," he said. "Follow me now."

心爱的 52 咱愛小

DAWN

Henri let the last of the scroll slip off the spindle and curl lightly around his hand. He smoothed it flat and read the final words again.

"The Tauri," he repeated. "These bandits were bad people ... everywhere they are mentioned in history it's always *kill and conquer.* They're referenced often enough, but sacked Rekeem? I hadn't heard of it before. Would the record tell of them ever being in Rekeem?"

The scrolls unfolded a story that needed an ending. Henri knew it, and he knew that the scribes knew it, else why include these words at all?

"There's another scroll in there," he muttered aloud, furrowing his brow to think.

"I couldn't see it with my mirror and light," he said. "What did I miss?" He rubbed the unshaven stubble of his chin and let out a sigh.

"I did look, I did, I looked everywhere with that light, as far up as I could see. There was nothing, unless it was in the shadows of the small vault. There must be a way ...."

Henri stood and looked through the large windows of the library toward the distant receiving garage. A lone light illuminated the sarcophagus in a soft yellow glow.

"What I need is a scope. That will do it. I will try again, but this time I will borrow one. Dr. Lincoln shouldn't mind, he leaves them around too much as it is—got himself scolded, yes, scolded for—for losing it? No, he misplaced it, that's right, he set it down and forgot, when was that? Just last Christmas. He set it down and covered it over with papers. Did they tell me $18,000? Things are so expensive now days, $18,000 for a scope. I will be careful, treat it carefully, and return it before he misses it. Yes, right now, before they see the panel underneath has been tampered with, and start asking questions."

Henri felt for his keys and started toward the door.

"Ah, how careless," he said as an afterthought, and returned to carefully roll the second scroll back to its place on the olive wood spindle.

"I will save this scroll for rereading later," he said, and left for the stairs leading to the offices in the west wing. "The good doctor won't mind if I borrow his special device just this once, he would want me to see if there is a third scroll stashed in there. Yes, he would want that."

End of Book 2

THE SAGA CONCLUDES IN BOOK 3,
"THE SEARCH FOR RASHA"

ABOUT THE AUTHOR

As a young child Paul B. Skousen grew up mesmerized by a faded Asian carpet that hung high in the main hallway of his family's home. It depicted desert nomads seated on a rug spread over sand, camped between palm trees, their camels pastured nearby. A couple of hunting dogs stood anxious, awaiting their meal, and in the background, rose the rolling desert sea of nondescript dunes, forever undulating toward the horizon, frozen in time. It was an era and destination he longed to see for himself—and over the years that followed, he did.

Skousen enjoys visiting the Middle East for archeology digs or just renewing friendships. He is a journalist by trade, finished graduate school at Georgetown University, worked as an analyst at the CIA, and was assigned to the Situation Room as an intelligence officer in the Reagan White House. He is a professor of communications at Utah Valley University and Salt Lake Community College. He's a married father of ten, grandfather to 32 at last count, and is the author of the three-volume Bassam series and several non-fiction books on politics and history.

www.ingramcontent.com/pod-product-compliance
Lightning Source LLC
Chambersburg PA
CBHW030358020726
47493CB00003B/868